W0018963

FIVE DAYS

ZOË FOLBIGG

Boldwood

First published in Great Britain in 2024 by Boldwood Books Ltd.

Copyright © Zoë Folbigg, 2024

Cover Design by Alice Moore Design

Cover Photography: Shutterstock

The moral right of Zoë Folbigg to be identified as the author of this work has been asserted in accordance with the Copyright, Designs and Patents Act 1988.

All rights reserved. No part of this book may be reproduced in any form or by any electronic or mechanical means, including information storage and retrieval systems, without written permission from the author, except for the use of brief quotations in a book review.

This book is a work of fiction and, except in the case of historical fact, any resemblance to actual persons, living or dead, is purely coincidental.

Every effort has been made to obtain the necessary permissions with reference to copyright material, both illustrative and quoted. We apologise for any omissions in this respect and will be pleased to make the appropriate acknowledgements in any future edition.

A CIP catalogue record for this book is available from the British Library.

Paperback ISBN 978-1-80426-951-0

Large Print ISBN 978-1-80426-952-7

Hardback ISBN 978-1-80426-953-4

Ebook ISBN 978-1-80426-950-3

Kindle ISBN 978-1-80426-949-7

Audio CD ISBN 978-1-80426-958-9

MP3 CD ISBN 978-1-80426-957-2

Digital audio download ISBN 978-1-80426-956-5

Boldwood Books Ltd
23 Bowerdean Street
London SW6 3TN
www.boldwoodbooks.com

For my sister Clare, the most brilliant woman I know

'Play is the work of childhood.'

— JEAN PIAGET

PART I

PART 1

1

DAY ZERO

Now

Time and space can be wonderous and magical: children become friends in a boisterous and busy playground; people fall in love at first sight across a crowded room; Olympic gold gymnasts can do a double-double dismount on a beam only 10 cm wide. But these simple forces all boil down to physics and chemistry: stars align, worlds collide, engines fail.

Minnie Byrne was getting her head around the fact that all the miraculous things she believed in could be put down to science, as she sat in a wing-backed window chair, *A Brief History of Time* on her lap, drinking iced coffee in a cafe-slash-book-slash-record shop she was trying to take ownership of. Minnie would not let a bad memory of a bad thing that happened there tarnish this coffee shop for her. It was a space she loved in a happier time, and it would be that way again.

Minnie's therapist had recommended she try new things: read books she would never usually dream of picking up (even if she was reading them in old haunts). Be more playful. Widen her friendship group. Learn a new skill. All baby steps she could take to 'get outside of herself' and bring back the carefree joy she'd felt as a child – Minnie was one of the lucky ones who'd had a happy childhood – and her therapist said it could help her heal as an adult.

She leaned back into the chair, her lungs and brain expanding with each deep, calm breath, each line absorbed. She was doing a good job of getting out of herself by reading all about black holes, white dwarves, time warps and the Big Bang. Despite her current lacklustre energy levels, due to her own personal quantum mechanics, Minnie was a gung-ho and positive person who liked a challenge. Growing up in a large family with five children, she had always done what her parents asked, however dull or however daunting the task seemed, because Minnie was a doer. A people pleaser. A glass half full. Minnie had liked to colour coordinate her parents' books before social media was even a thing on which to show off rainbow shelves. She liked to stack the dish-washer in what she felt was perfect formation (a challenge her father set her, so he didn't have to). She could recite the first line of all 154 of Shakespeare's sonnets in the correct order (a challenge she had set herself). At school, Minnie had relished homework and presented it as competently and as beautifully as she could, mainly because she wanted the teachers to like her. She wanted her therapist to like her too, which she knew was ridiculous.

Still, Minnie had picked up Stephen Hawking in the book section of Bondiga's Books & Records, not paid for it (another reason she loved this place; if she was careful with a book she could read it and put it back), and gone to find a seat in the window of the cafe area for some peace and contemplation.

She had just come to the remarkable realisation that there was a scientific explanation for everything, when a yellow object shot across the room in her peripheral vision. As Minnie gazed at the missile on its trajectory, she realised that her epiphany was about to collide with cata-strophe for someone else. She almost laughed and put her hand to her mouth as the ball struck a man, right on top of his head, and bounced on his mass of golden brown sticky-up hair. Space. And time.

It was a jolly looking ball. Small, yellow, bouncy. Even from Minnie's chair on the other side of the cafe, she could see that the ball had two black oval eyes and a curve of a smile, reminiscent of the acid house smiley face of the nineties. This ball had been manufactured to bring joy.

'Do you fucking mind?' said the man who had been struck, as he turned, exasperated, halfway through picking up his coffee. The ball bounced once on the table, almost in slow motion, with enough kinetic lift to land in the coffee he had just picked up. It sent a scalding splash of syrupy brown liquid all over his grey cotton shirt and lap.

'For fuck's sake!' the man lambasted, as he jumped up, placing the cup back onto its saucer on the table. Jesse was having a bad day. He was having a bad day before the ball struck his head and landed in his drink, and now he felt such searing anger, his hands were trembling. He was lucky not to spill any more. 'Do you *fucking* mind?' he repeated, louder this time, as he turned to the perpetrator, a little boy, frozen in the middle of the coffee shop.

The chatter in the room fizzled out as customers turned to look at the man and the boy. Only the distant sound of Leonard Cohen continued from the record shop in the adjacent room: Minnie's favourite coffee shop, book shop and record store were all owned by Alistair Bondiga and had been in his family for three generations, enjoying the gravitational pull of North London's book/record/coffee loving community since 1963. The book department of Bondiga's was always quiet and contemplative, but now the cafe was awkwardly silent too.

The little boy, whose eyes were both solemn and mischievous, looked back at the angry man, too scared to reply. The boy's mother, who had been lost in her own Instagram universe, looked up from scrolling on her phone, brought back into the room by the rudeness of the man and the commotion.

'Excuse me?' she said, her finger paused over a post she was deciding whether to deign with a like. 'What did you just say?' The woman stood and approached the man with the slow and predatory steps of a big cat, putting her paw protectively over the boy's chest as she pressed her legs into his back.

Kip, a man with green hair and an eighties shirt, who ran the coffee shop, came around from the counter with some paper towels and a cloth and wiped the table and Jesse's belongings down while Jesse felt the heat of his coffee, which he'd asked to be extra hot – Jesse always asked for his brew to be extra hot – hit his stomach and thighs.

'Do you need a hand?' Kip's colleague Steph asked, as she came from out the back with a sack of coffee beans. Kip shook his head and offered Jesse a paper towel for his shirt but Jesse was looking squarely at the mother.

'I said watch it!' he replied. 'Your kid has been throwing that thing all around the place – knocking into people – and now I'm burnt and covered in coffee. My notebook is wet. And I've got a really fucking important meeting and... thank you...' He trailed off sarcastically, as he put his palms in the air.

The woman looked aghast.

'Did you tell my son to fuck off?'

'No, I didn't.'

'Yes you did.'

'No I didn't. I said, "Do you *fucking* mind?"'

The woman was gobsmacked, and briefly looked to the other customers for support, to see if she was imagining the man and his rudeness. Most of them were keenly listening, but trying not to show it. Kip finished wiping down the table and pushed his little round glasses up his nose.

'Who the fuck do you think you are, swearing in front of my son?' The woman jabbed her finger into the space between them.

If Jesse weren't so stressed, he would have raised an eyebrow. Instead he looked at Kip briefly and took the paper towel with a small nod.

The little boy's bottom lip trembled. His wide eyes were like saucers. Minnie, watching from her chair, carefully put one flap of the book's cover into the page she was reading and placed it down. The boy *had* been annoying.

The relentless thud of the bouncy ball on the wooden floor had been making it even harder for her to focus on eleven-dimensional supergravity, and at one point she had had to reprimand him for almost going in her handbag to retrieve a wayward blueberry. His mother hadn't noticed, but Minnie's piercing green eyes had made the boy rethink.

'You need to go,' the mother, who had a grey bob and wore designer Converse, said as she looked Jesse up and down, her eyes landing on the portfolio propped up against the chair next to him. 'Jesse Lightning. You need to go. This is not a safe space for my son... You obviously know nothing about children and—'

That was the thing that stung Jesse more than the coffee. He was *not* a bad man.

'What?' Jesse scowled, still trying to pad his shirt down without making the stain worse. Kip handed him another paper towel and put some napkins on the table.

The boy's mother turned to Kip. 'You need to throw this man out and make sure he never comes back. Jesse Lightning. Make a note of his name and bar him—'

'Jesus Christ!' Jesse exhaled at the ceiling.

Kip looked a bit helpless.

'You're abusing my son!'

Minnie jumped up out of her chair by the window.

'Whoah! Hey, this is all getting a bit heavy.'

Jesse looked at Minnie, slightly shocked by her interjection and her face.

'How about cutting a little slack, on both sides, huh?' Minnie suggested. 'Fair dos – this gentleman was just minding his own business and now has coffee all over him; your boy... who I'm sure is delightful, didn't mean to cause any... but, you know, this guy didn't mean any harm either. I'm sure he's not the Child Catcher...' Minnie stopped wittering under the woman's withering glare.

The woman looked at Minnie territorially while she decided what to do, whether to escalate her complaint to management. 'Come on Orson, we're leaving,' she huffed finally.

'What about my ball?'

Orson looked at Minnie with a princely hauteur, as if she were his servant and he expected her to retrieve it for him before he would leave.

Minnie contemplated the man with the coffee stain on his shirt and wondered why he was still looking at her, perplexed, in the middle of his meltdown. For a brief, thrilling, microsecond, Minnie wondered if he might recognise her, before shaking her head.

That ship has sailed.

Jesse Lightning was in a slight trance, as if he were resisting the pull of a vortex he didn't have the energy to spiral into.

'Well?' Minnie asked. 'Are you going to let him have his ball back?'

Jesse stepped back to indicate 'Go ahead' and the boy put his grubby hand in Jesse's now-tepid coffee and fumbled for his ball, wiping it on his trousers.

'Fair dos,' Minnie said to herself.

The woman grabbed her bag, phone and son and left, turning and pointing to Kip and Steph as she stopped in the doorway.

'You'll be lucky if I ever come back!'

Minnie widened her eyes in a sarcastic *wow* expression, watched the mother and Orson leave, and then had another idea, as she turned back to Jesse.

'I have wipes!' she said helpfully, as she dashed to her bag in the window seat. 'Here, try these.'

Jesse was frazzled. Why was all this happening? Now? His face was hot. His shirt was stained. His crotch was wet. And he had a meeting with Maddie Feynman of the Fox & Feynman Literary Agency two streets north of *this* cafe of all places. He did not want more drama.

'Thanks,' he said, taking the wipes. He shook his head and mumbled, 'Little fucker,' under his breath.

'You can't say that,' Minnie gasped.

'I can.' He rubbed at the coffee, but it only seemed to widen and worsen the patch. 'But I shouldn't, I suppose,' he conceded.

'Here, let me get you another...'

Jesse looked at Minnie, puzzled. Why was this woman being nice to him when he'd just shouted at a kid?

'Nah I'm good thanks—'

Minnie didn't give him a chance.

'Kip, another...?' Minnie turned to Jesse as if demanding to know his order.

'A... a black Americano please,' Jesse said, unsure of himself, as Minnie went to the counter. 'Extra hot,' he mumbled, sheepishly, not sure this was a good idea. He'd already been scalded once.

Jesse sat back down and used the woman's wipes to clean his crotch under the table.

'And another Bondiga's blended iced coffee for me please, Kip.' Minnie waved her bank card.

'Don't worry about it,' Kip said with a smile that was halfway between pity and awe. He *did* recognise her. Kip's working days were always better when Minnie dropped in. 'It's on the house.'

'Oh, thanks!' Minnie smiled, pleased. Simple things, she remembered. Take the joy and the wins in the simple things. Free drinks. Free time. Space.

Minnie placed the coffee carefully in front of Jesse and sat down at his table without asking if it was OK. He glanced up as he finished with the wipe.

'Thanks, but you really didn't need to.'

'Oh I didn't pay for it.' She waved a hand. 'But, you know, "you're welcome".' Her laugh was slightly demonic.

Jesse studied the woman, getting a proper look this time. Her face was alarmingly beautiful. She had a short black bob with a cropped blunt fringe framing green eyes – a colour he couldn't put his finger on, it was so unique – and high cheekbones on pale, almost translucent skin. She looked like her face was her currency to getting her own way, although Jesse knew that wasn't true. No one always got what they wanted.

'Mind if I join you?'

'Looks like you already have.' He shrugged. 'I mean, sure... erm, it's just...' He looked at his watch.

Minnie carried on. 'My therapist recommended I meet new people. Go back to basics, be friendly, take leaps of faith. Just talk.'

Oh fucking hell. Jesse mentally rearranged his features, so he didn't look hostile. Too unapproachable. But he really didn't want to be anyone's therapy project and he really needed his meeting with Maddie Feynman to go well.

'Of course,' he said neutrally, gesturing to the chair the woman was already comfortably sitting on.

'I'm not crazy or anything,' she said, with a sparkle in her eye.

'Of course,' Jesse repeated flatly.

'Bad break-up. I'm seeing a counsellor who just suggested I meet new people. And, well, you're a new person!' Minnie said cheerily.

'Look, I'm...'

'Oh I'm not trying to hit on you by the way.'

'I wouldn't be interested if you were.'

They looked at each other in stony silence for a second.

'Charmed.'

'I'm sorry, it's just...'

'You're having a bad day.'

'I'm having a bad day.'

They said it at the same time and paused for a beat until Minnie broke the silence.

'Well, I've been having a run of forty-seven bad days and this week my therapist suggested I take action to end that run.'

Jesse liked the woman's exactitude, but didn't speak. He let her talk. He had a feeling she talked a lot.

'Get in touch with my inner child.'

Oh God. Jesse winced internally, trying to keep his face light. Minnie continued, in a low male voice that Jesse assumed was an impersonation of her therapist, except she made him sound like a geezer.

'"Ride a Chopper", "go runnin' in a field", "read a book you'd never pick up", "get out there and talk to people", "get off social media", "stop comparing", "stop adulting and go back to basics"...'

Jesse made a face as if to say that adulting *did* suck.

Minnie went back to her own, cheery voice.

'Just... talk and play, with the innocence and the joy that we had when we played as kids. No agenda, no beef.'

'Your therapist talks a lot for a therapist.'

'Well no, I talk at him and he gives me strategies.'

'Well, those strategies sound pretty sensible.' Jesse didn't want to sound like he was humouring her, but was aware he might be. They paused as she slurped her iced coffee through a paper straw that was already wilting and he inhaled the comforting scent of his coffee before taking a sip.

'Would you like to hang out and be friends?' Minnie asked, as she placed her drink down next to a brown paper napkin Kip had left on the table.

Jesse shuffled in his seat and glanced down at the coffee on his stomach. He winced apologetically and looked back up.

'I'm afraid I've got so much work... I have so much going on... I'm really...'

But her face was so earnest, her eyes so wide. Something about her made Jesse feel wretched. He put his hands up.

'I'm sorry, I'm an arsehole. I've just got the finishing touches to put to a presentation that's really important, for a meeting I have been trying to get for months, in just' – he glanced at the watch on his freckled wrist – 'in just half an hour, around the corner.' He looked exasperated. 'And I probably need to buy a new shirt first. I can't really be a good friend to anyone, or chat.'

Minnie looked downcast.

'Not since *fucking Orson* stitched me up anyway.'

Minnie forced a polite smile in defeat. She was becoming quite resilient when it came to rejection. She stood slowly and picked up her drink, leaving a dotted circle of condensation on the table, to return to her bag and book in the window chair.

'Fair dos. I'm sorry, I'll leave you to it. Good luck with your meeting.' She nodded, her smile fading as she turned away.

'Another time?' Jesse tried, not actually meaning it, and Minnie paused, almost paralysed, a flash of sadness on her face before she revived herself and said, 'OK!'

'OK good,' Jesse said politely, hoping there wouldn't be another time. He had no headspace for this.

'Let's play when you're not so busy,' Minnie said cheerfully.

'Play?'

'Yeah play.'

'Like a game? Like a boardgame?' Jesse frowned.

'No, let's just... play. Meet and talk. Like two kids at a park!' Minnie's idea was gathering pace, her enthusiasm returning. 'Do fun stuff. Hang out.'

Her sweetness was disarming and refreshing to Jesse, and perhaps she could have some answers for him, with all this therapy. Jesse's friend Andrew had recommended he see someone, although at the time it hadn't landed well.

'Erm, OK. I am pretty bus—'

'But rules. We'd need playtime rules. Tony would like that.'

'Who's Tony?'

'My therapist.' She said it as if it was obvious and then continued, planning out loud. 'Old school. No agenda. First names not surnames, fun and light. And we remember friendships used to exist *before* phones.'

'But Orson's mum just shouted out my name to the whole cafe, just to make sure I was barred.'

'Forgotten it already!' Minnie said happily.

Jesse doubted that – people rarely forgot his surname.

'Hang on, I need to write these down. Can I borrow your pen?' she said, nodding to the Sharpie next to Jesse's coffee-stained notebook. He handed it to her and she put her cup back down on the table and leaned against it, writing on the napkin in a blousy black scrawl. She wrote 'RULES' in capital letters and underlined it twice.

'Number one. First names only. No googling each other. There's no need for us to know anything more than what we decide to chat about, like kids in a playpark.'

For fuck's sake.

'Two. No exchanging of numbers. In fact, let's not rely on phones at all. People always make plans and then cancel them with a flimsy text. No tech. Just chat.'

Jesse didn't mind *not* giving this woman his number.

'Three. Do. Fun. Things.' Minnie said each word as she wrote it, and put three exclamation marks at the end. 'Like friends should do. Nothing taxing. I don't need taxing.'

'I don't either,' Jesse said, almost through gritted teeth.

'Sound good?'

She stood up straight and offered him the piece of paper.

I really don't need any more friends, Jesse thought. Except, as he thought it, he knew this wasn't true. He'd lost himself lately. His best school friend Will was talking about moving to America for love. His colleague Max was going through her own relationship difficulties. Just a few weeks ago, Jesse had nearly turned on the closest friend he had.

But this woman had a face he couldn't say no to.

He took the napkin.

'Deal,' he conceded, trying not to sound too unenthusiastic about it.

'Great!' Minnie smiled as she rose on the balls of her feet briefly. 'How about we meet on... Saturday? I'm not working Saturday.'

'I'm... erm... busy on Saturday.'

And then Jesse realised she had a face he couldn't lie to either.

'Actually I'm not that busy, I'm going to London Zoo, for research, but I was going on my own, so I could do some sketching.' He gently tapped his portfolio on the chair between them, making sure he covered his name with his palm, and remembered the time.

'Perfect! I'll meet you there! Say, 11 a.m.?'

Jesse felt like he didn't have much choice.

'Regent's Park, outside the main entrance?'

'Great,' he agreed.

'Oh, I'm Minnie by the way,' she said, extending a hand as she stood over him. He took it and she shook it effusively. 'Nice to meet you!'

'Hi Minnie, I'm Jesse.'

* * *

Jesse went to his meeting, where he impressed Maddie Feynman with his portfolio and she pretended not to notice the coffee stain around his navel. Jesse had an eager face she felt sorry for, she wasn't sure why, but his drawings and his ideas were beautiful. He didn't give Minnie another thought until that evening, when he was eating dinner with Andrew and Elena, and Andrew made a glib reference to their drug-taking past, which reminded Jesse of the bouncy ball with the smiley face on it. Then Orson. Then the woman from the cafe. But he kept it all to himself.

Minnie didn't give Jesse another thought until she was in the bath, writing in her journal, feeling proud of herself for having had a good day, learning about M-theory and superstrings, trying not to worry about work. And making a new friend. She made a mental note not to tell Tony that Jesse Lightning was handsome.

2

DAY ONE

Now

As Minnie walked along the leafy path of Regent's Park towards the entrance to London Zoo, she saw Jesse already waiting, one hand in his pocket, the other framing his eyes, as he gazed up to the sky as if he were looking for something among spring's cirrus stripes. He shielded his face from the glare of the sunshine as he took his phone out of his pocket and looked from the screen to the sky and back again.

'Hi, nice to meet you, I'm Minnie!' she said with a joke that belied and defied her nerves. She felt terribly anxious inside. This was a leap.

'Jesse,' he said, shaking her hand with his free one, conscious that his palm was warm.

'What you looking at?'

'Oh you know,' he said, infinitely less tense than he had been on Tuesday. Minnie could tell it from the softness of his shoulders. 'Just tracking something,' he added, casually.

'A planet?' she asked keenly. 'Did you see the moon move across Jupiter the other night? Five-per-cent-lit crescent moon. It was cool.'

Jesse looked at Minnie, puzzled. Was she an astronomer? He thought he'd seen a book about planets on her lap when he left the coffee shop with a polite wave.

He lingered for a perplexed second before answering.

'No, a plane. I have this cool app that shows you where all the planes in the sky above us have come from and where they're headed to, look...'

Minnie pulled in closer, relieved by how much more approachable Jesse was today.

'Lufthansa, going from Berlin to Chicago.'

He smelled fresh, of hair pomade and washing powder, giving Minnie a feeling of comfort, until she looked at his phone screen and winced.

'Makes me feel nauseous.'

'What makes you feel nauseous? My phone?' Jesse smiled. 'Is that why you said no phones?'

'No. Planes make me feel nauseous. Even thinking about them.'

'How come?'

'Oh you know... the crashes. The physics. How does a plane even get up in the air?'

Jesse raised an eyebrow.

'I know, I know, "science",' she said exasperatedly, using finger marks in the air.

Jesse smiled, slightly confused.

'Science is one thing, but sometimes you can't trust the universe. It can ruin everything.'

Jesse looked at Minnie and waited for an explanation, but it didn't come.

'Shall we go in?' she suggested, chirpily.

Jesse gestured to the entrance and took his wallet out of his bomber jacket pocket.

'Oh no! This is on me,' Minnie insisted. 'My idea. My shout.'

'Really?'

'For sure!'

They stood in the queue as the spring sunshine glittered through a vapour trail dotted in the sky and Jesse wondered what the hell he was thinking, agreeing to meet a stranger. A stranger with a freaky fear of aeroplanes, who was clearly going through something heavy, when he should be sketching on a quiet Saturday. He internally chastised himself for being shallow. Would he have agreed to meet Minnie if she didn't look the way she did? He was always drawn to what he deemed were good aesthetics. A cobalt and coral house exterior when he was travelling in Cartagena. A characterful hand-painted advert for a soda he'd never heard of on a roadside wall in Botswana. The packaging of a French luxury brand he had worked on, but whose clothing he couldn't afford.

Jesse cursed himself for judging her based on her beauty, as he put his wallet and phone back in his pocket.

'Let's do it!' she said cheerily, clutching two tickets as they walked through the entrance gate and into the zoo.

'Thank you,' he said. 'My turn next time.'

Minnie smiled to herself. Jesse was on board.

* * *

Minnie and Jesse walked self-consciously through the entrance gates and past a statue of Guy the Gorilla – that Minnie definitely would have suggested they sit on and pose for a selfie had they not just met – and past the gorilla kingdom, which was packed with young families.

'Are we sketching gorillas today?' she asked, looking for signs of Jesse's notepad and pencils in his Herschel backpack.

'No gorillas. My gorilla is already locked in,' he replied rather cryptically. 'I need birds mainly today.' He pointed the way towards an area he knew but Minnie clearly didn't. She didn't want to admit that in all her life living in London, she had never been to London Zoo. Her parents weren't keen on caged animals, and she couldn't even remember a school trip in the Rolodex of her memory. This was new and enchanting to Minnie so today she had her new and enchanting face on. It had been her standard issue resting face, until recently.

Minnie and Jesse were drawn to a lawn, where a birds-of-prey demonstration had just started to gather a crowd. They smiled politely at each other and silently agreed to join the group, who were watching a stout woman in green launch a tawny owl from her arm.

'Does anyone know how the flight of an owl differs to the flight of most other birds?' the zookeeper asked. A few people put their hands up and the woman pointed to a little girl next to Jesse. 'Yes?'

'They fly almost silently,' the girl lisped, almost silently herself.

'What's that?' the zookeeper asked. Minnie saw Jesse smile at the girl, encouraging her to speak up.

'They fly almost silently,' the girl repeated, a little louder.

'That's right!' the zookeeper said, into her microphone. 'And do you know how?'

The girl shook her head, looking like she knew, but was too shy to say so. The zookeeper explained to the group how the comb-like structure and velvety texture of owls' feathers in their wings dampen the sound of turbulence and flight, helping them hunt stealthily at night.

Minnie looked at Jesse as if to say, *wow*.

A pair of scarlet macaws, a toucan, a vulture and a harpy eagle all followed, with demonstrations and showboating from them all – apart from the vulture who seemed to be in a bad mood. Jesse needed to get a closer look at the scarlet macaws and made a mental note to find their enclosure afterwards. After some oohing, ahhing and cooing from the crowd, the zookeeper thanked the audience, asked them to support the zoo by signing up to become members, and the crowd petered out.

Minnie and Jesse smiled politely at each other before gravitating towards the owl habitat, where they ambled and stared into their cages. A great grey owl with a face so round and lined it looked like the shorn trunk of an 800-year-old tree, winked at Minnie with a piercing yellow eye. Minnie felt as if the owl were giving her a boost of encouragement.

Go on, you're doing OK. You're making a friend.

The owl kept staring, almost hypnotically.

'So clever,' she said to herself.

Jesse walked ahead, looking for the macaws, hands in his pocket as he watched an African eagle owl fly across its cage. He turned back to Minnie.

'Is it turbulence you're scared of? With flying.'

Minnie shrugged. 'I don't know, I've never flown.'

Jesse stopped in his tracks.

'What? Never?'

'No.' She laughed gently. 'My parents travel all over with work, so whenever they have down time, the last thing they want to do is get on a plane.'

'Really?'

'Yeah.' Minnie seemed surprised Jesse was surprised. 'When we went on holiday as kids, we went closer to home. Cornwall, Scotland or Ireland – both my parents are from Irish families, although they met in London.'

Jesse studied her. That made sense. Her pale, luminescent skin. Her black hair, its fringe so short it both framed her bright eyes while looking nervous to go near them. He could see the roots of her beauty as she tucked a strand behind her ear.

'We'd spend long summers in Galway, but always go by boat and car. Suited me!'

'And then... you just never?'

'Nope. By the time I was an adult and could go off on my own, I was too terrified to fly!' Minnie gave a laugh as if her fear were a wonderful and hilarious thing.

* * *

Minnie and Jesse meandered past a beautiful pink cockatoo, looking maudlin in its cage, which silently broke both their hearts, and then Jesse saw the macaws and peered in, taking photos on his phone.

When he finished he turned to Minnie, picking up where she left off. Jesse was the sort of person to mull over his words. He went at a slower pace than Minnie.

'That's actually quite impressive. Given what planes do to the planet.'

'It's cowardly, that's what it is. But I do sleep better at night for my footprint and all that.'

Jesse nodded.

'I have travelled beyond the British Isles. I'm not insular or anything. I went Interrailing with mates a few times. I've been island hopping in the Hebrides. Some beaches up there are more beautiful than the Caribbean, or so I've heard. I never felt like I was missing out.'

'No, that's brilliant,' Jesse said quickly. He didn't want her to think he was being judgemental, which he often was. 'Unless you ever let a fear of flying hold you back. If you ever did want to go further.'

'I'm good thanks.'

Jesse looked at her. Could a citizen of the world really get through modern life having never been on an aeroplane? She looked back and he raised an eyebrow, which she levelled with an explanation, not that she owed him one.

'Pan Am 1736 and KLM 4805,' Minnie reeled off, as she looked back at the macaws, who were squabbling on a branch in front of Jesse.

'What's that?'

'Worst ever plane crash, 1977. Well, worst after the Twin Towers.'

'OK...' Jesse wasn't sure where Minnie was going with this.

'Japan Airlines Flight 123, 1985; Charkhi Dadri mid-air crash 1996; Turkish Airlines 981, Paris 1974... I know too much now, I can't un-know this shit!'

'Shit, you really do. Maybe you need this app,' he said, wielding his phone before he put it back in his jeans pocket. 'You see that all those planes up there right now, they get to their destination without crashing! You know you're more likely to—'

'Yeah, yeah "die in a car crash on the way to the airport"... That just makes me nervous on motorways.' Minnie scrunched her face up and laughed. 'I don't drive either.'

'Wow, you are a catastrophic thinker,' Jesse observed, although she seemed to be rather jolly about it. Minnie nodded happily in agreement as they left the birds and headed towards Butterfly Paradise.

'So assuming you're not a truck driver or cabin crew or a pilot, what do you do for work? You said you weren't working today. Do you usually work Saturdays?'

'I'm an actor,' Minnie said, cautiously.

'Oh cool, what do you act in?'

'TV mostly. Well, TV *only*. A few ads while I was at college. Some voiceover stuff. Audiobooks. But I shot my debut series last year, an eight-part drama.' Minnie thought about the Marvel movie she'd auditioned for in February and how she was still waiting for a call back three months later.

'Will I have seen it?'

'Not yet you won't, possibly not ever. Legal wranglings.' She rolled her eyes. 'Something I don't understand between the author and the screenwriters. And scheduling wranglings with the networks. It's a shame because it was going to be fucking amazing. Big budget, from a bestselling book.'

'Wow, is it a book I'd know?' Jesse was intrigued.

'*Summer of Siena*?'

'Oh wow.'

He'd heard of it. *Summer of Siena* had been a global bestseller, possibly five years ago. He remembered seeing the stylish cover on the striped sunloungers at the beach in Antibes and liking the design. Jesse noticed book covers and liked the aesthetics of the beautiful ones; and loathed many. But he hadn't read *Summer of Siena*. Jesse was more into crime and thrillers.

'We started shooting this time last year, in Italy – I took the sleeper train – then we went to Norway – train and ferry – and shot studio stuff here. It was off the scale.' Minnie had the nostalgic look of someone reminiscing about happier times, longer ago than they were. A halcyon daze washed over her face.

Before.

'Well I hope they sort it out and the series gets aired. It sounds epic.'

'So do I. It was my big ticket.'

Jesse tutted in solidarity.

'But fair dos, it was a bit much to expect from my debut I suppose.' Minnie shrugged as she tucked her hands into her biker jacket. 'I went to drama school quite late. Tried to fight the calling with teacher training, but I couldn't hack it and dropped out in my NQT year.'

'Teaching is the hardest job in the world. My flatmate is a teacher.'

Jesse felt slightly disingenuous describing Elena as his flatmate.

'Although she left her classroom job to do private tutoring, it was so stressful in school.'

'I can believe it!' Minnie smiled ruefully. 'I left midway through my first year and arsed around, doing shop work and waitressing, which I did through drama school and still do. I call it my side hustle, but sadly acting is the side hustle.'

'Oh right. Whereabouts do you work?'

'Usually events. Corporate stuff.'

Jesse didn't go to many corporate events. He tended to go to creative events, art fairs and product launches. Minnie continued.

'I mostly work at parties or functions. You know, the faceless staff who walk round with trays of food...?'

Jesse nodded.

'No one sees us because they're too clenched about the canapés running out...'

'The canapé clench! I hate the canapé clench,' he confessed. 'The stress of it: "Will that tray come to me?" "Are those canapés the *one* food in the world I don't like?" Give me a proper burger any time.'

'Well there you go. Invisible me, contributing to your canapé clench!'

Jesse couldn't really imagine Minnie going under the radar.

'It pays the bills.' She shrugged, quietly embarrassed that she was privileged enough not to have to worry too much about bills.

* * *

By the time they got to the big cats and stopped to look at a beautiful tiger clawing at a tree, Minnie realised she had talked too much about the boring events she had worked at recently: a book launch, a *Eurovision* party, a construction industry awards ceremony, and cursed herself internally. She hadn't wanted to make a friend so she could talk at him about herself. She wanted to make a friend so she could show that she was listening to her therapist and taking his strategies on board. She wanted to go back to the innocence and happiness of her youth, when she'd felt comfortable in her skin and didn't even question whether she was good enough.

But this new friend was a little backwards in coming forwards. Jesse asked questions but didn't give much away about himself. He made her witter. She thought of what Tony might say if he could see them now, and tried to slow down her pace.

Deep breath.

'So what was your big meeting about? On Tuesday. What is it that you do?'

Jesse looked across at her. He wasn't an ogre, and nor was she. How hard could this be?

'I'm a designer.'

'Oh right.'

'Of numbers mainly,' he quickly clarified.

'What, like a maths whizz?'

Minnie pictured Jesse, a childlike version of himself making a guest appearance in his adult face. A prodigy wearing a bow tie, at one of those Rubik's Cube conventions where children beat world records and shock themselves as they press a buzzer to say 'Finished!'

Jesse laughed. He was not a maths whizz.

'No, graphic numbers. I design numbers and typefaces. In sport mostly. For football teams. Some branding. It's a bit niche...' He almost looked embarrassed, although there was no need to be. Minnie wore her enchanted face.

'I don't understand. Like, you come up with the number that a footballer will be?'

'No, that's the manager's job. I design the numbers, the typefaces, the fonts. So, say, Ronaldo wears a shirt with a number seven under his name. The style for that season, that font, that club, his name, his number – I might have designed it.'

Minnie frowned.

'I didn't realise that was even a job.'

'Well, someone does it! Although we don't get any credit for it. Not publicly anyway. It's just me and a few other designers around the world, either working for ourselves or agencies. I sort of work for myself.'

'But you get paid for it, right?'

Jesse laughed again.

'Yeah. I know the ethics of some sportswear brands are questionable, but I am paid. By the club or the organisation or the sportswear manufacturer or the brand. Whoever's commissioned me really.'

Minnie looked impressed.

'I have a little agency I run from a shared space near King's Cross. Just me and a friend from college. I do numbers and typefaces mostly. Sometimes I do product or packaging for brands but Max – my colleague – mostly focuses on that.'

Minnie sighed in awe.

'Well I have never met one of you.'

'I've never met an actor.'

Minnie shrugged. 'We're all actors.' She laughed to herself.

Jesse stopped and looked at the tiger, as he contemplated his own predicament. Was he acting too right now? Minnie continued.

'I will tell Tony that my new friend works in a whole industry I never knew existed or had given a second thought to. He'll be dead pleased.'

'You told him then?'

'Yep, saw him Thursday. I wanted a gold star. Which is half the problem. Sooo needy.' She shook her head and winced half in jest, as if it was one of her most unappealing traits.

'What did he say?'

'He said don't fall in love. I am absolutely not allowed to fall in love.'

Jesse stopped and leaned on the glass.

'Well you're safe with me. I am highly unavailable...' He peered through at a tiger cub rolling on its back as a heavy pause fell between them, and he reached for his camera phone again. Minnie looked at Jesse looking at the tigers and Jesse suddenly felt very aware of her eyes boring into him. He turned to her.

'I sound like a prick, don't I?'

She nodded. 'You do. But another of my therapist's recommendations is to look for the good in people. Like when we were young and not cynical, we would assume people were good like us, or thought the same way as us, you know?'

Jesse concurred, although he thought he might have been more suspicious of people than Minnie was as a child. She seemed like a nicer, more open human being.

'Tony told me to not assume people are pricks. So I'm not going to assume you are.'

'Thank you.'

'Shall we?'

* * *

They arrived at the Komodo dragon enclosure to see what looked like a prehistoric beast doing press-ups, its forked tongue darting out of its mouth every few seconds. Minnie put on her sunglasses and marvelled.

'What a creature!'

Jesse started taking pictures, crouching down to capture the contours of the side of its body; the ungainly gait as it propelled itself forward with its muscly arms.

Minnie watched him photographing the dragon, as if he were an exhibit too.

'So what was your meeting actually about, the other day?'

'Huh?'

'When I met you in the cafe. What was your big meeting? Number designs? Hey, did you ever design for Roy Keane? My mum and I both fancy Roy Keane.'

Jesse thought Minnie asked a lot of questions.

'He retired like twenty years ago! I'm old but I'm not that old.'

'I like an older guy. I mean – I'm the youngest in my family, I always hung around with older friends.'

Minnie thought of JP and felt sick.

Jesse raised a quizzical eyebrow before thinking it was best he got back on topic and returned to the reptile. He finished taking pictures and put his phone back in his pocket as he stood up.

'It was about something different from my agency work actually; you could call it my side hustle, I suppose.'

'Well, as you know, I am all about the side hustle!' Minnie sounded excited. 'What's yours?'

Jesse took a deep and contemplative breath.

'I was meeting a book agent. About an idea I have. Well, it's not really *my* idea.'

'Go on...'

'It's my dad's idea. I was hoping she'd want to take the book on and represent us, to try to get a book deal and get it published.'

'Oh cool. What's it about?'

'It's a children's book, set in a zoo. Paris Zoo.' Jesse looked at Minnie in the sunlight and paused, deciding whether to tell her more. She looked back with wide, encouraging eyes. 'My dad wrote it. He's more of a words man. I'm more about the pictures. So I was hoping to illustrate it, and, well, get it published.'

'Oh cool. Dream team!' Minnie said, but she could see a slight panic in Jesse's expression. 'Which is why you came to sketch...' She winced. 'I'm so sorry, I do have a habit of intruding. I don't have to stay long, I can leave you to it.'

'No it's fine,' Jesse said unconvincingly. 'I'll take videos and photos today, on my phone. I've got some in the bag already.'

'Guy the gorilla?'

'*Georges* the gorilla!'

'Cute.'

'There are specific animals I need to find, characters, but I need to re-read it first to be honest.'

Minnie studied Jesse's face. She had a feeling he wasn't being totally honest with her, and he wasn't. He knew every word of the book inside and out. But he didn't owe her an explanation. And now he was talking, she didn't want to interrupt.

'There isn't a Komodo dragon in the manuscript anyway.' He shrugged. 'Maybe I could add one in, it's very impressive.' They both observed the beast doing another set of press-ups.

'Have you ever published a book before?' Minnie asked.

'No, but I've been wanting to do something different for a while.' Jesse looked almost guilty for not braving it sooner. 'To put my design to different use. Have my name attached to a project for once. My name never appears on the football kits or fashion brands I design for.'

'You design for fashion brands too?'

'Packaging and typography, yes. The actual clothes, no.'

'I suppose Paul Smith packaging has to have Paul Smith written on it and not Jesse... there, I've forgotten it already!' Minnie laughed, not being totally honest either. 'So the meeting went OK then?'

'Yeah, Maddie, the children's book agent, she loves the concept and she's taken it on. She thinks she can find a publisher, once I come up with some more detailed illustrations. Something more final.'

'Oh, congratulations!'

'Thanks, I'm really pleased.'

'*Fucking* Orson didn't blow it for you then.'

'Nope, maybe I even have *fucking* Orson to thank for it. Getting me all hyped up and in the zone.'

'Doubtful.' Minnie rolled her eyes then looked around. 'This calls for a slushy.' She walked to the drinks stand next to the reptile enclosure where bright blue ice was whirring in a machine behind the counter.

'I'll get them.' Jesse nodded, ordering two and tapping to pay. 'But Maddie said the kids book market is pretty brutal if you're not already a celebrity.' Again he felt a flash of fraudulence, as if he weren't being entirely honest.

'It's like that with acting,' Minnie rued, thinking the same. 'But nice that your dad and you are working together.'

Jesse's throat tightened and he couldn't get any more words out, so he looked up at the sky again and quickly at his phone. BA 278 was coming into Terminal 5 in four minutes. A young man with curly hair put the frozen blue drinks on the counter and Jesse took a swift sip. It felt like reaching the sea after running on hot sand.

'Anyway, cheers!' Minnie toasted, raising hers and knocking her plastic dome into Jesse's. 'Congratulations on the book!'

* * *

As they sipped their slushies and meandered past the reptile house, a comfortable silence fell over them. Minnie finally relaxed into the quiet, stopping wittering and letting Jesse speak, if he wanted to. Jesse warming up and asking less superficial questions.

'How about you? Do your parents support your acting?'

'Oh totally! They're supportive of all of us.'

'"All of" you? Cripes, how many of you are there?'

Now Minnie held back, which was most uncharacteristic.

'I can't tell you much.'

'Why?'

'Because that would break the rules.'

'Why would it break the rules? Playground buddies talk about their families.'

She gave a sheepish look. 'It might give away stuff about me.'

'You're not a royal are you?'

Minnie laughed, her mouth blue if not her blood.

'No. But I *am* a queen.'

They slurped their drinks and paused to watch a snake uncoiling itself, as they both considered why Minnie had stopped slaying of late. Jesse dared to ask.

'So what – or who – was this ratbag who caused you to end up in therapy?'

'Well that was me, it was my doing really.'

'That sounds like you're being a bit harsh on yourself.'

'No I'm not saying it for a pity party, but I lost myself a bit. Forgot myself for someone not worthy of my heart.'

'Who were they?'

Minnie was surprised by Jesse's candour. Then a thought flashed across her mind as she looked at Jesse looking a little vulnerable himself. Might Tony disapprove of her using Jesse to help with her therapy? Maybe it wasn't fair.

'He was a he, and he was a shit really, but I'm only just coming to terms with it. It all happened pretty hard and fast.'

'Oh dear, I'm sorry.' The silence was more awkward now. 'I don't mean to pry.'

'No that's OK, I *always* mean to pry, I'm really nosy.' She smiled, before her face dropped to a frown. 'We met at a party, last December.

He was very impressive. A "Lord Business" type. Loved his car, loved the Cotswolds, we hooked up. He liked to brag about me at parties, that my show was going to be the next *Normal People*. He hadn't seen either *Normal People* or one scene of *Summer of Siena* – he hadn't read either book of course – but he kept bragging about me to his friends. Made me feel special.'

'Is he in TV?'

'No he's a restaurateur, owns a chain of "upscale fish restaurants" he called them, which made me laugh at the time. What does that even mean?'

'I guess it means he doesn't run a jellied eel caf in Peckham.'

Minnie laughed.

'No. Most of his "properties" are in Central London, Fulham, South-west London... he's opening one in the bloody Cotswolds.'

'What's your beef with the Cotswolds?'

'Oh, I don't know. Just that *he* went on about them I suppose. Bragging that he'd been to the Beckhams' place or Soho Farmhouse. I should have dumped him in the Cotswolds on New Year's Eve when I had the chance. Anyway, I didn't, and then he blindsided me. Said I wasn't so sexy when I was down. And then I went *really* down. Until I realised just how much I had lost myself in a short few months. Because of a "confident" man. Confident my arse. All small dick energy.'

Jesse frowned. He really didn't want to think about the guy's dick.

'He didn't even dump me for a younger, hotter, more successful model. Turns out he had about four of us on the go, and I was the most "disappointing". The one he let go.'

'What a dick.' Jesse shook his head.

'You know the worst thing?'

'What?'

'I was so dazzled by him, I felt fortunate to be in his company, to the point that I can see why I was disappointing. I would have stopped fancying me, being so... grateful and needy.'

'Well you're better off without him, smarmy fucking slug.'

'You know the guy?' Minnie joked, nudging Jesse on the arm.

Jesse knitted his eyebrows together in a frown. No, but he could picture him.

'Because that's *exactly* what he is,' Minnie confirmed. She thoughtfully drank the last of her slushy. 'Is my tongue blue?' she asked, sticking it out.

Jesse laughed. 'Very. Which means mine is too.' He stuck it out at her briefly, then blushed. 'There you go! You wanted to go back to the simple days. When we didn't know just how much chemicals and shit were in blue drinks...'

'Elephants and marmalade sandwiches!' Minnie mused, nodding to a solitary grandad with a young boy next to him, unwrapping lunch from a brown paper bag.

Jesse laughed and Minnie was serious for a second.

'Look, I'm sorry, you don't need to pick me up. I wanted you to be my friend. But you're a busy guy with a book to draw, so I'll leave you to it at the giraffes. Surely there's a giraffe in your book?'

'Genevieve.'

'Genevieve. She sounds lovely.'

Jesse's phone beeped in his pocket and he rushed to take it out. He looked up to the sky, and down at his phone.

Landed.

'So what *is* the one food you don't like on the canapé tray?'

'Huh?'

Minnie was very good at darting back and forth into conversations her friends had thought they had left.

He pondered his answer before making his declaration.

'Pallid mushroom vol-au-vents. They taste of cardboard.'

'Urgh, yeah, gross. I wouldn't mind if I never saw another mushroom vol-au-vent!'

* * *

They got to the giraffes and Minnie felt it was time to go.

'Look, I'm going to head off, you've got all these characters to draw and I'm just in the way.'

'It's fine—'

But she talked over him again.

'Who's the main character?'

'Huh?' he asked.

'What's the most important animal you need to sketch? Genevieve?'

'Remy. Remy the red panda. The book is called *The Amazing Adventures of Remy the Red Panda*.'

'Ahhh Remy! I love the sound of him already.' Minnie stopped at the map next to the giraffe enclosure and looked for red pandas on it.

'But they don't have them here. I went to Whipsnade Zoo a few weeks ago and sketched there. Today I need macaws, giraffes, penguins, elephants, zebra...'

'And what's Remy like?'

'He's nosy actually!' Jesse almost nudged Minnie back but stopped himself. 'A friendly little detective, solving the case of the stolen krill from the penguin enclosure, or the case of the zebra with the missing stripes.'

'Who turns out to be a horse...?'

'Plot twist! You got it,' he said with mock shock.

They laughed as Minnie drew her finger along the board, mapping her way to the exit. She tapped it twice.

'That's me. I'll head off and let you sketch.'

'You don't want to see the penguins?'

'Nahh it's fine. Penguins smell, I imagine. I'm outta here. Although...' She studied the board again. 'I have never seen an actual regular panda in real life.' Minnie narrowed her eyes as she scoured the map.

'No giant pandas here either I'm afraid.'

'What?'

'They don't have them at Paris Zoo either, and there isn't one in my dad's story yet, but I'm thinking of adding one in, you know, if it turns into a series. Maybe do one on a monochrome theme.'

'Ever the designer!'

'Yeah.' Jesse rolled his eyes.

'So how will you study a giant panda?'

'I'm going to have to use some artistic licence with that.'

Minnie looked shocked that such a rule could be broken.

'Google is my friend,' Jesse said mysteriously, as if he were giving away a trade secret.

'Well, there are like *millions* of videos of cute pandas on YouTube.'

'True. I would like to go to Edinburgh Zoo to see giant pandas for real. I read there are two up there. Only ones in the UK. But that's OK, I can take a trip one weekend. Anyway, my daughter won't forgive me if I see a giant panda without her.'

3

MINNIE

Six Months Ago – December

'Mushroom vol-au-vent or smoked salmon blini, sir?'

A man with thick fingers and wet lips picked up a small beige pancake with some anaemic salmon and a limp sprig of dill placed on top of it and sniffed.

'No disrespect, love...' he said, like a man who was absolutely about to be disrespectful. 'But you're catering an awards do for the restaurant industry and you're serving up this shit?'

Minnie was shocked. She was so used to being invisible at these events. Twirling and turning, her face obscured by a large black tray or a shiny silver platter. Ignored at work, when this summer, only a few months ago, she was filming in Norway and staying in an idyllic summerhouse on a fjord. Having a little no-frills fling with her co-star Dexter. Now she was at The Dorchester, on the restaurant industry's biggest backslapping night of the year, and someone was actually engaging with The Help, even if he was being rude. To Minnie's utter surprise she found the blunt man with a bullish face and a crinkled nose refreshing.

'Hey, don't shoot the messenger,' Minnie said, lowering her tray so she could look him in the eye. 'If it were up to me I'd be serving my granny's colcannon and beef stew. Artfully plonked on top of ridiculously small pancakes of course.'

The man liked Minnie's sass and held her eye. She wasn't tall but she was as tall as him.

'Now you're talking,' he said, licking his lips.

'It's stick-to-your-bones good,' Minnie said, as if she were passing on the recipe. 'None of this bollocks.'

She continued on her round as if she were mid-Viennese waltz and the man grabbed her arm with brazen fingers, his appetite whet.

Minnie wasn't sure what it was about the man. He wasn't as handsome as the German guy she had dated at drama school. He wasn't charming like the politician's son her parents had tried to set her up with. He was definitely not as sexy as her co-star last summer. This man was probably double her age and had chins that held anecdotes of excess and bonhomie, but he certainly had a spark about him. Maybe it was his confidence. Maybe it was the award he was clutching in his other hand, like an Oscar.

'Congratulations,' Minnie smouldered.

Minnie liked pretending she was someone different at these events. A spy or a mistress. A thief or a showgirl. When really, she felt completely split down the middle. Half of her felt proud to be grafting when she didn't have to; the other half of her was embarrassed that she, Minnie Byrne, daughter of Geraldine and Jeremy Byrne and part of the Byrne acting dynasty, was invisible.

'What did you win that for?'

'Best newcomer. Which is a bit of a joke at my age.'

'What's your restaurant?' Minnie held his gaze.

'Well it's a chain. First time a chain has won best newcomer, that's how fast we're rolling out.'

Minnie knew she was meant to be impressed by this, so she raised her eyebrows flirtatiously. Tonight she was pretending to be a call girl, even though she had no intention of sleeping with anyone.

'Will I have heard of it?'

'If you haven't, you will by tomorrow. We'll be all over the papers.'

The man's Essex accent sounded charming. 'Sexy Seafood. We're a chain of upscale fish restaurants.'

'What does that mean?' Minnie pictured a Japanese chef in a sleek commercial kitchen, massaging a fish's belly in a certain direction to bring out some kind of undiscovered, coveted flavour.

'It means it's fancy innit.'

Minnie didn't think this bolshy man's fancy restaurant would be as fancy as her best friend's understatedly fancy restaurant in Camden – in fact she was miffed Hilde wasn't here at all, but not many independents were. Although Hilde not being here did give Minnie a little freedom to do whatever the hell she wanted tonight. Maybe she would come back around again for this guy. She could do with cutting loose.

'Oh, right, fancy...' Minnie winked as she twirled into the darkness to carry on with her job. Thrilled to know that the man, tongue hanging out and little eyes spellbound, was watching her weave away.

4

JESSE

Six Months Ago – December

'Why are you upset?'

'What?' There was a brief and tense pause at the small kitchen table. 'Why am I upset?' Jesse was dumbfounded.

'No, sorry,' Hannah said quickly. She looked like she'd forgotten. Among the box files, folders and wine glasses, lit by the screen of the laptop she kept staring at, her face gave all the tells that she had, for a second, forgotten.

Hannah had been doing that thing Jesse hated but never pointed out: when she pretended to listen while stealing longing glances at the email she was partway through writing or the text she was trying to read. She looked away from the screen and up at her husband while she tried to suppress her resentment. She had a lot going on too.

'Look, if you need to go, go. I can ask friends to help.'

Jesse wondered who those friends might be. Hannah didn't have many friends out of work. All of the friends they'd made through parenthood were friends Jesse had cultivated. He had been the parent who was able to go to the baby groups, the sing and sign classes and the toddler jams around his agency work, while his co-worker, Max, had held the fort. It was impossible for Hannah to do all of the 'toddler treadmill' stuff, she called it, with her job and her busy life.

'I do need to go. I need to be with her.'

'Then go!' Hannah added a smile to downplay the undertone of snappiness, and stole a quick glance of her screen. 'I can call in favours for a few days. We had the twins over for a playdate a couple of weeks ago, I'm sure Andrew and Elena will help out.'

Jesse had had the twins over a couple of weeks ago. It was a playdate Jesse had managed. He had looked after Ida, Oscar and Fred one day in half term while Oscar and Fred's parents, Andrew and Elena, went to the West End to choose their wedding outfits. Jesse had taken the day off work so he could play Hungry Hippos, go to the park, and cook spaghetti Bolognese for three six-year-olds, before clearing up the chaos of the aftermath in their flat. Jesse had told Andrew and Elena to take as long as they needed, so they went to Randall & Aubin in Soho for champagne and oysters to celebrate outfits well-chosen and talk about their upcoming February wedding; plan their epic honeymoon to Australia. It was a rare day for them. Hannah had joined them at 8 p.m. after a corporate dinner nearby, and all of them had arrived back at the flat in an Uber at 10 p.m., the twins asleep on the sofa while Ida was in her bed.

'I don't think we can call in that many favours. I was thinking of going for a couple of weeks.' Jesse swept breadcrumbs off the kitchen counter as he spoke.

'What?'

Panic washed over Hannah's face. She didn't sort the breakfast chaos, the packed lunches or the school run. She didn't know the after-school club routine the way Jesse did. *He* had the luxury of working for himself and managing just one person in a shared space on Gray's Inn Road. He was his own boss and could fit his work around Ida. Hannah had fifteen direct reports and multimillionaire clients. This was the deal.

'How am I supposed to—'

'I'll take Ida with me, it'll just be a fortnight then I'll be back for... the service... and for Christmas.'

Hannah looked aghast. She took another sip of red wine while she processed it.

'You're going to go for two weeks? In winter?'

'France keeps running in winter, Hannah.'

'No but—'

Every summer since Hannah and Jesse had got together in their teens, she had enjoyed the ochre-hued buildings and the lavender-bursting fields of his parents' holiday home in the South of France – which had become his parents' permanent home when Jesse went off to university. But Hannah had never seen the Luberon valley in its stark-ness. The curved stone walls of the abbey at Sénanque looking heather grey under a cloudy sky. The dry brush of the lavender fields out of season. The boarded-up houses and cafes with signs saying *fermé*. Some-thing about Ida seeing the South of France in a new state, without Hannah knowing what it looked like, without being able to picture Jesse and Ida there so clearly, gave her a sense of panic. A feeling of being out of control.

'School will understand,' Jesse reasoned. 'Given the circumstances. What do they do in December anyway?'

Hannah's brow creased as she took another large sip from her glass next to the laptop. Jesse, standing, topped them both up. She looked back at her screen, trying not to read an email while Jesse tried to read her face. Then a wave of relief washed over Hannah's angular features. One that Jesse could understand. *This could work*. Hannah was good at making things work.

She softened as she realised she wouldn't have to feel bad about missing all the Christmas activities – the school play she didn't want to go to anyway. She could get as blotto as she wanted at all the dinners she was expected to go to. She could live free and not feel guilty about work taking priority, for one joyful fortnight.

'You can join us for the funeral, and we can all travel back to London for the service,' Jesse suggested.

That put a dampener on things. Hannah rearranged her features.

'OK.'

5

MINNIE

Now

Jesse Lightning... Jesse Lightning.

Minnie was so tempted to google him.

'No!' she whispered to her phone as she sat alone at a restaurant table in a lull between services. This was her game, her rules; it would be morally wrong to google him. It would give her an upper hand and Minnie liked to play fair and square and always had done. When Minnie's brother left his deck of cards on the table to go to the toilet, she wouldn't look, even if she were tempted. When she sat on her sisters and tickled them until they almost wet themselves: if they shouted stop, she would stop. When Minnie's best friend's boyfriend told Minnie in Year 10 that he liked Minnie more than his girlfriend and tried his luck, she told him to back off. 'If you don't tell Lotte, I will,' she had said to Matthew Mroz outside the chemistry lab. Minnie played fair and square. *Fair dos* was one of her most commonly used expressions.

So why hadn't Jesse said he had a daughter sooner?

Minnie's friend Hilde slid into the seat opposite, her chef whites grubby, and glided a plate from her palm into the space under Minnie's nose.

'Swiss kohlrabi, lacto fermented with wild blueberries and greens from the garden kitchen. Try it.'

Hilde was the five-foot-zero birdlike kickass chef at Alpine NW1, the restaurant she had opened with her brother Martin two years previously. The restaurant served thoughtful modern Swiss dishes on pretty vintage blue and white plates their ancestors had collected for a century, not knowing that their precious china would be used by AI engineers and UX writers over in London. Hilde was Minnie's flatmate, except she was rarely at the flat on account of breaking her back to serve the diners of Alpine NW1 their very beautiful, highly ethically sourced food.

'You're ridiculous,' Minnie declared, as she studied wafer-thin rectangles of vegetable, tinged pink at the edges from the pickling process, dotted with tiny trumpet chantarelles, blueberries, pea shoots, and pink and orange flower petals. 'This is too pretty to eat!'

And too small, Minnie thought, but she didn't have the heart to say. She didn't really understand this fine dining malarkey. Her mother regularly served her granny's recipes of boxty, coddle, barmbrack and hearty stews at their large family dinners in their large homely house at the top of East Heath Road in Hampstead. Minnie's parents were actors; three of her four siblings were actors, and Minnie had done everything she could to swerve and evade the inevitable. To do her own thing.

Rosie, Minnie's eldest sister, was a theatre actor. Lillia a stuntwoman. Caleb – the first boy and the middle child – was a data analyst, and Anthony, the next child from Minnie was currently a TV detective. Minnie, the youngest of the five children born into the Bohemian Byrne circus, had fought the calling to join the 'acting dynasty' they were often called in the press. She wanted a normal job like Caleb, which was why she'd done teacher training before her first school placement put her back on the path to the family business. Besides, acting was what Minnie was best at.

She'd had the whole auditorium in the palm of her hand as Miranda in *The Tempest* at school at King Alfred. She had dazzled as Maria in *West Side Story*, so much so that a Puerto Rican parent in the audience couldn't believe her accent wasn't her own; and after three years of study at Mountview in Peckham, with some TV ads and voiceover work in the bag, last summer Minnie had filmed her big-break TV drama, in London, Norway and Tuscany.

Hilde drew Minnie's phone away from her, so she could give the plate the full attention it deserved, and saw the name 'Jesse Lightning' in the Google box at the bottom of the screen. Search as yet incomplete.

'I thought you weren't going to—' Hilde stopped as she watched Minnie take a bite. They sat in silence while Minnie swallowed faster than she meant to and nodded in appreciation.

'Clever woman. Stunning.'

Hilde smiled.

'It could do with some—'

'Soda bread,' they both said in unison, Minnie giving an impish smile, Hilde rolling her eyes.

'Anyway I'm not searching him, I didn't press it, see? I was just tempted. For a split second.' Minnie narrowed her thumb and forefinger as if she were carefully forcing fighting magnets together. 'I just didn't expect him to have a kid.'

'Why not? You don't know the guy. You only met him on Tuesday, Min.' Hilde looked concerned. She had been worried about Minnie meeting a stranger at the zoo when Minnie explained the whole story to her, late on Tuesday night. Minnie had recently hit rock bottom. At the start of April she had spent an entire week in bed, crying, unwashed, sad. Lying on her side, staring at smudges on the wall, patches of newspaper fingerprints, wondering how they came to be on her bedroom wall. Hilde had come home from the restaurant one night and gone to check on her.

'What's the point?'

'What's the point of what, sweetie?' Hilde had asked.

'What's the point of trying.' It wasn't even a question.

Hilde had made her tea and toast and tried to get Minnie up, but she just lay on her side, staring at the wall. As Hilde ran Minnie a bath, she looked in the bathroom cabinet, and their usual shared stockpile of paracetamol and ibuprofen had disappeared. She found them all in Minnie's bedside drawer, decanted into a little bowl, like mints.

Minnie didn't get up and have the bath Hilde had run, she fell back asleep, but Hilde lay next to her all night, just to keep an eye on her. The next morning she called Geraldine and Jeremy, who came round, binned the medication, insisted Minnie take a bath, changed her bedding, opened her curtains and put in a call to Tony, a therapist their friends recommended after their son saw him for OCD.

What if the man from the cafe took advantage of that? What if he turned out to be a psychopath? He had shouted at a kid for no real reason.

So Hilde was especially glad to see Minnie alive now and assumed their London Zoo date that *wasn't a date* hadn't amounted to much, otherwise, why would she be in a closed restaurant at 5 p.m. and not having animal-inspired sex back at his flat?

Oh yeah, because he had a kid, apparently.

'And why wasn't he taking his kid to the zoo?' Hilde asked.

Minnie looked blank. She hadn't got that far. When Jesse had dropped his daughter into the conversation, Minnie had made an even hastier path to the exit.

'I know,' Minnie said. 'And it's *fine*. We're new friends, it *wasn't* a date. Why would he need to tell me he had a kid?'

'But he *did* tell you he had a kid.'

Hilde was very matter of fact. There was no messing with her. If her sous-chef Keenan hadn't plucked the pea shoots at the right point, she'd tell him. If a restaurant customer made a complaint on Tripadvisor, she would leave them a one-star review in return and call them out for being rude or awful diners. If Hilde didn't like Minnie's outfit choice, or boyfriend, or thinking, she would tell her.

'I know,' Minnie conceded. She just hadn't expected to be so thrown by it.

'I need to prep the Alpine miso,' Hilde said, as the not-terribly-Alpine soundtrack of three police cars and their sirens sped up the high street. 'Wanna help me?'

'Hmmm, I think I'm going to go home and do some journalling.'

'Good, you'll only distract Keenan if you stay. Get outta here.'

Minnie finished her plate and grabbed her biker jacket.

Jesse Lightning.

She shook her head as she left the restaurant, annoyed that she wanted to know everything about him and his bloody daughter.

Jesse Lightning

She shook her head as she left the restaurant, annoyed that she wanted to know everything about him and his bloody daughter.

6

JESSE

Now

Jesse walked into the corner office of the grand shared workspace building on Gray's Inn Road, through a glass Crittall door with a sign saying Lightning Designs on it in an abstract font. No thunderbolt on his logo. Too obvious. The ground floor office had just two desks, one looking out onto the hustle of the buses and people walking up the road to King's Cross or down the road to Chancery Lane; the other desk facing an exposed brick wall with a screen on it. There was a tiny round meeting table behind both desks, by the door. It was small but light and airy, made more so by the cascades of plants tumbling from rope hanging pots Jesse had attached to hooks in the ceiling.

He nudged the door with his shoulder as he carried two coffees in glass cups that were kept behind the bar marked 'Jesse' and 'Max' in black marker on cream masking tape, nodding a thank you to the barista as he opened the door.

'I got us both one,' Jesse said as he placed Max's regular flat white in front of her.

'Ah, thank you,' she said, gratefully hugging it with her hands. 'I was desperate but no one was in when I arrived.'

'Wow, you were early.'

Max looked a little flustered. Her face was usually a picture of seren-ity, her movements always slow and thoughtful.

'I wanted to get ahead on the GrowPots packaging this week,' she said, then took a grateful sip. This was only a half-truth. The whole truth was that she'd wanted to get out of the flat before her husband Liam woke up. He'd been at his worst all weekend.

Seeing Jesse, his kindness and his extra-hot coffee, was a cruel reminder for Max that it didn't have to be like that. Why was she putting up with it?

'Good weekend?' she asked, shifting the focus. 'How was the zoo?'

Jesse hadn't told Max that he was meeting a stranger at London Zoo because he thought it would sound weird and inadvisable in his situa-tion. That was his half-truth. They knew each other well enough to know when and when not to bother with all of it. When Max said Liam had had a heavy night, Jesse knew the subtext and would gently ask if she was OK. Max would usually say yes, even though she knew some-thing had to give.

Jesse and Max had met at college in Reading, on the same Graphic Communication and Design course, when Max had been getting a grilling from a particularly harsh lecturer about her work for a fabric softener brand they were inventing. Jesse had put his hand up, disagreed with the lecturer, and said he thought Max's design was great. It hadn't gone down well, neither with the lecturer nor Max, whose usually serene and smiley face was thunderous.

Max had scowled at him as they'd filed out of the tech room. 'I don't need rescuing,' she'd said, with a quiet shake of her head.

'No, but I could have done with some help,' Jesse had replied. His designs were being critiqued after Max's, and boy had the lecturer torn his work apart. Max hadn't stood up for Jesse, and then felt terrible about it. She had thought his work was exceptional, so she bought him a Coke and a panini in the canteen by way of a thank you and an apology. Six years later, Jesse started Lightning Designs, specialising in sports typography, and two years after that he employed his best girl friend Max to take on more of the packaging and product side of things. Max had been at Jesse and Hannah's wedding in Richmond Park; Jesse had been at Max and Liam's more recent wedding at Hackney Town Hall, but he'd taken Ida instead of Hannah because she was on a work trip.

'The zoo was good thanks. I didn't get as much sketching done as I should have.'

'Too weird without Ida?'

'Yeah,' Jesse said noncommittally, as he went to his desk with three big computer monitors on it, with photos of Ida dotted around the screens' edges, slumped into his seat and sighed. 'Everything is too weird without Ida,' he said sadly. Max's eyes almost filled up.

'Want to talk about it?' she asked, taking another sip of syrupy coffee.

'No.' Jesse smiled gratefully. 'Do *you* want to talk about it?' It wasn't often he raised the elephant in the room. How Max's honeymoon period had been anything but. How she seemed to want to spend more time in the office than she did at home. She shook her head gently and swivelled her chair back to the drawings in front of her.

Jesse put the radio on and awoke his screens to remind him what he had been working on before the weekend. Before he'd thrown himself into *Remy*, the zoo, and the crazy lady from the coffee shop.

A football kit. A brand story. A mission statement. A club that had just been promoted to the Premier League. His comfort zone. His happy place.

He looked at one photo of his daughter, pinned to the screen in the middle. Golden brown curls, blue eyes, cheeky face.

Deep breath.

7

DAY TWO

Now

'Nice to meet you, I'm Minnie!' Minnie said, with an ebullient handshake as she arrived outside what looked like a warehouse that might have once been a bingo hall. If it had, it was now being turned back into a bingo hall on the first Saturday of every month.

'Good to meet you, I'm Jesse,' Jesse said, confused but going along with it. It wasn't that funny, but Minnie delivered her sort-of-joke so wholeheartedly and enthusiastically, he relaxed into her hearty greeting.

'Are you feeling lucky?' she asked.

'Not really.'

'Great! Let's do it!'

Minnie and Jesse walked into the venue like the couple at the Oscars who were too cool to dress up. Or like they hadn't got the memo. Or like friends on a Saturday afternoon, because they definitely weren't a couple. Minnie was wearing her leather biker jacket over a short floral dress and ankle boots; Jesse wore neat jeans and a bomber jacket with an elasticated neck. All around them, women, men and drag queens were dressed to the nines in confections of gold sparkles, silver sequins and gunmetal lamé. The room was positively bursting with flammable clothing, dotted with people wearing sparkly cowboy hats, feather boas and fake tiaras.

This was not what Jesse was expecting at a Mile End bingo hall at five o'clock on a Saturday afternoon, so they scanned their tickets with the bouncer and made a beeline for the bar. They leaned up against it side by side as Minnie picked up a drinks menu on a laminated sheet of A4.

'How did you hear about this?' Jesse asked as Minnie studied the cocktail list. 'And *why* didn't you tell me to wear something a little... jazzier?'

Minnie laughed, half in apology, half in excitement.

A man resembling Jay-Z wearing a full tux and sunglasses walked through the room to a small cheer and weaved through the audience, greeting people with slaps on the back and fist bumps, as he headed to a stage at the front of the hall. The place looked more like a community centre than the Kodak Theatre.

'My sister Rosie came here on a hen do, said it was hilarious,' Minnie said as she looked from the drinks menu to the room.

'It is,' Jesse laughed. 'I just feel woefully underdressed.'

'You're all right,' she reassured him. 'Fair dos, we weren't to know.'

Jesse was one of the few men in the room without make-up, glitter or dripping in jewels and he felt terribly self-conscious.

'What are you having?' he asked Minnie urgently.

The bingo hall was buzzing with hen parties and groups of friends arriving to celebrate thirtieth birthdays, fortieths and possibly a seventieth judging from a group of golden girls at the front. A heavily pregnant woman was celebrating her baby shower, and she looked like she might give birth at any moment. All these people had one thing in common, they were coming out for Beyoncé Bingo on an early summer's evening in a grimy hall. The game where you 'slay all day', according to the poster outside – well, from 5 p.m. to 10 p.m. anyway – and prizes included anything from a Beyoncé mug to a bottle of champagne. And cash of course.

'What shall I go for? A "Bloody Becky" or a "Long Island Iced Tease"?' Minnie pondered.

'I'll get one of each,' Jesse declared. 'See which you like the look of best – I'll have the other.'

'Thanks.'

'And a beer please?' Jesse added to the barman.

Minnie studied Jesse's profile as he ordered. His golden stubble lit by cheap lighting. His sincere face and light eyes studious as he flipped the menu over and looked at the back. 'Oh and a basket of Houston Fried Chicken, right?' he asked Minnie. 'Or are you veggie?'

She waved a hand.

'Bey's favourite? Count me in.'

* * *

The man dressed as Jay-Z stopped at a piano on the stage and lifted the mic.

'I got ninety-nine problems...' he teased as he stroked the curves of the ball machine on top of the piano, and looked at the audience over his sunglasses. Pockets of partygoers cheered. 'Actually I got ninety in *my* cage.' He gave the balls a spin.

Minnie laughed as the barman pushed their gaudy looking cocktails, complete with plastic pink flamingo stirrers, towards them. She picked a cocktail up at random; Jesse lifted the other and his bottle of beer.

'If you take a wooden spoon, someone will bring your food over,' the barman said.

'Great, thanks.'

'Come on, let's find some seats!' Minnie said eagerly.

Jesse had a feeling it was going to be a wooden spoon sort of night as Minnie hurried away and he followed in her wake. She was going so fast he had to be careful not to spill any of his cocktail. Minnie turned around and looked at him and he had this strange feeling of being in a ridiculous, hopeless place, with someone who was so open to it, he laughed quietly to himself. Her enthusiasm was infectious.

'Here!' she said, grabbing them a spot between two big groups. They sat side by side facing the stage, squeezed in, and looked at the cards and dabbers in front of them.

'Are we gonna win big tonight?' Minnie smiled.

'No,' Jesse said.

'Fair dos. But you gotta have faith that the balls will roll in our favour.'

The lights dimmed, Jesse and Minnie sipped their drinks – Minnie content with the Bloody Becky she had landed – and 'Gay-Zee' introduced himself while he rapped something about liberté, égalité and Beyoncé, and explained the rules of Beyoncé Bingo (much the same as regular bingo but with different calls: eighty-eight would be 'two curvaceous queens' in *this* bingo hall). Gay-Zee then called for the lights to be dimmed further, and the raucous cheers to rise, as he introduced his better half, 'Bingoncé', who would get the balls rolling.

A stout and stunning woman in a gold fishtail dress sashayed on stage to 'Crazy in Love' and rapturous applause, revellers getting up on their feet to the blaring horns and sass. Many of the crowd had clearly been before and knew the drill.

'How y'all doin'?' Bingoncé said as she started singing. Kent tones pushed through her Texan accent; her smoulder more Broadstairs than Bel Air. But Bingoncé and Gay-Zee made such a dazzling couple, Minnie and Jesse could not stop smiling in awe. 'Get up and join me!'

Minnie stood up and started dancing alongside the women next to her, arms in the air.

'Come on you!' she said, raising both hands in a motion to tell Jesse to get up. Jesse slowly and self-consciously got out of his seat and joined her, although his movements were more of an awkward sway than Minnie's gay abandon, dancing as she looked at the performers on the stage. He really needed to drink, and quickly.

'God this is funny!' Minnie said, clutching her middle as she turned to Jesse.

He nodded cautiously.

'I mean, we're stood here like two idiots on a Saturday afternoon – and I'm not even drunk! When you've probably got better things to do!'

They both thought about his daughter, Jesse knowing every freckle on her face; Minnie not even knowing how old she was.

The whole hall was dancing to 'Crazy in Love', even the golden girls at the front.

'Sit down, sit down y'all!' the queen commanded at the end of the track. 'Put on your sitting britches, bitches, and have yourselves a drink. I'll be back to get these balls rolling in just a coupla minutes...'

Bingoncé sashayed off.

Minnie sat down and saw the relief on Jesse's face as he sat too and slurped his Long Island Iced Tease.

'I'm sorry, you don't look like the sort of guy to drink silly cocktails from a plastic glass...' she said as she flicked the flamingo.

Jesse took a big sip.

'This is actually quite nice,' he said, appraising it. 'Who knew?'

Minnie laughed.

'I mean, I'm not one for audience participation so she'd better not get me up on stage...'

'Don't worry, I don't think she will.' Minnie looked around at all the people who would catch Bingoncé's eye before she would land on Jesse, and then felt a bit guilty. 'But you know, you gotta be game, roll with the punches... If she calls you up, then you need to get up there and do a kitty-kat crawl or a lick lick lick.'

'What the fuck is a kitty-kat crawl and a lick lick lick?'

'Little Beyoncé dance moves. I'd demonstrate them for you, but I need more cocktails.' Minnie looked around. 'And I need more space.'

Thank fuck for that, Jesse thought, then *he* felt a bit guilty.

'Give way to Bey, Jesse!' Minnie joked, hitting him on the arm, as if she could read his mind. 'The risk of being pulled up on stage is part and parcel of being in the presence of that *amazing* dress I'm afraid. Lighten up! It's going to be fun.'

'I guess...' He shrugged.

'Anyway what's the worst that can happen if she does call you up?'

Jesse frowned.

'Yeah, I don't like the stage the way I think you like the stage.'

'You might love it.'

'I doubt that.'

'A bad thing can turn into a good thing, I know that.'

Jesse's brow crinkled. He didn't really think that was true. Some terrible things had happened to him in the past six months, and he struggled to find a single good outcome in any of them.

'The night I met JP and had a doomed relationship? Bad. Making a new friend in a cafe because JP landed me in therapy? Good! Tenerife 1977? Definitely bad. Never flying because I'm too scared? Good and freeing in many ways.'

Jesse frowned again, more playfully this time.

'Beyoncé Bingo, well hopefully it's going to be good, I have a feeling...'

'Or maybe it's going to be so bad it's good?' Jesse offered cynically.

'Yes!' Minnie clapped her hands together excitedly.

Jesse took another long sip of his Long Island Iced Tease and put it down on the plastic tablecloth.

'Anyway what happened that was so bad in Tenerife? Apart from my first lads' holiday...'

Bingoncé returned to the stage and started singing 'Irreplaceable', her final number before 'eyes down' she had said, and started shimmying towards the ball machine.

'Tenerife 1977? Did we not talk about that at the zoo?'

'Well...'

'Worst ever plane crash.'

'Twin Towers aside,' Jesse said, quoting Minnie, who looked briefly impressed. He had been listening.

'The Tenerife airport disaster of 27 March 1977... *Everything* conspired that day.'

'Like what?'

'Two Boeing 747s collided on the runway. A KLM flight was trying to take off while a Pan Am plane was still taxiing. Everyone died in a fire on the KLM, only sixty-one survivors from the front of the Pan Am made it out alive. Almost six hundred people died – the deadliest incident in aviation history. Until—'

'Until the Twin Towers,' they both said in unison.

'But you know what the weirdest thing about that day was?'

'Not just the highly unlikely chance of disaster... which hasn't happened on a scale like that in nearly fifty years...?'

Minnie smiled as if to say, *I know I know, I'm ridiculous*, but carried on, her momentum gaining pace.

'Neither plane was meant to be there!' She looked as if she'd just delivered an awesome card trick.

Jesse looked blank.

'A terrorist bomb set off by Canary Island separatists had exploded in Gran Canaria, so all these flights had been diverted to Tenerife.'

'Well isn't that even more reason to believe in the safety of aviation? Neither plane suffered jet failure nor malfunction. No broken wing or bird in the engine. It was just pure and simple shitty circumstances, like terrorism, or a depressed co-pilot. The likes of which are so miniscule.'

Minnie's eyes widened in horror.

'Does that not make it easier for you to get on a plane?'

Jesse obviously had no clue, Minnie thought.

'Japan Airlines Flight 123?'

'What?'

'That was "structural damage" causing 520 deaths. Second most deadly aviation incident caused by technical failure. And it was crazy circumstance.'

'Oh God, do I want to know?'

'You *should* know, Jesse! Might make you think twice about flying. August 12 1985. The plane was flying from Tokyo to Osaka when the tail broke off and it crashed. But – get this – the crash was later found to be down to an incident *seven* years earlier, when the tail was damaged coming in to land at Itami Airport, and it wasn't repaired properly.'

'So what's your point? Other than never get on a plane. Or maybe stop reading up on this stuff.'

'My point is a positive one actually...' Minnie said it pedantically. 'Tony says all this is out of our control. A bomb could go off on another island or a tailstrike repair could come unstuck. You have to just roll with it. Good *and* bad. And try to find the good where you only see bad. Lots of things led me to working that event where I met JP. I might have been filming. Or going to a friend's birthday party. I had no plans, so I worked a crappy event at The Dorchester where I met a man who managed to unravel me within a matter of months.'

'So what's the good in that?'

'I met you, didn't I?' Minnie said it so sweetly, Jesse looked at his lap and smiled. 'And I am learning from it. I am learning not to ever forget myself. To remember my worth. To find the good in the bad, and to not sweat all the cosmic stuff I have no control of.'

'Wow, your therapist is gooooood.'

Minnie smiled proudly, as if she had just passed a test.

'So why don't you do it? Take a holiday further afield. Prove you can. If you have to give in and submit to the universe... book a flight!'

That reminded Jesse. He awoke his phone. The flight he was tracking was halfway to Lahore.

Minnie's shoulders slumped again.

'It's just all so... well it's so brutal when you're talking about a disaster in aviation. Or heartbreak.'

'I guess...' Jesse said, as he put his phone to sleep again.

'Why do you look at all those planes anyway?' Minnie shout-whispered, as Bingoncé hit the vocal gymnastics on the last note, took a bow to huge applause and whistles, before an excited hush fell over the room.

Jesse didn't answer. Instead he studied his card to familiarise himself with his numbers, and picked up a dabber.

'Good luck!' He smiled.

* * *

'Number thirteen, Galentine's Day...'

'Seventy-three, Queen Bee...'

'Two curvaceous queens... eighty-eight!'

'Sixty-eight, "Amazing Grace"...'

'Twenty-two, two little twins...'

The pace of Beyoncé Bingo was as fast as the woman herself, and Jesse's red splodges were landing on the card in an aesthetically pleasing formation.

'Look!' he said, nudging into Minnie. 'One more and I get a line!' He looked pleased with himself, then glanced at the card of the woman on the other side of him. She didn't have as many red splodges. This *was* fun.

'Hang on—'

'Eighty-two, "Déjà Vu",' called Bingoncé.

'BINGO!' bellowed Jesse, taking himself by surprise as he punched an arm in the air. Everyone in the hall turned to look in his direction, surprised by such timely success.

'I've got a line!' he called, and looked around at a room full of blank faces. 'Do you get something for a line?' he asked Minnie under his breath, now self-conscious as the atmosphere had gone so steely.

'Ooh, we have a winner, that was quick!' Bingoncé cooed. 'Stand up, honey, let me see you...'

Jesse looked around and stood up gingerly. Minnie looked up at him, ignoring the golden hair on his taut stomach where his jacket and T-shirt had risen up.

'OK, baby, read out your numbers please and Gay-Zee will check them back...'

The woman's American accent was waning.

'Five.'

'Uh-huh.'

'Thirteen.'

'Yeah.'

'Thirty-five.'

'Correct.'

'Sixty-eight.'

Gay-Zee nodded.

'Twenty-two...'

'And...?'

Jesse looked at his card and up again, his cheeks starting to burn.

'That's it.'

'That's it? Honey, I said we playin' for a full house.'

Quiet ripples of relief and laughter rolled over the bingo hall.

'We don't do lines here, do we, baby?' Bingoncé said.

'Nuh-uh.' Gay-Zee shook his head sanctimoniously. The audience chuckled.

'Oops,' Minnie said through gritted teeth. She gently tugged Jesse's sleeve, beckoning him to sit down.

'Sit ya handsome ass down, honey, and let's stop stealing my spotlight, huh?' Bingoncé said, eyeballing Jesse flirtatiously.

There was a raucous cheer – the game wasn't over.

'Sweet dream or beautiful nightmare?' Bingoncé pointed and winked at Jesse. 'Take a bow, honey, let's get on with the show.'

The crowd cheered louder and Jesse took it on the chin, turned to face the majority of the room, and took a humble bow before plonking himself down, his face tomato red. Minnie patted him on the arm.

'Don't worry,' she whispered. 'I'm sure it happens all the time!'

Jesse took a hearty swig of his beer and the game continued. A basket of Houston Fried Chicken finally arrived, and when a woman at the back of the hall later shouted 'BINGO!' she *was* a winner.

'Fair dos, never mind buddy,' Minnie consoled, as they each stabbed popcorn fried chicken with a wooden fork. 'Two more cards, two more chances to win.'

Jesse loved Minnie's optimism.

* * *

At the break a drag artist called Queen B came on stage and sang 'If I Were A Boy', while Minnie went to get Jesse another beer and herself a gin lemonade, sips of which helped her ask the question that had been hovering at the front of her mind but the back of her throat since they arrived.

'So what's your daughter's name? How old is she?' Minnie asked, as she straddled the bench and sat back in, placing Jesse's beer in front of him. 'I can't believe you didn't tell me you were a dad!' She internally cursed herself for sounding weird about it, when she absolutely wasn't weird about it.

'Should I have done?' he asked with a smile.

'We're mates, I'm intrigued!'

Jesse's face lit up as if he were pretty intrigued too.

'Her name is Ida. She's seven.'

'Ahhh, Ida. Beautiful name.'

Jesse's face dropped a little. 'She lives with her mother, in our flat in Kentish Town.'

'Oh, Kentish Town, that's near me!'

'I have her every other weekend – which is why I can't easily meet on a Saturday.'

As Minnie had hastily left Jesse at the zoo two weeks previously, and suggested Beyoncé Bingo, they had agreed that meeting fortnightly might suit the rhythm of their diaries. It was only twice a month, Jesse figured. He could commit to twice a month for a few hours while Minnie needed to do what she needed to do for her therapy project.

'Oh, you're divorced?'

'Separated,' he replied swiftly.

'How long have you been separated?'

'A few months. Just a trial thing though, while we work out what we want.' As Jesse said it, he wondered why he was lying. What difference would it make? 'I'm staying with my mate in West Hampstead for a bit.'

'My parents live in Hampstead!'

'Nice. You grew up around there?'

'Yeah.' Minnie nodded, but she didn't want to make this about her. She wanted Jesse to finally open up. 'So who's your mate you're staying with? Is that the teacher?'

Minnie had noted when Jesse referred to his flatmate as a teacher that *she* had left the classroom to do private tutoring. Perhaps the flatmate was a new girlfriend.

'Yeah Elena's a teacher. A private tutor now though. I'm staying with her and her husband Andrew. And their twin boys. They're the same age as Ida. We met through Ida actually, when they were all babies.'

'Ahh nice.'

Jesse made a face.

'Not nice?' she countered.

'It's pretty fucking soul destroying actually, living with kids who aren't yours.'

Minnie's pale nose crinkled. 'I bet. So what happened?'

'Just a rough patch, you know... baby comes along and you don't have a proper conversation for seven years.' Jesse said it so vaguely as if it wasn't really happening to him.

Minnie didn't know what it was like. There had been five kids in her childhood and her parents always seemed to be talking. It was a happy, vibrant and loving home.

'What's she like?'

'Hannah? Or Ida?'

Minnie couldn't help but bristle at the name Hannah and she didn't even know why. Hannah might be the nicest woman in the world and Jesse might be a shit husband or an awful father. He didn't give off that energy though, despite first impressions.

'Your daughter.'

'Ahhh she's amazing. Coolest kid I know. Gorgeous – of course. Obsessed with marsupials. Can tell you any fact about any Australian animal you could ever want to know.'

'Ooh does she know about quokkas? Those funny animals people take smiley selfies with? I see them all over Instagram.'

'She has a quokka calendar on her bedroom wall.'

'Cool!'

'Yeah, she wants to go to Australia – now *that's* a flight.'

Minnie winced.

'The twins, Andrew and Elena went to Australia a few months ago, brought Ida back a cuddly wombat. She loves it so much, she takes it everywhere.'

Minnie smiled at the sound of it, at the look on Jesse's face.

'It took the edge off her friends going to Australia while she had to stay here and go to school.'

'Well she sounds intrepid.'

'She is. She wants to go to Nepal. I don't think I'd heard of Nepal aged seven.'

'I definitely hadn't! She's a smart cookie.'

'She wants to be a red panda when she grows up actually, although that's ambitious.' Jesse winked at Minnie, and she felt a strange and surprising crackle inside, which she buried, while he continued. 'My dad said Remy the red panda was inspired by Ida.'

Jesse smiled to himself and smoothed out the next bingo card in front of him.

'And Hannah? Is she a flight attendant? Or a pilot? Is that why you're always on that tracker?'

'Hahaha no!' Jesse measured his features. 'She's an accountant. She had – she has – a proper job. Number crunching with CEOs and CFOs and all that stuff.'

'Wow.'

Queen B left the stage and a group from a hen party were crowding around Gay-Zee as he started tinkling the notes of 'Empire State of Mind'.

Minnie studied Jesse. She had a thousand questions a mate would ask a mate, but for some reason, none of them could make their way from her brain to her mouth. For once, Minnie Byrne had clammed up. She stopped talking, stopped wittering, stopped asking questions. All of a sudden it felt like it was a no-go area and too intrusive. So she changed the subject.

'Ooh, I have cool news!'

'What's that?'

'I have an audition at the end of the month. In Paris. For a movie!'

'Wait, what? That's like *three* really cool pieces of news. Take me through them, one at a time.'

'Well Devon – my agent – he's got me an audition after a bit of a lean few months, so it's great, but I feel out of practice.'

'You'll be awesome I'm sure.'

Minnie nodded. 'It's exciting. It's at a hotel in Paris. Wim Fischer is directing.'

'Wow, Wim Fischer? That's so cool.'

'I know right? He's on the junket juggernaut promoting his new film, so his casting director and he are having meetings for his next movie while he's in Europe.'

'That's incredible Minnie. Congratulations!' Jesse raised his bottle and Minnie met it with her gin lemonade.

'And I don't have to fly, just out and back on the train in a day.'

'Even better!'

'I probably won't get it of course.'

'Of course,' Jesse joked.

'But getting the audition is the first hurdle.'

'It's amazing. Well done.'

Minnie looked as if it was no big deal, even though she knew it was.

'What's the role?'

'Her name is Veronica Valla. She's a cocktail waiter by night and an assassin by... well, also by night. She's part of this European organisation of spies blah blah blah but she's kickass and I'd love to play her.'

Jesse suddenly noticed a very kickass sparkle in those green eyes of Minnie's.

'Well...' he said with consideration. 'I think you've already nailed it.'

Bingoncé came back on stage singing 'Cuff It' before calling eyes down for a second round and Minnie increasingly felt, with every sip of gin lemonade, like fucking up the night.

8

DAY TWO

Now

'Come on, let's go celebrate!' Minnie said, clutching a manila envelope of cash and a bottle of Sainsbury's prosecco she wasn't *entirely* sure Mrs Carter would drink. Minnie had won big on the third game, bellowing 'BINGO!' ten times louder and prouder than Jesse mistakenly had.

They walked through Mile End Park, appreciating the early June chill after having danced to 'Survivor', getting sweaty at the end of the night. Jesse had had little choice in dancing after one of the women in the fortieth birthday group dragged him to his feet. He'd looked terrified, but survived, and Minnie rescued him by joining in. The blast of air now made him slow down as they got to Mile End Tube.

'You know I can't,' Jesse said, slightly relieved he had a genuine out. 'It's the twins' birthday tomorrow – my friends' kids – so I said I'd help prep the party. Ida's coming.'

Oh, boring! Minnie wanted to sing.

'Nice,' she said instead.

'Yeah it's a bit of bonus time on a non-Ida weekend.'

Jesse looked genuinely excited and Minnie suddenly realised how different their lives were. That perhaps a forced friendship with a temporarily single dad wasn't the best idea.

'Ahhh that's sweet,' she said, as enthusiastically as she could muster. 'I should probably get home anyway, start looking at the script for my scene.'

'Paris calls,' Jesse said hopefully.

There was a slight awkwardness, a mutual deflation in the air, as they made their way down the stairs to the platform to head back west. A train was already in the station, which gave them a distraction, a reason to rush. They made it and sat next to each other on tatty upholstered seats while the train doors beeped and the tube left the station.

'My mum lives in France,' Jesse said, breaking the impasse.

'Oh cool, Paris?'

'No, in the south.'

'With your dad?'

The noise of the train rose, howling through tunnels and the open window at the end of the carriage, as the tube raced through London's Saturday night underworld to Stepney Green. The sound hit the carriage like a scream, a muffler, which gave Jesse the freedom to say what he hated saying out loud, as loud as he could manage.

'No, my dad... my dad died.'

Minnie looked at Jesse sharply, glad the screech of the tube on the tracks silenced her gasp.

'I'm so sorry.'

She sat examining Jesse's face while he stared at an advert for well-woman vitamins above the heads of the passengers opposite. 'How long ago?' She wanted to put her hand on his arm but couldn't now. She suddenly had a horrible feeling. 'It wasn't a plane crash was it? Oh G—'

Jesse shook his head.

'No. It wasn't a plane crash.' He gave a brief and rueful smile. 'It was a common-or-garden-variety heart attack. He was in his garden, actually, in France.'

'Oh no.'

'He loved his garden,' Jesse said, as if it made it easier.

'When did he die?'

Jesse cleared his throat as the howl in the tunnel quietened. It was hard enough to say it to Minnie, he didn't really want the other passengers in the half-empty carriage to hear too.

'Early December. Before Christmas. He was putting pots away for the frost and... he just fell down, in his greenhouse.'

'Last Christmas gone?'

He nodded.

'That's only six months ago,' she said quietly. 'I'm so sorry.'

Jesse smiled as if to say thanks, because he couldn't speak. The tube stopped at Liverpool Street and more people got off and then on. Neither Jesse nor Minnie noticed a single thing about any one of them.

'What about the book?' Minnie asked.

'Well, this is the reason I need to get on with it. My dad wanted me to draw it when he was alive, but I was so caught up in work and Ida – and Hannah...' He shook his head. 'I always pushed the book project to the bottom of my to-do list. I thought my dad was immortal – he was always so strong.' Jesse turned to Minnie. 'Like yoga-obsessed strong.'

'Wow.'

Minnie thought of her own dad. Watching him on stage when she was a little girl and being both bored and immensely proud at the same time. She remembered being in his arms while he had thick stage make-up on, and wanting to wipe it away so he looked like her dad again. She remembered how she treasured every bit of one-to-one time with him as a teen. The thought of losing him washed over her in panic and fear. It was unthinkable to imagine she and her siblings would have to go through it one day.

'Do you have any brothers or sisters?'

Jesse shook his head, feeling that he had sobered up. Thinking that that was probably a good thing.

'Just me and Mum now, but she's so far away.' The guilty hue on his face deepened and he half winced.

As the tube slowed into Moorgate, Minnie realised she needed to change lines.

'This is me,' she said, briefly squeezing his arm before straightening her bag on her lap. She didn't really want to leave him now. 'Thanks for a fun night, I'm going to go and blow my fifty-three-pound winnings on a Balmain dress.'

Jesse laughed.

'And swap this shit for Cristal...' she said, wielding the bottle as she stood up.

'You want me to see you to your flat?' he offered.

'No! You're good, I'm not far from the tube, my flatmate's restaurant is even nearer. I might stop off for leftovers en route.'

'Oh really?' Jesse felt bad; he should have ordered more than a bowl of fried popcorn chicken, but the night had been so unexpected he hadn't factored in food.

'Yeah, I like to hang out there and make a nuisance of myself anyway.'

'In which case, let me sort out the next meet-up...'

Jesse called them meet-ups; Minnie called them playdates, as if she was the parent out of the two of them, as if the word *playdate* was part of her vernacular.

The tube was pulling into Moorgate and Jesse felt an urgency, realising he had about thirty seconds in which to come up with a plan.

No phones.

Minnie stood in the centre of the carriage holding the handrail, giving a little wiggle to straighten her dress.

'Two Saturdays' time yeah?' he said, looking up. Not sure whether to stand too.

'Yeah groovy,' Minnie said casually, a hunger rumbling in her stomach. 'Where?'

The tube stopped. Jesse panicked, stood, and kissed her on each cheek to say goodbye. She felt his imprint, and it pleasantly surprised her.

'Oxford Circus, Nike Town?'

'Like we really *are* kids,' Minnie laughed, as she walked towards the doors. 'Finally! You got the hang of this!'

Jesse smiled.

The doors opened.

'Cool. Nike Town, 7 p.m.?' Minnie said.

'See you in a fortnight.' Jesse waved, and slumped back down in his seat.

The doors slammed closed.

9

MINNIE

Five Months Ago – New Year's Eve

'My gewl Minnie has *just* finished filming a stunning new drama for the BBC – or is it Amazon – haven't you, babe?'

JP laid a hand on Minnie's thigh and squeezed it, as he angled his cigar to the other side of him and blew a plume of thick smoke into the air. Minnie hadn't remembered the names of everyone sitting around the dining table of the Cotswolds country pile on New Year's Eve – she had met so many friends and business associates of JP's in the past month she couldn't possibly remember everyone, and actually all that mattered was this brilliant man and how... safe he made her feel.

She really did enjoy how much he adored her.

'Ooh do tell us about it!' an artist friend of JP's said keenly, her blonde bob not moving as she shook her head and widened her eyes.

Minnie was sitting around a grand candlelit dining table with a vet (Nathan) and his artist wife (Clarissa); a swimwear designer (Emilia) and her investor husband (Timothy); a property developer (Nick) and his interior designer husband (Diego); and JP's wine buyer (Kiki) and her husband (Paul), while an assortment of their children seemed to be charging around upstairs like a herd of elephants. The names of

everyone had all come so quickly, JP had flown through the introduc-
tions when they'd arrived. Minnie wasn't even sure whose house it was
as they sat down for dinner and caterers glided through with Chilean
bass and black truffle butter. But everyone seemed to hang onto JP's
every word, and most of them seemed eager to hear more, even if they
weren't. They looked at Minnie, forks poised, keen to be charmed. Some
smiles of intrigue, some of exasperation, as if they couldn't be bothered
to remember her name either. It made Minnie feel both thrilled and
vulnerable.

'Well, it wrapped in the summer...' She said the word *wrapped* as if it
didn't fill her with enormous excitement and pride to say it. As if she
were her parents and she had *wrapped* on a thousand projects. 'From the
bestselling book – do you know *Summer of Siena*?'

Half the guests gasped, the other half looked blank.

'Oh I loved it!' said the swimwear designer, her accent American.
'You remember honey, in Mykonos, it was like, the book on every third
towel was *Summer of Siena*. Too funny.'

The husband looked sniffy, as if he wouldn't have deigned to read
anything popular.

'I loved it too,' confessed the interior designer. 'You're playing *her*
right?'

Minnie nodded proudly.

'She is gonna go stellar, aren't ya, babe?' JP gushed.

Minnie smiled, trying to downplay it, but God how she hoped. She
had fought the urge by doing every distraction she could: waitressing,
partying, teacher training. Her first year of teaching had been so bleak,
the school she had got a job in so underfunded and the staff on their
knees from working until eleven o'clock at night, then bumping into
pupils and their families at the foodbank at the weekend. One teacher
cornered Minnie in the stationery cupboard and almost burst into tears
as she implored her, 'Don't do it. I wish I hadn't left banking for this.'

The stress of teaching at a failing primary school, teamed with the
dazzle of seeing Rosie on stage; Lillia's stories of being Emily Blunt's
stunt double on set; and seeing Anthony on the cover of *Radio Times* at
the supermarket checkout, kept pulling Minnie back to the family busi-

ness. She wanted a piece of the pie that *could* be hers if she was prepared to graft for it, to go to drama college, prove her name, and learn all the disciplines of the trade. Minnie went to Mountview and loved every second.

'She's got a Marvel audition in a few weeks,' JP said proudly, looking around the table. 'My Wonder Woman.'

'That's DC,' said Kiki, JP's wine buyer, flatly. She wasn't impressed by any of it. Kiki remembered the days before she'd met her husband, when JP used to show *her* off.

'And you know who her parents are, right?' JP bragged. 'It's foregone innit, babe? Foregone.'

Minnie blushed. She was both extraordinarily proud of her family while also being annoyed that JP had brought them up.

As Minnie asked the artist about her work, her styles and disciplines, she noticed that the vet husband kept looking at her chest. Minnie's breasts were small and the lace collar on her shirt was Victorian, but still the guy kept looking as if she were there to be ogled. JP had presented her as such, she supposed.

'My ingénue...' JP later said, as they were all sitting on the sofas around a large fireplace, waiting for the countdown. As he said it, he pressed the end of Minnie's nose with his forefinger. Minnie looked at him adoringly, falling already, as she thought about him in bed, how they would be soon, and how thrilling it was. His mass on top of her felt powerful; when she straddled his sweaty body and felt him between her legs, she would wonder if it was just another role she was playing, as she looked down on herself.

'My ingénue I call her,' he chuckled again to himself as he beckoned a member of the house staff to top up his glass. A French word that sounded funny in a thick Essex accent, but it was endearing, sweet even, however clumsily JP said it.

'Ooh, countdown's coming!' said Emilia, as everyone stood up and staff walked around with trays of champagne, topping everyone up. Minnie took hers and smiled at the waitress, knowing she must be desperate to finish her shift and see her own friends and family; relieved that she didn't have to work tonight. Minnie hadn't accepted a wait-ressing shift since she'd met JP a few weeks ago.

'Ten... nine... eight...'

JP pulled Minnie in, his arm strong around her waist.

She felt a pang of treachery for having ditched the Byrne family party in London – a Hampstead tradition – in favour of a guy she had only just met; or not helping Hilde out at her New Year's service and lock-in.

'Seven... six... five...'

Minnie suspected JP had lots of offers and options on where to spend his New Year's Eve. He didn't have to turn up anywhere alone if he didn't want to, but he'd invited her. *His* ingénue.

'Four... three... two... one...'

'Happy New Year, babe,' JP said, pulling Minnie in even closer and pressing himself to her. Minnie kissed him as if no one were watching.

'Happy New Year,' she said breathlessly before breaking away from this new and crazy whirlwind, a man unlike any she had never known. 'I love you.'

10

JESSE

Five Months Ago – January

'How's it going?' Jesse asked, as he answered the FaceTime call he was anticipating. He was walking around the flat searching for Ida's cuddly koala as he took the call. He picked up cushions and looked under the sofa, again.

'Good thanks,' Hannah replied efficiently, staring into the screen at her own face rather than Jesse's. 'Everything OK?' Vague questions. She could only ever steal a few minutes during a client dinner, a quick text or a phone call from the loo. She always hoped Jesse's answers would be just as expeditious.

'I couldn't find Kling – can't find him anywhere.'

'Oh dear.'

'She must have left him at school – so we had a bit of a meltdown at bedtime.'

'Oh dear.'

Jesse threw the cushions back on the sofa, plumped them up and positioned them. Even halfway through a cuddly toy disaster, he liked his mid-century modern sofa to look aesthetically pleasing.

'Yeah, I only just got her to sleep. She was all over the place about

Kling. Probably overtired from going back to school. *Magic Animal Friends* did the trick.'

Jesse could tell Hannah didn't have much time so he stopped talking about the bloody koala, gave up on him, and peered through the crack in the bedroom door. His daughter was curled and calm, facing the wall. He went in quietly, just to see the soft rise and fall of her cheek, which he showed Hannah on camera before retreating, gently pulling the door to, so the noise of Mummy on FaceTime wouldn't wake Ida straight back up.

'I can't really talk, dinner is running on.'

'Oh no.'

'*Such* a bore...' Hannah bemoaned as she stared into the camera from what looked like a cramped cupboard but was probably some opulent restaurant bathroom cubicle. The occupational hazard of being an accountant in the hospitality industry was it involved a lot of corporate dinners, which in turn involved a lot of Jesse ending up eating on his own or finishing Ida's macaroni cheese leftovers. 'The client has just ordered a bloody round of limoncello shots for Pete's sake; I've just escaped to the loo to see how things are.'

'Well yeah, it wasn't great but she's OK now. I'll ask Miss Sullivan in the morn—'

'Did she do her Times Tables Rock Stars?'

Jesse wanted to tell Hannah he'd sacked off the times tables because the game was making Ida cry, and that was *before* they realised Kling was missing. They put on *Just Dance* instead. Horsing around to the 'William Tell Overture' always lifted her mood. But it was easier to say yes. He'd explain it in the morning.

'Yep all good here.'

Little lies.

He could feel Hannah's eyes scrutinising the screen from her Face-Time corner.

'OK great,' she said, as if she was only half listening anyway. She had work on her mind.

There was a knock on the toilet door.

'Yup, hang on a sec!' Hannah hollered, sounding stressed.

'OK well Ida's asleep, I'm about to have a beer, no need to rush,' Jesse conceded. 'I'll watch a *Peaky Blinders* and clear up.' Hannah hated *Peaky Blinders*. And *Narcos* and *Planet Earth*. So Jesse caught up on all of the programmes she hated when she was out schmoozing, which was usually a couple of nights a week.

The person knocked on the cubicle door again and Hannah looked flummoxed.

'Go! Enjoy the dinner. Eat their profits,' Jesse assured her.

There was a knock again, more frantic this time.

'Hang on, I won't be a second!'

'High-end restaurant with only one ladies' loo? Jesus. They need to get more toilets.'

'Yah this is more of a gentlemen's club. Again.' Hannah rolled her eyes. 'I've got to go. See you later, bye.'

'Bye, honey.'

Jesse assumed Hannah had already left the call as he felt cut off by a sharp change of angle and the sudden disappearance of his wife's face. He was about to press the red button on his phone when he realised Hannah's phone had fallen somehow, its camera now facing the ceiling. A ceiling that looked much bigger and much more ornate than a ladies' bathroom cubicle.

The camera was still on and the call was still running. Jesse thought Hannah would be mortified if he heard her on the toilet, she always shut the bathroom door to pee, even after sixteen years together, after eight of marriage.

'Hannah?' Jesse said, almost in a stage whisper. Hazy silence. Then he heard a click. Voices in the distance, getting louder. Muffled ruffling. Jesse went to say Hannah's name again, but something stopped him, so he muted the already-low sound of the news on the living-room TV and slumped on the sofa, on the cushions he had just rearranged, eyes still on the ceiling that was showing on the phone screen. A familiar voice spoke in an unfamiliar tone.

'I'm so sorry, darling, just tying everything up at home.' Hannah didn't sound like a frantic accountant in a small toilet cubicle any more.

She sounded relaxed. The voices became indistinct again, then he heard a mumble, a groan. An in-joke, a laugh.

Jesse sat on the sofa of their stylish but small two-bedroom Kentish Town apartment, his eyes piercing the phone screen, dreading what he might hear.

'I want that pussy and I want it now,' said a male voice.

Jesse planted his hand over his mouth as he choked, remembering he might be audible even if he were invisible. He looked around his living room in shock. Sophie Raworth was looking back at him sympathetically as she read the news.

He glanced down at his phone, wanting to throw it across the room, yet he felt compelled to listen, like a prairie wolf, ears alert, his throat ravaged with thirst on the precipice of a discovery.

A thick voice. A zip.

Big lies.

A gasp. A groan.

A hairy arm came into view, a hand pushing a phone away until it was covered and muffled by a sheet, a cushion or a pillow. But still, Jesse heard the familiar cries of his wife's pleasure, bubbling up from somewhere in his past. He ended the call before anyone could hear him cry.

11

JESSE

Now

'I wanted the blue piece!' Oscar protested through thick, lispy lips, prodding his finger at a towering Minecraft birthday cake fashioned out of blue and green blocks.

'What's wrong with that green one?' Elena asked, although she knew what was coming.

'It's small.'

'It's not small. It's a big piece of cake, you're a very lucky boy.'

'I want a blue piece!'

Oscar's twin brother Fred, who had the same narrow blue eyes and curly hair, although his hair was dark brown to Oscar's sandy blond, looked down at his own plate, quietly pleased with how the cake cutting gods had favoured him.

Oscar glared at his twin, the temptation to take his plate searing through him. Fred gave him a *don't you dare* stare.

'If you argue then neither of you will have any cake!' Elena said sharply.

'I'm not arguing,' Fred said in a matter-of-fact manner, not taking his eyes off his brother, who was so close to grabbing Fred's plate, or worse, flipping it up in the air.

'Oscar why don't you choose another piece?' Elena suggested, as calmly as she could, but the boy was locked in a silent standoff with his brother. It was the twins' birthday, and Elena had just realised that seven-year-old boys might be the most selfish creatures on the planet. Still, she did her best not to lose her cool and declare it in a rage, today of all days. 'Look, Ida hasn't even had a piece and you're complaining about yours!'

Elena, knife in hand, looked over at Ida and Jesse, coiled together on the sofa. 'Would you like some cake, sweetie? This piece has a chocolate number seven on it.'

'No!' the boys shouted in harmony, surprising even themselves, united by their mutual greed.

Ida clung to her dad's middle, arms wrapped around him as they slunk into the sofa, and shook her head.

'No thank you,' she said in a little voice. A sadness had washed over Ida that even cake couldn't counter.

It was getting to *that time*, when she would have to unpeel herself from her father, for a reason that didn't even make sense.

Why was her daddy living with silly Oscar and Fred and not her?

Elena softened with Ida's sadness.

'Are you sure, lovely girl? I can wrap some up for you to take home...?'

That made Ida feel even worse. She didn't want to go home because then this day would end. She squeezed her dad tighter.

'It looks yummy, my love, let's take some with us yes? You could have it in your packed lunch tomorrow. Or – shhhhh – for breakfast!'

Jesse tried to make light of the fact that his heart was breaking too.

Andrew popped his head around the door of the living room. Its high ceilings and clean Georgian lines muted by a grey June Sunday and the post-party mess and detritus. Twenty children, aged six and seven, had trampled their way through the house before Safari Steve turned up to tame them, with his boxes of tarantulas, beetles, a boa constrictor, meerkat and an owl. Only Fred had been brave enough to wear the boa like a scarf.

'Just nipping out for a bit,' Andrew said casually.

Elena, still wielding a large knife, looked at her husband in disbelief. 'For what? The shops are probably shut.'

She had almost lost her shit at 11 a.m. when Andrew sat reading the *Observer* while she, Jesse and Ida threaded pineapple and cheese chunks onto cocktail sticks and pierced them into a cucumber crocodile. It was now 4.30 p.m. and the relief at the party having gone well was countered by the mountain of mess that needed clearing up.

Andrew looked across the room as if to say, *And?*

'You're going out now?'

'Yeah, I need to get my steps in and decompress.'

Andrew and his bloody steps, Elena and Jesse both thought.

Andrew left the room as quickly as he had entered.

Jesse had become accustomed to Andrew's weird walks at inappropriate times, but they didn't always seem fair on Elena. Sometimes he'd go to get a paper and end up walking for an hour or two, returning home empty handed, saying he got lost in a podcast, expecting Elena to be pleased he'd got an extra 5,000, 8,000 or 10,000 steps in. When the twins hassled their parents to get a dog and Andrew protested, Elena reasoned that it would be a guaranteed way for Andrew to get all his bloody steps in. Except she knew she would end up walking it, and she was a teacher, she didn't have time to walk a dog around Hampstead Heath three times a day.

Ida yawned and sprawled further across her dad, locking him into place with a little leg. Maybe her golden-brown tendrils could pin them both to the sofa and neither of them would be able to get up and go, although she *did* want to be back home. She just wanted to be there with her daddy, sitting on the end of her bed, reading her a favourite *Magic Animal Friends* book and not going anywhere.

The twins were still frozen in silent combat, staring each other down over Fred's blue piece of cake being bigger than Oscar's green one. Neither dared make a move.

'Just choose another one, Oscar, for goodness' sake!' Elena said. 'And bring your cake into the kitchen, you boys need water to counter all that sugar.'

The front door clicked and Jesse and Elena heard Andrew whistle as he flew down the stoop.

'You sure you don't want any?' Jesse asked Ida, to distract from Andrew's selfishness more than anything. Andrew had always been prone to it. When the baby group lot would get together and have a picnic on the Heath or Regent's Park, Andrew would serve himself a big plate first and go and sit on the nicest looking rug while Elena tussled with the twins. It irked Jesse, even though there were many reasons he liked Andrew. He was funny. He was gregarious. He had given him a roof over his head, although Jesse suspected it had been Elena's idea.

Ida shook her head again.

'No thank you.'

'Come on, boys, let's eat in the kitchen, leave Ida in peace. I'll start the bath.'

As quick as a flash Oscar grabbed the cake on Fred's plate while Fred, rather than lose it, smashed it into Oscar's Minecraft T-shirt, twisting the plate in circles just to really be sure it couldn't be eaten.

'Wahhhh!' cried Oscar.

'Raaaa!' raged Fred.

'Get upstairs, now! Both of you! It might be your birthday but NO CAKE NOW!' Elena bellowed, while Fred made a run for it and Oscar chased him up the stairs.

'I'm so sorry,' Elena mouthed to Jesse, although he felt bad for being there. He always did. He had to find a solution soon, whether it was to go home or find his own flat. He just about had the means. This was only meant to be a stopgap.

Jesse gave Elena a grateful nod, then stroked Ida's hair and tucked a curl behind her ear. It reminded him of the way Minnie tucked strands of her short black bob behind her studded ear, and he felt weird to have thought about her right here, right now, while he was with Ida.

* * *

Jesse had got back from Beyoncé Bingo happy and merry, pleased that they had evolved from the polite chit-chat at the zoo to something deeper, talking about their fears, work dreams and grief. It had surprised him that he was pleasantly surprised by the shift. Even though he felt self-conscious dancing to 'Survivor' with Minnie, he liked the fact that he never would have foreseen it at the zoo. Even less so in the cafe at Bondiga's. But the conversation on the tube about his dad had been enough to gently sober him up, and he felt content on the walk back to the house and able to wrap a pass the parcel gift for the party while Andrew popped out to get ice from the off licence. While they wrapped presents and chatted, Elena said she thought Beyoncé Bingo sounded fricking amazing, but was more intrigued by who Jesse had gone to the bingo with, given it didn't sound like something he would have chosen to do by himself. Elena had been terribly worried about her adorable Jesse; life had been so cruel to him and she still couldn't bear to talk to Hannah. If Hannah posted something on Instagram, or sent a message on the baby group mums WhatsApp, Elena would internally curse and not respond.

'Oh just a mate I'm helping with some work,' he had said, which only piqued Elena's interest more.

'You know you don't owe Hannah anything,' she said with a sage look.

Jesse smiled, gratefully, as he wrapped Starburst sweets into layers of paper and tried not to cry.

* * *

'Can I stay here tonight?' Ida asked quietly. Jesse's heart broke into a million little pieces all over again.

'With those crazy boys?' Jesse asked, pointing to the ceiling. From the living room they could hear the stampede from Elena chasing the twins into the bathroom.

'Oscar and Fred get to have sleepovers with you.'

Jesse felt a sharp pain in his chest.

'They're not in my room, darling. I'm just in the spare room.'

'No but they see you at night and in the morning and have breakfast with you. You're *my* daddy.'

'I am, and I always will be. This isn't for long.'

'Why does Janey babysit me? Why don't you babysit me?'

'Who's Janey?'

'She looked after me last night.'

'Last night?'

For fuck's sake.

Suddenly Jesse felt terrible about having been at Beyoncé Bingo while his daughter was being babysat by someone new. Janey wasn't the first babysitter Ida had mentioned in the past few months. Hannah had booked their neighbour's daughter Daisy to look after Ida a few times – she had even trialled a girl called Leonor to be a nanny Jesse didn't want Ida to have – Jesse had been devasted when he'd found out.

Why didn't you fucking ask me? he'd asked Hannah in a hastily sent text. *I'm her dad. I'd give anything to sit with her on a Saturday or a Tuesday night – and you're paying some teenager who doesn't give a shit?!*

Please, give me room, Hannah had responded.

Jesse scoffed. Surely he should be the one needing room after what she had done to him.

Then there was Freya – Jesse didn't know where the hell she'd come from. And now Janey. When Jesse's real question was: why did Hannah keep going out on the Saturdays she had Ida anyway? Jesse treasured his weekends with his daughter.

It felt like another treacherous move.

'What's Janey like?' Jesse asked, as neutrally as he could.

'I don't know, she didn't talk to me, she was on her phone.' Ida then cupped her hand over her mouth and whispered, 'I think to her boyfriend.' Jesse saw a flash of Ida's mischievous smile reappear before it fluttered away again.

'I'll talk to Mama, see if I can babysit instead.' Jesse shuffled. 'I want to be with you, more than anything, I promise.'

Ida said nothing as they listened to the thud of the boys running along the landing to the bathroom and Jesse sat up, unpeeling Ida from him so he could get up. 'Come on, let's wrap a few pieces for you. Breakfast, lunch *and* dinner tomorrow,' he said with a cheeky grin.

12

MINNIE

Now

'How are we doing?' Tony asked, crashing back into his chair, clipboard teetering across his jeans. Tony wasn't the image of the therapist Minnie had conjured before she'd met him eight weeks ago, when she'd been ready to tell him her heart was broken after a passionate and intense short-lived relationship. That she was struggling to get out of bed and had even contemplated going to sleep for ever. That she was struggling to feel any self-worth. Angry – *so* angry – at herself for letting someone break her heart. She had expected Tony to be a slight man in a turtle-neck with wispy hair and intellectual glasses. But Tony looked more like Action Bronson or Rag 'n' Bone man than the stereotypical therapist she had expected. He had tattoos up his forearms, a bald head and bushy beard, and he wore band tees, jeans and trainers.

Minnie liked that Tony surprised her. She liked that he challenged her. She had enjoyed his suggestions to return to the passions of her mostly happy childhood – she liked the inner-child work they had done – and she'd taken most of his suggestions on board, although she hadn't ridden a Chopper or gone running through a field yet, but she had made a new friend and she had mostly got off social media.

Tony's first question always amused Minnie though.

'How are *we* doing?'

He said it in his gravelly Camberwell voice.

Minnie didn't know anything about Tony Critchley other than he liked Biffy Clyro, N.W.A. and Death Goals (if his band T-shirts were anything to go by). And that he liked ink. She also knew his professional qualifications, which were proudly displayed on the wall. She knew from his online profile that he was a Cognitive Behavioural Therapist who offered support for anxiety, depression, OCD, PTSD, substance abuse and broken hearts. She wanted to know what he got up to at the weekends, what made him tick – for all she knew he could have just come down from a psychotic episode, or be feeling bleak and full of self-loathing himself, but she didn't want to chip into her £110 an hour fee asking Tony about Tony. Plus she liked the mystery and the edge of him as they sat in his office, just off Marylebone High Street. A plain little room for such an opulent area, with three chairs, a desk with a laptop in the corner, and a Chinese money plant that lifted the room with its fronds of bright green circles. When Minnie was trying to answer tough questions she looked to the Chinese money plant. It reminded her of an installation she had seen at the Tate and brought her calm.

'Yeah good thanks. I went to the bingo at the weekend, won big.'

She said it so Tony could tell it wasn't going to be life changing.

There was a pause, while Tony waited for Minnie to say more.

Shit.

Part of her felt like a naughty child for holding something back. She didn't want to tell Tony she had been with Jesse, having such brilliant fun, because then Tony might think Jesse meant more to her than he did. And she was already embarrassed about how hard and fast she had fallen for JP. So she held back. Hid behind sarcasm. Then stayed silent for a few seconds. A concept that always threw her.

She bit her tongue.

'And how have you been feeling this week, generally?'

'Ummm, OK, I think. I feel proud of myself for taking on board some of the actionable strategies.' She couldn't *not* tell him.

'Which strategies were they?'

'I went to the bingo with the new friend I'd made, the one from the cafe.' She said it as if she had made a hundred new friends in the past few weeks.

'That's great.'

Tony didn't ask any more about the friend. Perhaps it wasn't an issue, which gave Minnie a small sense of relief.

'And how's your anger been? Last week you touched on anger right at the end.'

Minnie's brief sense of relief dropped. His question floored her. She was still angry, and she realised it as she looked Tony in the eye, a searing rage and sense of injustice pummelling her.

'Yeah, still there,' she conceded.

'I was thinking we might do some chair work this week,' Tony said.

'Chair work?'

'Yeah, it's a good way of letting go of someone from your past. It could be especially helpful for you, given the circumstances. The unfinished business and loss of control. Get up...' He signalled, and rearranged the third, empty, chair in the room so it was placed opposite Minnie. Tony moved his seat alongside Minnie's, a few metres apart.

'I thought that was for couples' counselling,' Minnie joked nervously, nodding to it.

'Oh it is. I have a messy divorce in next...' Tony deadpanned. 'But for now...'

He pointed to the space. 'Would you like to give it a go? If not I can sit there and we carry on.'

Minnie nodded and looked at the chair.

'What do I do?'

'I'd like you to imagine...' Tony looked down at his notes to remind himself of the awful ex's awful name. 'Imagine that JP is sitting in front of you right now.'

Minnie took a deep and nervy breath.

'When you can imagine him, I'd like you describe what he looks like, what he's wearing, what the expression is like on his face...'

Minnie bristled at how easily she conjured him as she kept her eyes open and stared at the void.

'Erm, he's wearing a black shirt, black trousers, black shoes. He has a little smirk on his face, like he's wondering why I brought him here. The fucker.'

Tony nodded and smiled. He liked Minnie. He didn't always like his clients, but he liked her sense of humour and her gumption, although she did need to stop making light of everything that was causing her pain. He cleared his throat.

'I'd like you to tell JP why you want to speak to him.'

Minnie wasn't sure that she did. She felt so humiliated by him. By the way he'd reeled her in. By the very public way in which he'd dumped her. By his lack of concern or care. By the way he'd shut the door so brutally and finally on their relationship, when she had given him all of her.

'I don't want to talk to him,' she said, frowning.

Tony sat quietly, watching Minnie as she looked at the Chinese money plant, and then the floor. Then she found her voice.

'Actually, I do.'

Minnie looked back at the space, feeling one part ridiculous and one part empowered. She straightened her spine, played with her fingers. The dark grey nails she had painted hastily before meeting Jesse on Saturday night were now chipped and worn.

'I'm so upset!'

She looked to Tony with caution.

He nodded.

She looked back at the chair JP was sitting on.

'How could you do that to me? I don't fall for people lightly! I gave you all of me and you just let me down. I want to move on... but I can't.'

'And how do you feel when you look at him?'

'How do I feel? I'm angry!'

'Tell him.'

'I'm angry. When you dumped me it felt like someone had died. I fell apart. I hate you for that!'

'Tell him again.'

'I hate you! I want to be free of you!'

Minnie broke her gaze with the empty chair and started to cry. She then looked at Tony and apologised for being silly.

'Don't be daft,' he said, handing her a box of tissues from his desk. She took three out with vigour and wiped her eyes. Tony waited for a moment, then continued.

'You mentioned how you gave all of yourself to JP, can you tell him more about that?'

Minnie frowned at Tony, who gave her a gentle and encouraging nod as he straightened the hem of his sock and smoothed the laces of his adidas Gazelles. Minnie looked back at the space in which she had conjured JP and took a deep breath.

'I gave you so much! I put loads of faith in you. I gave you loads of my time and let you totally dictate to me because I loved being with you. I thought you loved being with me, but it was bullshit. You're a total bull-shitter! I was just one of many!'

The silence was amplified by the noise outside. The mid-morning traffic.

'Is there anything else you'd like to say to him?'

Minnie thought of Jesse and whispered, 'I want to move on with my life. I want to stop feeling sad about you. Stop being annoyed with myself. Accept it's over.'

'Tell him again, but say it with more power.'

'What?'

'You have the power to be clear, and forceful and distinct. Tell him.'

Minnie looked back at the chair. At JP.

'I want to move on. I want to accept it's over.'

'Louder.'

'I want to move on. It's over. I want to say goodbye!'

'Then say goodbye.'

'Fuck off! Goodbye.'

Minnie gave a nervous laugh and looked back at her hands as tears of heartache and relief tumbled onto her lap.

Tony gave her a minute, took the empty seat back to the corner and rearranged his so he was sitting at a diagonal to Minnie, facing her.

'Well done, eh?' he said, like a guy encouraging his kid at Sunday football. 'You're the one responsible for saying goodbye now, not him. You're empowering yourself to do that.'

Minnie sniffed into the tissue.

'How do you feel?'

Minnie's brain was scrambled. JP had just been in the room with her and she had come so far. It felt liberating. It felt good. Yet what she really didn't want to admit to Tony was that she was starting to think about someone else.

13

DAY THREE

Now

Jesse raced up the stairs, two at time, and into the lights of Oxford Circus. Even though the sun still lit the sky at 7 p.m. in the middle of June, the illuminations of the shopfronts, buses and adverts still stood out and made Jesse narrow his eyes to adjust. Nike Town was in front of him, and under a giant swoosh stood Minnie, chewing the inside of her cheek as she looked to all four corners of the circus, almost missing what was right in front of her.

Jesse was two minutes late; he didn't like being late.

'So sorry!' he said with a flustered smile.

'Ah!' she said in relief. 'I'm Minnie, pleased to meet you!'

Jesse didn't have time for that today, plus he thought they'd moved beyond it, so he nodded and smiled quickly.

'Sorry, I got stuck on the Central Line and—'

'Oh! Don't worry! I hadn't noticed.' Minnie was just pleased by how keen Jesse looked, how miffed he seemed to be late. An anxiety had started to creep in during the latter half of the two-week gap between saying goodbye to him on the tube and meeting him tonight. A fear that he might back out of their agreement; it was so hastily made. But he was here, and he seemed like a very different man to the one she had met in the cafe a month ago. He looked like he gave a shit; that he wasn't just humouring her any more.

'The thing I booked started at seven; sorry, it was the best I could find.'

'"The best you could find"? This sounds intriguing...'

'Well, I don't know about that.'

To Minnie's complete surprise, Jesse looped his arm loosely through hers, so he could guide her across the road, looking both ways hurriedly, south to Regent Street.

'Where are we heading?'

'This way...'

He was half-running half-walking as Minnie kept up by running on her tiptoes.

'Hang on!' she laughed, as if she couldn't keep up, when she could. 'Where are we going?'

He didn't answer; his focus was on Regent Street and getting across that, as they dodged couples, families and tourists. They dashed past the Apple shop and Burberry, Jesse leading them, Minnie laughing, as he weaved them into a side street tucked between Regent Street and Mayfair. Jesse was so worried about missing the start, he hadn't even realised their arms were looped together as they stopped outside a bar in a courtyard with 'The Sinking Heart' written over the door in a red font. He quickly let go.

'What are we doing here?' Minnie asked cheerfully.

'Cocktail class,' Jesse declared. 'To help with your audition.'

* * *

Minnie and Jesse pushed through a set of double doors that opened to carpeted stairs going down to a plush-looking bar with illuminated circular 'windows', each lit with frosted glass, as if it were the sky and they were on a cruise ship that had been abandoned before its maiden voyage. At first sight the place seemed closed, but at the bar to the left of the bottom of the stairs, Jesse and Minnie saw a small group of people and a man with silver cropped hair wearing a floral waistcoat.

'Ahh, our last couple!' the man said as he looked to the foot of the stairs and pressed his palms together.

'Er, yeah we're not a coup—' Jesse went to say.

'It doesn't matter!' Minnie whispered, hitting Jesse on the arm as she skipped down the bottom step. 'This is great!'

'One of you must be Jesse?'

'That's me,' Jesse said, raising a hand as he peeled off his jacket and slung it on a nearby banquette. Minnie followed suit and did the same; her leather biker jacket was far too warm for today, and she slung it on top of Jesse's.

'And you are...?' the man said, studying Minnie with enchantment.

'Minette,' she said, formally.

'Minette?' Jesse said under his breath, giving her a double take.

Minnie responded with a look as if to say, *and what of it?* A face that sat somewhere between indignation and flirtation.

'Minette, I must say you have the face of the Absinthe fairy,' the man said.

Minnie wasn't sure if the man had paid her a compliment or not, but she said, 'Thank you,' all the same.

'Jesse, Minette, these are your fellow cocktail crafters today. I'm Thomas, your master mixologist here at The Sinking Heart, a ship where your troubles and your misdemeanours will drift to the bottom of the sea.'

'Sounds good,' Minnie said, quietly and agreeably.

'If you look at your colleagues' lapels you will see I have put each person's name on a sticky label – don't worry, it will not ruin your chic clothes – and if it does, white spirit will do the trick!'

One of the women in the group said, 'I hope not,' only half in jest.

'The labels act as a convenient prompt so we all know whom is whom.'

Minnie stifled a laugh. This was going to be fun. Jesse was more apprehensive, worried that the class he'd booked would be disappointing.

Thomas pointed to the other end of the group.

'We have Greg and Kathleen, James and Maya, Alison and Michelle and here we are, Jesse and Minette, how wonderful. Are we all couples today?'

'We're friends,' Jesse and Minnie said, at the same time as Alison and Michelle said, 'We're sisters.' Alison and Michelle looked nothing like each other, and were used to having to explain they were related. Thomas didn't seem to care much; he needed to get on before the bar started to get busy, so he began with some mixology basics.

'There's a reason classic cocktails have endured,' he said sagely. 'No gimmicky names or "twists on twists" in *this* class...' Jesse and Minnie looked at each other guiltily after their Beyoncé bastardisations of a fortnight ago.

'I won't tell if you don't tell,' she leaned in and quietly whispered under her breath.

'We will be starting with the most requested cocktail in the world. Anyone know what that is?'

Easy, thought Minnie. She'd worked too many events not to.

'The margarita,' she said, rising on the balls of her feet and smiling.

'Well done you,' Thomas said, like a proud uncle.

As Thomas demonstrated how to make the perfect margarita, he imparted wisdom that went beyond the four key ingredients (tequila reposado, ice, fresh lime juice and triple sec... the salt rim was optional, he conceded). He was obviously very particular about his cocktails and the methodology in making them: alcohol was the most important ingredient and ice second; mixers were something to heed – cocktails should contain alcohol, ice and fresh natural ingredients; flavours should be balanced; and if you didn't make your cocktail look appealing, there was no point in making one.

'It absolutely *has* to look covetable and drinkable. Anyone can throw together some ingredients but the *art* of making a cocktail is to make the imbiber feel special,' Thomas declared with a haughty smile, as he raised his demonstration margarita.

Minnie and Jesse watched him take a showy, ceremonial sip and both suddenly felt terribly thirsty.

When the group broke to make their own, Minnie made a mental note to change her audition tack: she had imagined herself as a flamboyant flairer of a cocktail shaker, like Tom Cruise in *Cocktail* but killer. But the more she observed Thomas, the more she could envisage a cooler, calmer, more understated audition playing out, and she felt grateful to Jesse for this priceless insight.

'Thank you,' Minnie said, as she pressed lime halves on a juicer. Thomas had advised them to squeeze half their limes on a juicer, and the other half with their fingers, to really *feel* the difference in how their nectar was procured. ('Machinery yields more; but to really taste a cocktail you have to *feel* the ingredients,' he advised ostentatiously.) Minnie was looking down at the zingy liquid and pulp gathering in the juicer, almost blushing at the thoughtfulness of Jesse's playdate activity. 'This really is kind of you.' She kept her gaze down lest he see how much she cared.

'No problem,' Jesse said, happy he had made her happy. Bubbling at the anticipation of tasting their beautifully crafted drinks.

Once each of the group had blended their own margarita, Thomas asked them to reconvene in their semi-circle in front of his trolley, coupé glasses all poised in varying shades of pastel yellow, pale gold and green.

'Now, what are we drinking to?' Thomas asked eagerly, starting at one end of the line.

'My Christmas present!' Kathleen said, taking a large slug. 'Only took us six months to get some childcare,' she quipped. Greg drank to that.

'Our wedding anniversary,' James said, as he looked at Maya and smiled. 'Seven years,' they both said in unison as Maya raised her glass back and Thomas moved down the line.

'The end of my treatment,' Alison said boldly. 'I rang the bell on five months of chemo last week.'

'Oh my goodness,' Thomas said softly. 'This group! Alison my darling, cheers to you.' He raised his glass again and took a sip. Jesse and Minnie, standing next to the sisters, smiled, as they saw a tear loaded with heartache and relief run down Michelle's cheek.

Minnie didn't know how to follow that, and she didn't want to have to explain her audition and jinx it. She paused and looked at the ice cracking in her glass before raising it. Jesse noticed her margarita was the same colour as her eyes.

'To friendship,' she said, turning briefly to Jesse as her lips met her glass. Her margarita actually tasted good.

Thomas looked to Jesse at the end of the line expectantly, who glanced down at his trainers for a second. A flit of a frown creased his face as he galvanised himself and looked back up.

'To my dad.' Jesse raised his glass gently. 'It would have been his seventy-seventh birthday today and it's very weird this being the first birthday without him. Without seeing him clock up another year.' He gave Minnie a quick guarded look, then swallowed hard to gather himself. Minnie could see his Adam's apple bobbing.

Deep breath.

'And it's Father's Day tomorrow. Another reason I'm drinking to him.'

Jesse raised his glass and looked up to the ceiling before taking a sip. Minnie drank to Jesse's dad as well.

'Cheers,' she said quietly.

Minnie didn't realise Jesse's dad had been so old. Her dad was only in his late fifties and he had five children, but they had started young. She felt terribly sorry for Jesse's loss, and pictured his lonely and quiet childhood with an ageing father. For a brief second Minnie wanted to squeeze Jesse's hand so badly. So she did.

*   *   *

The second cocktail was a Manhattan, first mixed in 1870 at the Manhattan Club by the mother of Winston Churchill of all people, Thomas said, as if it was a surprise to him too. Jesse's lacked finesse and Minnie's was a bit too strong for her liking. The third was a French Martini, during which Thomas invited Minnie to come round to the other side of the bar to make hers. This helped Minnie get into the character of Veronica Valla – and everyone except Jesse wondered why Minette sneered and smouldered a little as she shook her stainless-steel cocktail mixer.

By the fourth – an espresso martini to wake them up – and

Thomas' only nod to modernity ('Created here in London, by the don Dick Bradsell...') – Jesse and Minnie were both starting to feel drunk: their 'cheers' were more slurring, their eye contact lingering, the energy shifting. Was it the cocktails or a suppressed sizzling feeling inside?

'Thank you,' Minnie said, again, to Thomas, and the classmates dispersed into the bar with their espresso martinis and the other Saturday night revellers. Jesse and Minnie pulled up a plush stool each, put their drinks on the high table in front of them, and made themselves comfortable. 'That was really lovely of you.' She squeezed his hand, and not for the first time that evening, he felt it like a shot.

'You're welcome,' Jesse said, taking in his drink. He licked the coffee-coloured foam from his top lip. 'I'm just sorry the bartender wasn't hot. I was hoping for Tom Holland for you, he was more like Tom Baker.' Minnie felt his deflection like a punch in the stomach.

Friends. Absolutely not allowed to fall in love.

'Huh?' Minnie said, buying time, still trying to get her head around this fact – this handsome friend, who had been holding her eye so beautifully and was going through his own shit and turmoil, had been trying to set her up with a barman.

'Tom Baker. You're probably too young. He played Dr Who.'

'I know who Tom Baker is!' Minnie scoffed a little zealously, lest she show her disappointment. Of course she knew who Tom Baker was. Doctor Who number four, national treasure, and her eldest sister's godfather. 'And I'm not much younger than you, I don't think...'

'Thirty-one,' Jesse said. 'Almost thirty-two.'

'Wow you look older!'

'Thanks,' Jesse laughed. 'People always say that. I think it's just my bad dad hair.' As he said it he ruffled his temples. He didn't want to ask Minnie how old she was.

'Well people always think I look younger than I am, which pisses me off when I'm going for kickass female roles.' She took an inelegant drink of her espresso martini. 'Which is why I *reallllly* want this one. So thank you.' She put her glass down and pressed her palms together.

'You're welcome.'

'Oh!' Minnie remembered with excitement. 'I almost forgot in the rush to get here! *Summer of Siena* has been given the green light.'

'No way!'

'Yes! Amazon Prime are showing it in their autumn schedule. All legal issues are resolved.'

'Congratulations, that's amazing. And that'll help boost you with your Paris audition surely, no? Saying you're the star of a hot new Amazon show...'

'Maybe.'

'So what happened with the legal issue?'

'Oh I don't really understand, but the publisher realised that their author will do much better for it airing than with legal wranglings holding it back.'

'I bet.'

'It's going to be international – they're launching on Amazon Prime in the US at the same time as the UK!'

'That's brilliant.' Jesse smiled to himself as he took another sip. He was genuinely happy for her. 'You'd better start flying then, get over there.'

Minnie curled her nose and tucked her hair behind her heavily studded ear. 'Buzzkill!'

'Sorry.'

'Don't worry,' she said dismissively. 'I'm pretty sure the launch party will be in London.'

'Or it could be LA?'

Minnie gave him a mock scowl. 'Most of the cast and crew live in London or Europe. I'm sure they'll do it here.'

Minnie put her little finger in her drink to chase the decorative coffee bean out of the glass so she could eat it.

'Have you ever been to America?' she asked, curiously.

Jesse had. A few times.

His parents had taken him to Disneyland when he was a child, tagging it on to a work trip of his dad's. He was quite an anxious boy and didn't like the theme park rides, but he did love going to an observatory with the best views of the Los Angeles cityscape, glimmering in the twilight. He'd loved how beautiful the lines of the city looked, lit and transient, as if the grids and the skyscrapers might move at any second.

Jesse went back one summer during university with Hannah; they flew into Los Angeles and took Greyhound buses all the way to New York, stopping at different cities across the Union. Visiting the Grand Canyon in Nevada, the Book Depository in Dallas, Beale Street in Memphis and Pennsylvania Avenue in Washington along the way. Hannah hadn't wanted to see Jesse's view of Los Angeles from the observatory. She'd told him to stop going on about it. The city felt hot and grimy and she just wanted to get the hell out as soon as they could.

Jesse glossed over that part but told Minnie about Disney, about Los Angeles in the glittering twilight. About how he'd travelled across the US by Greyhound, which could be practical for her except for the whole getting to and from America part. He told her how he had been to New York for work a couple of times.

'*La La Land*,' Minnie said smiling.

'What?'

'That view from the observatory. Griffith?'

'That's right, it was Griffith Park.'

Jesse remembered how beautiful the lines of the observatory building were too.

'It's where they dance in *La La Land*. You know?'

Jesse hadn't seen the film but his friend had designed the poster. The Deco font. The yellow dress. It looked stunning. He hadn't realised it was set at the observatory he had been to as a child.

'Oh, right.'

'And *Rebel Without a Cause* was filmed up there,' Minnie said with authority. 'It's classic LA, apparently.'

All Jesse knew was that his parents had driven him up to Griffith Park at sunset and they had stood on the white terrace enjoying the most magical view of his life. He remembered his dad placing a loving palm on his shoulder blade; he recalled being terrified of his father dying, even then. He realised he must have known he wasn't immortal.

Jesse broke himself from his dark and sad spiral.

'Well now it feels wrong that I've been there and you haven't,' he said.

'No, no! I like hearing about places I won't fly to. What else did you see there?'

'We did walk the Walk of Fame...'

Minnie looked down at her drink. She didn't want to tell Jesse that her mother had a star there, it would ruin the game.

'I remember looking for Harrison Ford and being really hungry, and then being confused by how excited my parents were to see Angela Lansbury's star.'

'What's not to love about Angela Lansbury?' Minnie gasped, as if it were obvious.

Jesse laughed. 'Well I'll know your name soon! Minette...?' Jesse lingered on the question mark.

'Whoa whoa whoa that's against the rules! You still have the napkin, don't you?'

Jesse patted an imaginary pocket against his heart.

'I do.'

'Good.'

'Anyway, I'll take a picture of *your* star next time I go to LA.'

Minnie wondered if he perhaps he was flirting.

'Cheers to that!' she said, as they clinked their almost-empty glasses and their heads drew in together. Jesse looked at her and held her gaze for a fraction longer than either felt comfortable with within the parameters of the game; with the mess and confusion in their hearts.

What are you playing at mate? he thought.

Do not fall for anyone. It's against the rules. Minnie was a stickler for the rules.

'Food!' Minnie said sharply. 'We need food!'

'Yes, yes...' Jesse was flustered. 'I should have sorted something to soak up the cocktails, especially after last time.'

Minnie batted her hand as if it hadn't mattered.

'Shall we go and get some dinner?' he suggested. 'There are some nice places over the road.'

Minnie shook up her hair.

'I have a better idea. My friend's restaurant in Camden Town. It's the prettiest food you will ever see on a plate in London.'

Jesse thought that sounded wonderful.

14

DAY THREE

Now

It was 10 p.m. when Minnie and Jesse arrived at Alpine NW1 and the Saturday night service was coming to an end. Which meant they were just in time for a just-vacated table, and just in time to eat whatever it was Hilde had remaining in the kitchen.

'Lemme go check,' said Camilla, a Danish waitress with a joyful smile. She came back with two plates of Swiss water buffalo tartare and crispy salmon tostadas with pickles and yuzu mayo; Hilde herself came out of the kitchen with the last portion of Swiss lamb with herbed panko crust and kimchi fermented cucumber, and a bowl of strawberries marinated in homemade elderflower syrup.

'Here you go, you scrounge-ah!' Hilde said, noticing Minnie wasn't alone. 'Jesse L—'

Minnie stood up abruptly and shouted 'Hiya!' to stop Hilde in her tracks. They hugged, Minnie whispered something in Hilde's ear, and sat back down.

'Jesse, L-ove, welcome to Alpine NW1,' Hilde said as she slid her dishes onto the table and joined them.

'Hey,' Jesse said, and Hilde gave Minnie a sharp and admonishing look as if to say, *you didn't tell me he was hot.*

'Jesse this is Hilde, my flatmate and the owner/chef here.'

'Hi Hilde, lovely to meet you – your food looks incred—'

Hilde held up a palm to stop him.

'When my friend said she was going to meet a man at London Zoo, I thought perhaps you were a serial killer.' Hilde had a way with words; she could say anything with a smile.

Jesse laughed; Minnie winced.

'None taken.'

'But it's nice to know that you aren't. I assume you aren't, is that right?'

'That is correct. Turns out we're both 100 per cent completely sane and normal, eh Minnie?' Jesse said, turning to her, as if he were shouting hallelujah at the heavens. Minnie loved the sound of her name on his lips, so much so that she stayed silent.

'So what's this?' Jesse said, rubbing his palms together. 'They all look incredible.' He pored over the plates in front of him as Hilde explained them, appreciating the aesthetics of each crafted dish, the way they sat on pretty blue and white patterned china.

'Well that should be served with grilled baby gem lettuce and anchovy but we're out of that now,' Hilde said, pointing to the water buffalo tartare, as if Jesse might spot that. He looked like he had a good eye. 'And these strawberries should be served with wild sage flowers but my brother Martin is still foraging in the Alps...'

Jesse liked Hilde's perfectionism.

'It all looks stunning, thank you.'

'You're welcome!' Hilde said, surprised that she was so pleasantly surprised, as she looked at Minnie and felt a flash of worry for her and her fragile state of mind. JP had been an entirely different kettle of fish, but still, she needed to recover and be single. This guy needed to not be anything more than a friend. 'Ah excuse me, some regulars...' she said, getting up deftly as she went to help some customers who were leaving. Hilde helping anyone with their coat was a sight to behold given she was so small.

'Clever isn't she?' Minnie beamed proudly. 'Although I'm more of a steak and ale pie girl.'

Jesse turned the plate around, to take in the intricate textures and colours at all angles, although the dim lighting wasn't helping.

'So clever. God, it's an art.'

'Do you cook?' Minnie asked genially.

'A bit, but I overthink it. I try to make everything look nice – not this nice of course – but I don't have that ability some people do, to just throw ingredients together. I stress too much about how it's going to look on the plate. And you know, Ida's tastes are pretty limited.'

Jesse said it as if Minnie knew her.

'What did you get up to last weekend?'

'With Ida?'

Minnie nodded.

'I took her to the Twist Museum, have you been?'

'No, I've not heard of it.'

As they ate, Jesse told Minnie how he and his daughter had run around rooms of light displays and optical illusions at a museum designed by neuroscientists to explore the way the brain interprets reality. Ida had loved pretending to be a giant with Jesse in diminutive form in a monochrome room that looked like it was designed by Bridget Riley.

'Sounds wonderful!'

'Yeah it was cool.' Jesse's face dropped a little, his smile unconvincing.

Minnie tried to stick a fork in some pea shoots. 'Wasn't it?'

'Oh the museum was. And we had ice cream in Hyde Park.'

'What went wrong?'

The greyness that swept over Jesse's face said it all.

'It ending?' Minnie suggested carefully.

He nodded.

'You just have this pit of dread in your stomach all weekend, like a countdown timer, and although I shouldn't even think about that on a Friday night or Saturday, and I know I should live in the moment, I can't. And I don't want my feelings to filter through, but they do, so... so Ida feels this dread too.'

'Oh man.' Minnie had been desperate to ask what happened with his wife. Was it actually over?

'Is there no hope of you moving back in?' she said, acting as hopeful as she could.

Jesse shook his head but couldn't speak. Minnie wasn't sure how she felt about it. Terrible for him that his marriage looked over; terrible that a fractal of her felt some relief when she had no right to. She had no personal investment in his marriage, but God she fancied him as she watched him eat.

What the hell happened?

'So what can you do? Get more time with her?'

Minnie noticed the background music was cranking up a notch with each guest who left. Casual fine dining looked like it was evolving into a traditional Saturday night lock-in.

Jesse shook his head, trying to smile through his lack of ideas.

'I don't know. I don't often have her at Andrew and Elena's... only on the Friday night if we do, but it doesn't really work with their twins. It's *their* space. I need to get a place for myself, but... you know. I miss our home. I didn't want to have to be the one to move out.'

Jesse stopped himself from saying more. He was so hideously embarrassed by what had happened. Worse still since he'd discovered an extra layer of deception.

Minnie noticed the stress on *our* home. This was a guy she would never know as well as his wife knew him. But that was fine, they were just friends.

'Where does your daughter stay when you do have her?'

'We do the odd overnight hotel when it's my weekend.' Jesse hated that he spoke in terms of *my weekend*; in terms of on-and-off parenting. 'We stayed in the countryside when we went to Whipsnade. We did a night in Brighton last month. I take her out so we're not treading on anyone's toes.'

Jesse felt like such a loser, he could barely meet Minnie's eye.

'It's not sustainable.'

'It's not! It's sounds rotten for you.'

Camilla came back and placed two beers on the table and Jesse and

Minnie smiled their thanks to her. Jesse wondered how to pay for all this, or whether it was on the house. He felt terrible that he'd only bought rounds of drinks and a basket of fried chicken at Beyoncé Bingo.

'Can you stay at your flat on the weekends you have her? Is there somewhere your... your ex can go?'

'That's what we did last weekend. Hannah went to stay with friends.'

He tried not to sound bitter or loaded.

Minnie looked at him expectantly, as if to say *go on*.

'And on Sunday teatime, when Hannah came back and it was time for me to go, it all kicked off. Ida screamed. She was raging. Clinging to me. Hannah thought it would be better if I just ripped off the Band-Aid and went. She was shouting at me to go, which didn't help. But I couldn't. Ida was screaming for me.'

Minnie felt sick for him.

'Oh dear, that sounds awful. What was she screaming?'

'She was saying, "I love you but if you go I'll hate you." She got herself so worked up she was raging. It was hideous.'

'Uff,' Minnie exhaled. 'It sounds it.'

'I had to put her to bed, hysterical, and just lie with her, to regulate her breathing.'

'God, Jesse, that sounds traumatic.'

Jesse looked at Minnie across the table, her eyes filled with empathy and sorrow, and gently smiled, a flash of gratitude on his face.

Minnie held his gaze. She wanted to ask him a thousand questions; she thought of Tony and how he might broach them. She wondered if she should broach her new and confusing feelings for Jesse at their next session.

How are we doing?

But this wasn't about her, this was about him. And Minnie thought Jesse sounded like a wonderful dad; she felt terrible for him.

Jesse spoke as if he'd read her mind.

'I want to go for full custody.'

Minnie smiled but internally winced. These things didn't tend to work in the dad's favour, did they?

'I've been Ida's primary carer for most of her life. I'm not saying that in a judgy way – it's the way that worked best for our family. Hannah's job is demanding, she didn't want much time off. I could work it easier with...'

Jesse was going to say Lightning Designs, but couldn't remember if she remembered his name or not. 'With my company. I used to draw in the evenings and during her naptimes as a baby. My assistant Max could pick up other stuff. Client meetings became a bit easier for me in the Zoom era, but Hannah's always pretty much needed to be in an office. Her job is more corporate and big finance. Plus she loves the social side of it...'

Jesse cringed internally, remembering the phone call. The sick feeling when he eventually saw his wife with her lover.

'Well it sounds like you have a good case for full custody then,' Minnie said hopefully.

Jesse shook his head. 'I moved out. I think that was a mistake. I should have sat tight.'

'So what happened?' Minnie finally found the courage to ask. 'Why *did* you move out?' But a mis-timed cheer distracted them.

'Yayyyyy! Minnie!' bellowed Keenan, Hilde's assistant chef, as he came out of the kitchen, face shiny and eyes alert, relieved to have finished the busiest shift of the week. The Alpine NW1 staff worked hard and they partied hard. He swaggered over to the table, not entirely happy to see his crush eating the food he had prepped with another man.

'How are ya?' Keenan's Irish accent was thick, his face mischievous. He gave Jesse the most cursory of glances.

'Good thanks.' Minnie beamed up at him.

'Special lock-in tonight!' he said, as he closed the doors on the last of the guests and pulled the window blinds down. 'Joining us?' he asked, looking at Minnie and not Jesse. 'It's my birthday. Here!'

It's my dad's birthday, Jesse thought.

'Ahhh, I didn't realise! Keenan, this is Jesse...'

Keenan placed a shot glass in front of Minnie, and reluctantly went to get another for Jesse.

'There you go, mate,' he said with disinterest.

'Thanks.' Jesse raised his glass and downed the amaretto.

'Happy birthday!' Minnie said, standing to hug Keenan. She wrapped both arms around his neck and gave him a tight and hearty hug. She pulled back and put her palms on his cheeks.

'You don't look a day over thirty!' she joked.

'Fuck off,' Keenan replied.

Jesse watched as Keenan's tattooed fingers gripped either side of Minnie's waist and he felt that maybe it was time to go home.

* * *

Half an hour later, the restaurant was bustling again, with Keenan's friends dropping in to wish him a happy birthday on their circuit of after-work after-parties. Hilde didn't mind the hedonism and turned a blind eye to drugs, as long as she didn't see anything untoward going on herself. Minnie was oblivious to it – she had always been scared of drugs and was a happy enough tipsy drunk – and she danced with Keenan and his mates to UK garage while Jesse watched, remembering songs from his first school disco.

Camilla slid in next to him and pulled her ponytail out of its band.

'Uff, I am tired. How these guys can party like this is beyond me!' she said through a wholesome smile. She took a swig from her bottle of beer.

If Camilla felt old, Jesse felt older, creepy even, as he took a sip from a small tumbler of craft beer, which didn't sit well on top of all the cocktails and amaretto, as he and Camilla watched Minnie and Keenan in the centre of the restaurant. The life and soul. Surely none of this lot remembered this music from the first time around?

'Hey, can I just tap and pay for what Minnie and I had?' Jesse asked Camilla. 'I need to go...'

'Oh that's not necessary, I think Minnie comes in a lot and finishes up.' Camilla laughed. 'Like, whatever's left in the kitchen.'

Jesse wasn't sure.

'At least let me get the drinks.' He handed his card over the table between them. 'Can you just tap like a hundred?' Jesse asked. He had a feeling this might be the last time he saw Minnie. 'I don't want to take the piss.'

'Hmmm, well, if you're sure...' Camilla said in Scandi-sounding English. She got up and went to the terminal behind the small bar while Jesse watched Minnie, laughing as she danced. Her infectious, wonderful, intriguing laugh. How relaxed she seemed. He couldn't remember seeing Hannah laugh so wholeheartedly in a long time. He couldn't remember Hannah laughing like that at all come to think of it. While Minnie's laugh lifted him, he was being brought down by something he knew he had no right to feel. He didn't like the way Keenan's hand rested on Minnie's lower back as he leaned over her to whisper something into her ear; Jesse didn't like how it agitated him.

The cocktails felt like they were curdling under the beer in his stomach. He couldn't feel sick tomorrow. Tomorrow was Father's Day and he had a bonus couple of hours with Ida for the occasion.

Time to go.

Beyond the dancing he saw Hilde shoot him a look through the people in the middle of the room. She was drinking what looked like neat whisky or dark rum, and she raised her glass to Jesse, giving him a sympathetic smile. Jesse could tell Hilde felt sorry for him.

I'm such a loser.

He looked back at Minnie and Keenan grinding. Camilla returned with his bank card.

Beyoncé came on the playlist, 'Alien Superstar', as Jesse picked up his jacket and tentatively shuffled to the makeshift dance floor. He wasn't the type to leave without saying goodbye.

'Eyyyy!' Minnie cheered, looking for Jesse, but he wasn't at the table any more. She spun around again, not noticing he was making his way into the crowd.

'Hey!' Jesse struggled to get Minnie's attention as her back was to him and Keenan's shoulder was doing its best to block him.

Why the fuck am I getting sucked into this?

'Hey!' he said louder, towards Minnie's ear. 'Hey, look, I'm gonna go!'

Minnie turned around sharply and pressed her palm onto his navel.

'What?'

'I'm gonna go, I've got loads on tomorrow.'

'On a Sunday?'

'Yeah. It's Father's Day.'

Jesse didn't want to admit he was mostly free tomorrow. He could see his daughter for a couple of hours, special dispensation, and then he would be sketching. He didn't want to admit that he had no interest in watching a young, free, single woman he had no right to feel jealous over, or intention of falling for, dancing with a young, free, single (ripped) guy he had no right to feel envious of. He needed to go back to West Hampstead and google his legal rights as a dad who might want custody. He needed to plan what he was going to say in what was going to be a very difficult conversation with Hannah, which he would leave until after Father's Day, so as not to make it harder.

'But I haven't shown you my lick lick lick...'

Minnie looked at Jesse in the dim, red and pink lights of Alpine NW1, almost provocatively, holding his gaze, her tongue poised. To Jesse it felt like a punch in the chest.

'What?'

'Or my kitty-kat crawl.'

'Eh?'

'My Beyoncé moves!'

'Oh yeah.' Jesse gave a half-hearted smile. 'I have to go. Sorry. You'll get home safe, yeah?'

'Yeah, I'm just up the road, I'll go when Hilde goes.'

'Great stuff,' Jesse said functionally, as he kissed her on each cheek and turned away.

Minnie studied him in the melee and the darkness. This wasn't the way either of them had wanted the evening to end. A tense and sudden goodbye while the dancing around them intensified. Minnie grabbed Jesse's hand before he slipped away and he stopped and turned around. She pulled herself into him, an anchor, as she steadied her restless legs.

'Why don't you come with me?' she said, almost nervously, to his neck, her hand still clutching his, sparks of electricity no scientist could explain shooting between them. He paused and looked down at her. He felt a longing he didn't like.

'What?'

'Why don't you come with me? To Paris? Thursday week. Just for the day. You can go to the zoo while I do my audition?'

Jesse was a little bewildered. Through the cocktails and the beer and the fog clouding his brain, he tried to think. Ida. Work. Max. He could see Keenan looming behind Minnie. Jesse was tall and strong, but something about Keenan's youth, his energy, his intoxication, made him seem like a behemoth.

'Erm, I dunno, I'd need to che—'

'Great! I'm booked on the first train out of St Pancras. See you there?'

Jesse leaned in, kissed Minnie's cheek once this time, and left, as he heard Keenan bellowing over Beyoncé.

15

MINNIE

Four Months Ago – February

'I know he's Mr Billy Big Balls and all that...' Hilde's English was a strange mixture of East London vocab spoken in a Swiss German accent, which often enabled her to be more forthright, for blows to be delivered without people realising. 'But I think he might be a little bit... how do you say it... toxic?'

'What?' Minnie's face was aghast. She stopped threading a long earring through one ear as she stared at her reflection in the hallway mirror of their maisonette flat. She turned around to look at Hilde.

'He just sent me a really fucking expensive dress, wrapped in a really fucking expensive box.'

'Yeah but that's what pimps do, bae.'

Hilde rummaged through a cascade of jute and cloth bags shut in an understairs cupboard, looking for the one she'd left her wallet in.

'What?' Minnie had been getting ready for the car that JP was sending, to pick her up at 5 p.m. and take her to the BRIT Awards, where he'd bought a table for him, Minnie and a group of associates he was trying to impress.

'He sometimes talks to you like you're a kid, right? I mean, he sent you that dress and told you to wear it. He touches you on the nose like I touched Doris.'

Minnie struggled to get the earring through, a scowl creasing her face.

'Who's Doris?'

'Our Bernese.'

Minnie fixed her earring and looked back at her reflection. She wiggled to straighten the fabric. The dress JP had sent was a black, tight, short Saint Laurent number with shoulder pads and a plunging neck that showed a vast V of alabaster skin from her collarbone to her navel. She felt pretty special in it. Her mother rarely wore expensive dresses unless she had to. Geraldine Byrne was known for her Bohemian aesthetic. Her flea market kimonos and her deep red hair, wild and curly, now grey at the temples. Although the family lived in comfort, material objects hadn't ever been desirable to Minnie's mother. She'd wear designer clothes to the Olivier Awards or the Oscars, but was happiest free of stage and film make-up, barefoot on a beach in Dog's Bay.

'You really think that?'

Hilde's face flashed with relief to find her wallet, as she picked up her parka. She nodded.

'Remember that scene in *all* the romcoms? When the rich guy sends the ditzy woman an expensive dress and we're meant to feel excited for her about this?'

'Yes!' Minnie said excitedly.

'Eww!' Hilde looked horrified.

'What?' Minnie was shocked that Hilde didn't agree with her.

'Remember your Bechdel test, babe.'

Minnie nodded and tapped her temple with her finger, as if to say *noted*.

'I mean, fuck that shit. No one tells you what to wear!' Hilde sounded both outraged and amused.

Minnie looked back at herself and ran her fingers through her short black fringe.

'I know, I know. But if I didn't think I looked awesome in it, I wouldn't wear it.'

Hilde had to give Minnie that. She nodded appreciatively as she put her parka over her chef whites. Anyway, Minnie didn't have time to be outraged or offended, the driver was going be here in ten minutes.

She hadn't had time for much lately. She'd turned down waitressing work to focus on hanging out with JP and a big audition she had last week for a Marvel movie. Minnie had been working out to try to build some muscle, using the gym in the basement of JP's Holland Park home. Getting up after he'd gone to the office, working out, then trying not to snoop around his epic four-storey bachelor pad before going home, changing, then meeting him again for dinner in one of his restaurants.

Minnie felt a buzz of nervous anticipation about tonight. Not only because she was going to the BRIT Awards, but because she was hoping to run into her sister, Rosie, there. Rosie was married to a folk-rock musician called Teddy, who the family all adored, and whose band had been nominated for Best British Group. Minnie wanted to celebrate with Rosie, Teddy and the band but she also thought it would be the perfect place for her to introduce Rosie to JP, when JP, the wide-boy raconteur, would be in his element schmoozing. JP wasn't like the guys Rosie and Teddy hung out with – he was double her age and not exactly rock-star handsome – but Minnie hoped JP's charm and sparkle would win through and permeate her sister, as it had her. Rosie's approval meant a lot to Minnie. It always had. She was ten years older than Minnie and they were close, despite being Byrne bookends. Rosie was pregnant with her first baby, and if she didn't click with JP then at least she and Rosie had the pregnancy to talk about, although Minnie didn't think JP would be very interested in that. She wondered how a man like JP had got to his fifties without having any children, but she liked the George Clooney edge of it... even though JP looked absolutely nothing like George Clooney.

Tonight seemed like the perfect way to segue JP into the family, through Rosie.

She roughed up the back of her short black bob so it looked artfully tousled and tried to look at herself objectively. It really hadn't crossed her mind that JP was treating her like a hooker. She felt like a princess the way he put her on a pedestal.

'There's nothing toxic about having fun,' Minnie said, standing firm. 'And JP's so supportive. He's let me work out in his gym.'

'Someone's gotta use it I guess...' Hilde joked to herself, but Minnie gladly ignored it. She was proud of her man and all he had achieved.

'He's been helping cheer me up while I wait on Marvel. And anyway, he's a money man, he throws bling at a problem, I'm down with that.'

'You're not a problem though. There is nothing to fix.'

Minnie levelled Hilde with a sarcastic look as if to say *that's not what I meant.*

'You're a fucking *queen* as you are. And you'll always be a superhero, whether Marvel want you or not.'

Minnie smiled gratefully. 'Thank you.'

'Anyway, I got to get to the restaurant. I'm meeting a geezer about some Swiss Black Angus, like, twenty minutes ago.'

Minnie laughed.

'Have a great night.'

'I will.' Minnie smiled, as Hilde opened the flat door. 'Harry Styles is meant to be going!' she called, as the front door slammed. Minnie knew Hilde wouldn't give two hoots about whether Harry Styles was there or not. All Hilde cared about was tonight's service. And her friends. She was a fiercely loyal friend.

Minnie leaned in to her reflection and pressed the tip of her nose in the mirror, like JP did. Perhaps it did feel a bit condescending.

16

JESSE

Four Months Ago – February

In a large airy room in Fulham Palace, the wintry trees of Bishops Park looking like spectres through the window, Jesse and Hannah sat side by side, waiting. Waiting for Andrew's bride to arrive, waiting for an explanation, waiting for a solution, waiting for an answer to their deadlock.

Oscar and Fred tugged on Andrew's jacket and played with the rings; Andrew's brother Justin tried to keep them occupied by doing a trick where he pretended to slice his thumb in half using the forefinger on his other hand.

'That's stupid!' Jesse saw Fred say to his uncle, although Jesse couldn't hear it under the sound of the string quartet.

As they had taken their seats and nodded to Andrew, Justin, and the boys, Jesse had said he wished Ida could have come to the Valentine's Day wedding. Even though it was a school day.

'I'd have taken her out of school for this,' Jesse said, leaning into Hannah but without looking at her. Ida had known Andrew, Elena and the boys all her life.

'I wish we'd had a no-child policy at our wedding,' Hannah shot back quickly.

Jesse looked at her, surprised.

'What? Bloody Wilbur cried all the way through the vows!' she snapped in justification.

Jesse and Hannah had got married eight years ago in Richmond Park, near where they had gone to school in Surrey. Jesse had wanted to get married in the South of France but Hannah wanted to be closer to home, so he'd traded the purple lavender of Provence for a wisteria-covered Georgian mansion in the middle of the park in spring. They had exchanged vows in a room not dissimilar to this one, not dissimilar to a hundred weddings they seemed to have gone to lately; they ate lamb and rhubarb crumble and danced to 'You Are So Beautiful' by Joe Cocker.

Jesse looked around the room, taking in the touches he recognised. Bow-backed chairs and a flower arch at the front. The nervous groom and his best-man brother, although Jesse had asked his dad to be his best man.

He knew if Ida were invited, she would have sat impeccably next to him in a pretty dress, or her fanciest 'explorer shorts' as she called them.

He smiled to himself as he watched the boys, pretending to be amused by them while feeling the force between him and his wife, noting that no part of his body touched any part of Hannah's, despite the chairs being crammed in. It was like an air lock separated the gap between their seats.

Jesse looked at Andrew ruffling Oscar's hair then trying to tame it before smoothing down his own nervously. Why was he so nervous? This was a brilliant idea. Waiting until their twins were six to get married, so their kids could be there, so they could witness and remember their parents' declaration of love. Giving their relationship and parenthood time to settle, to really think about their vows before making them. Hannah had clearly made hers in haste.

Maybe we were too young.

They had only been in their early twenties.

Jesse leaned in to Hannah, their shoulders briefly touching. He felt her almost flinch.

'I'll move out,' he said quietly. Hannah looked at him sharply, then down at her skirt as she swiped a loose thread from it. She was shocked, both at what Jesse had just said, and for choosing now to say it, of all times, as if he had planned it. To announce it in a crowd, while a string quartet played 'Marry You' by Bruno Mars. Minimal chance for an argument or a scene.

Jesse had been sleeping on the sofa ever since the night Hannah came home last month, apologised for smelling of garlic, blamed her PA Tara for having put the dinner in the diary in the first place, apologised that the client had talked for too long and said they had all got a bit carried away. She said she desperately needed to pee before she put her bag down. Jesse was sitting on the sofa, elbows on his thighs. She hadn't even stopped to look at his harrowed face.

'I know what you did,' Jesse had said, the words like vomit he couldn't hold back. 'The client got more than a bit carried away.'

Hannah had stopped suddenly in the doorway, hoping desperately that he didn't know. She didn't have time for explanation and retribution.

'I heard you, on FaceTime.'

She turned around, her face almost angry as she looked at Jesse, although she couldn't meet his eye. A suppressed outrage, as if her husband had been spying on her. She closed her eyes, let out a huge sigh and leaned on the door frame in defeat.

'I can't do this now,' Hannah said, as she kicked off her heels, took her Nike trainers from the shoe rack by the door, put them on, and headed straight back out. She hadn't stopped to go to the loo.

Jesse sat on the sofa for another forty-five minutes, thinking, *Is that it?* Wondering if Hannah had just left him without even bothering to tell him. Wondering still who the man was who'd made his wife groan. Who the man his wife was repeatedly calling a *naughty boy* was. Wondering what the hell was going to happen to their beautiful daughter. Then Hannah came back to the flat and deigned to offer Jesse an explanation.

'It didn't mean anything.'

Didn't. Past tense. A one-off? It didn't sound like a one-off.

'I'm not in love or anything.'

Hannah didn't notice the look of total confusion and bewilderment on Jesse's face. *Not in love with her lover, or not in love with her husband?*

'I need time to work out what's going on in my head.'

Jesse wanted to shout, *What the fuck* is *going on in your head?*

'Who is he?' Jesse asked, but Hannah just ignored the question.

How could you do that?

'It doesn't matter,' Hannah snapped after a third time of asking. Jesse was taken aback by her righteous rage.

My dad just died.

'What matters is the *reason* it's happened. *Who* is irrelevant.'

'No it isn't. Who is he?'

Hannah stayed silent and stony faced.

'How long has it been going on? You seem pretty comfortable together.'

They knew their way around each other's bodies.

'Were you fucking him when I went to France? When my dad died?'

Hannah managed to look both mortified and livid, her thin lips creeping into a trembling line. She took a deep breath.

'Look – I'm not happy. You're not happy. We need time.' As she said it, she held up her hand, as if she were scared of Jesse. He did make her flinch. That was the most hurtful thing. Loving, doting, kind Jesse made his wife flinch. She'd rather talk dirty and get fucked by a faceless man than look at her husband, who had just lost his dad.

Jesse slept on the sofa, and the next morning, when Ida saw him, eyes ringed and red by the double blows of grief, she asked him if he was playing hide and seek. 'No my sweet girl, I was snoring too loudly, Mummy couldn't sleep.'

'Koalas snore loud, Daddy,' Ida replied without question. 'It sounds more like a burp. You can sleep in my room if you want.'

* * *

After a month of sleeping on the sofa, of living in a pressure cooker, where Jesse felt he wasn't allowed to mention the situation or raise it, he realised it was all too much. Too much sadness, too much betrayal, too much grief. He was grieving his dad, and he was grieving his marriage, and everything he thought he knew about his wife. All the things he had thought highly of her – how clever she was; how driven she was; how go-getting she was; how beautiful she was – had come crashing down. He couldn't tell his friends. He'd only told Max last week that they were having issues when she'd found him asleep at 6 a.m. in the office, in a sleeping bag on the floor. He definitely couldn't tell his mother given what she was going through right now, although Jesse did tell Elena. He was doing some branding for the private tutoring company she was planning to start up, and they'd met for a coffee when she was near his office, to chat through designs. Elena Apfel Private Tutoring. He did put an apple on her logo, even though he refused to put a lightning bolt on his – she was a teacher, it was a gift.

'Are you OK? You look awful!' Elena had said. And then Jesse couldn't keep it in any longer.

'Do you know about Hannah's affair? Has she told you?'

Jesse could tell from the horror on Elena's face that she knew nothing, before going through a torrent of emotions and questions, about who she was sleeping with, how she could do that to Jesse, how awful everything must be at home. The branding fell by the wayside that day.

'What are we going to do about the wedding?' Elena had asked, horrified. 'Shall I uninvite her? I'm not sure I can look at her.'

Jesse shook his head.

'Keep it all normal. It might all blow over in time.' As he said it, he stole a sideways glance at Elena and they could tell from each other's expressions that this wasn't the sort of thing that would just blow over.

A few days before the wedding, Elena had an idea: she convinced Andrew into them offering Jesse their home, housesitting while they went on honeymoon to Australia. The twins' half-term break was being extended to three weeks, and Jesse could live freely in their West Hampstead town house while the family were away, giving him and Hannah time to work on their marriage. Elena was so livid she couldn't bring herself to speak to Hannah in the run-up to the wedding. She put her lack of communication down to being too busy with the last-minute details. Andrew agreed and told Elena they could offer Jesse a place to crash, but otherwise he wanted to keep out of it. It was none of their business.

* * *

The string quartet started to play 'Halo' by Beyoncé, Jesse not knowing he would be dancing to a rendition of it sung by a drag queen a few months later. Heads started to crane, to see whether this was Elena's entrance music. Hannah looked quickly, but the bride wasn't there yet.

'Where will you move to?' she asked hurriedly, as she looked at Andrew and the boys at the front. Oscar was teasing Fred and stealing the ring he was in charge of. Justin told them to calm down. Andrew looked tense and kept his gaze at the floor.

Jesse nodded towards the front. 'They said I could have their place while they're in Australia. Said I could stay longer if need be.'

Hannah almost choked. '*What?*'

'Shhh...' Jesse whispered, calling for calm as he pressed a horizontal hand down through the air. Hannah didn't flinch now. She looked panicked and alert.

'It makes sense. Three weeks. It'll be healthy.'

'That's ridiculous!'

'Why? They've got the space. I can watch the house, put the bins out, feed Rocky.'

Hannah looked like she was the one who'd been betrayed.

'I think it makes sense,' Jesse said again, as coolly as he could, about a prospect that sickened him.

Hannah shook her head as if it were a firm no.

'It doesn't make any sense!' She paused. 'What will Ida think? You living in Oscar and Fred's house and not with her?'

'They'll be in Australia.'

'No but—'

Jesse turned to Hannah and actually looked at her, his eyes piercing.

'Well do *you* want to explain it to her?' he said, as harshly as he had ever spoken to his wife in their lives together. He rubbed his face in disbelief. He felt so tired, his eyeballs so sad they hurt.

He couldn't understand why Hannah was quite so incredulous. *She* had been the one to blow apart their marriage. How many men had she slept with anyway? Was it one special guy, or something she did regularly to get kicks with clients? She still wouldn't tell him who he was. Why wouldn't she say who he was if it was over? Did she really not love him? How reckless to ruin your marriage for someone you didn't love. How could she kick him when he was at his lowest ebb, heart already torn and hollow from the emptiness of grief?

Jesse took a deep breath and out of habit he went to feel in his pocket, before remembering the keyring his dad had gifted him after a trip to India wasn't there. He had lost it one month before his dad had died and it haunted him. A little brass statue of the goddess Saraswati his dad had picked up at a tourist shop and was so taken with her, he gave her to Jesse, and Jesse had treasured it for years. Until he lost her. His pocket was empty.

'Would everyone please stand?' the celebrant said with a warm smile. Jesse slowly rose; Hannah stood abruptly, flustered, her bag dropping to the floor and its chain strap clanging to the metal of the chair underneath her, making people look. Then Jesse had an epiphany.

17

MINNIE

Now

'Another Pimm's?' Minnie asked the city boys, shiny faced, wearing thick ties and cream linen suits. She'd seen their type all week. On a jolly from Deloitte or JP Morgan; Hearst or Procter & Gamble.

The men looked at each other in their corner of the busy corporate hospitality tent, ruddy from a day at the tennis. The taller one, with black hair, blue eyes and emergent freckles shrugged. He'd had enough, he could feel sugar on his teeth, but he didn't know how to say no to the waitress wielding a glass jug of the stuff in each hand.

Regardless of their response, Minnie was going to top them up anyway. Once she got rid of this round, she was clocking off. She needed to prep for Paris. Run her lines one last time and work out what to wear. Midsummer in Paris was looking pretty warm.

'There you go!' she said, filling the man's glass almost to the top.

'Whoa!' he said, heeding caution, but Minnie was careful to offload as much of the stuff as she could without spilling a drop.

She looked expectantly at the freckled man's friend, who was blonder, wider and ruddier. He stood with an empty pint glass and wolfish eyes.

'Go on then...' he said, thinking Minnie would get him a fresh glass, one more suited to Pimm's, lemonade and fruit. She filled his pint until one of the glass jugs she was holding was satisfyingly empty, gave them a smile, then waltzed off to the adjacent kitchen tent behind canvas screens.

Once Minnie was out of sight, she stopped behind a canvas partition, tilted the lip of the almost-empty second jug to her mouth and drank Pimm's and lemonade like a hamster from a bottle. She was mindful not to choke on any cucumber, strawberries and mint mulch at the bottom of the jug.

'Job done!' she said to herself cheerily, as she continued into the kitchen and handed the empty vessels to the boy who was washing up.

'There you go!'

The boy didn't say thanks, as Minnie went to her locker and grabbed her jacket, bag and phone. Her phone was already ringing as she picked it up and her blood ran cold when she looked at the screen. JP. The photo she had assigned him when she had the privilege of being his lover. Small blue eyes sparkling at the camera, tumbler in one hand, cigar in the other, and Minnie, arm draped around his neck as she kissed his cheek adoringly. How dare he invade her space when she was doing so well? She hadn't spoken to him since he'd dumped her in the cafe of Bondiga's Books almost three months ago. Yesterday, at her session with Tony, JP's name barely came up, which felt liberating – but then nor had Jesse's, and she had wanted to sense check her changing feelings for him with her therapist. *Next time*, she had thought.

'Fuck,' Minnie said, ignoring the call but letting it ring, as she nervously looked at the screen.

She took off her lanyard and handed it to the guard at a makeshift table in the staff security tent and weaved out to the exit, conveniently shielded by an American tennis star, his huge racket bag and his entourage. It felt a bit dramatic for dodging a call and Minnie chastised herself for caring. For hiding. What did she have to hide from?

She walked out of Queen's and down the stuccoed streets of West Kensington, back towards the tube station, her white shirt, skirt and black tights making her feel clammy. She made a mental note: definitely no tights tomorrow. Paris was going to be even warmer.

Paris. Keep the focus on Paris.

Minnie's phone rang again.

Fuck.

If only she'd been in the tube already.

She thought it was unlikely to be JP – he didn't chase or leave messages. She dared to look at the phone she clutched like a hand grenade, and saw that it was him calling again.

Shit.

What did he want?

I don't have to answer.

Why now?

You can do this.

'Hello?' Minnie answered, cautiously.

He will not steal my power. He will not break my soul.

'Hey, kid, how ya doin'?'

Kid.

Minnie took a deep breath.

'Yeah not bad thanks.' *Keep it breezy.* 'How's tricks?'

'Yeah all right thanks, all right.'

What do you want?

JP didn't have time to call for pleasantries. In the four months he had ricocheted through her life like a pinball, he had never called her to chat. He was too busy with his restaurants to chat on the phone. He liked to talk at dinners or in bed after sex, but if he ever did call her, it was to make a plan. To confirm she'd be where he wanted her, when. To request that she come to whichever restaurant he was having a meeting in. In fact, Minnie realised then that JP only made phone calls when he wanted something urgently.

Fuck.

She had a terrible feeling he was nearby, in one of his West London 'properties'.

There was a pause. JP never paused.

'What's up?' Minnie asked.

'I was just thinking about you. Wondered how you was getting on.'

Minnie took a deep breath.

'Yeah I'm fine thanks.' She smiled into her phone, as if to convince herself. Until she remembered she *was* doing fine.

'I'm off to Paris tomorrow actually, for an audition.'

'Oh great, what's it for, TV?'

'No, a movie. A Wim Fischer movie.'

'Fuck me,' JP exclaimed.

'I'm meeting his casting director tomorrow.'

Don't sound grateful, Minnie. She thought of Tony's listening face. She thought of the empty chair. She thought she might throw up into the gutter but perhaps that was the Pimm's. She knew better than to swig it like that just to finish a shift.

'Good for you.'

The patronising pleasure in JP's tone made Minnie feel defensive. Her throat tightened. She felt like she couldn't speak. She *couldn't* speak. He'd taken the wind out of her sails again.

I'm doing so well. I have earned this audition.

'Actually, Min, you was on my mind – I read in the paper about *Summer of Siena* coming to screen. All legal scores settled. That's great news, babe.'

Minnie exhaled in relief. Relief that she understood. She was desirable again. On the up. Not some sad waitress who didn't get a call back from Marvel. Not the disappointment whose famous parents hadn't seemed as charmed by him as he thought they should. And in one conflicted, constrictive clash, Minnie regretted telling JP about Paris. It wasn't his business.

She was scared of being desirable again.

'My ingénue,' JP said proudly.

18

JESSE

Now

'Hey, do you need me for the GrowPots thing tomorrow?' Jesse leaned back on his chair and interlocked his fingers behind his head as Max turned around. 'Because I might be out of the office. But if you need me...'

Max tried to measure Jesse's face. He didn't usually tiptoe around her about meetings.

'No I think I'm good to go with it all – if you wanted to look at it before I...?' Max sounded unsure of herself, and leaned over to her in-tray where her drawings for a new brand of healthy children's ready meals were sitting on top of the brief.

'No, no you're way better than me on this!' Jesse released his fingers and waved a hand. 'I was just thinking of going to Paris tomorrow, that's all. Wondered if you needed me here.'

'Paris? Wow, how come?'

'But not if you need back-up.'

Max looked at him, puzzled. Jesse was a good boss; they worked beautifully independently, and comfortably together on the clients they did coincide on. He was supportive, no nonsense and didn't play games, so it was unlike him to sound so uncertain about something.

If the boss of a sports brand was ever shitty with Jesse, he'd politely stand his ground and remind them of the brief. If another designer got a little too close to Jesse's style with a new typograph or design, he'd send a courteous but strongly worded letter, as if to say *I'm onto you mate*. Jesse wasn't shy to speak his mind when it came to work, or take a day to do something if he needed to. It was only in his marriage that he had been woefully voiceless. His indecision now confused Max.

'I don't need back-up, I feel ready and the client is lovely. What's Paris for? More fashion?' Maybe that's why Jesse was looking for an excuse.

'No, no,' Jesse said, with some relief. The fashion work was Jesse's least favourite because the clients were the most precious. Jesse preferred the numbers, the football teams, shaping the look for a generation of footballers and their fans, in clothing that would hopefully go down in history as the greatest in their club's era.

One of Jesse's earliest memories was of Manchester United winning the treble in 1999. He was six. He wasn't a Manchester United fan, but that shirt: the piping, the collar, the font. One look at it would capture a moment in time and a moment of glory. Like the Dutch national kit of 1988 (faded orange chevrons). The France kit of 1998 (classic stripes). AC Milan's *invincibli* kit of 1992 (simple and chic). Juventus 2015 (away; classic salmon pink and red clash). Club America 1995 (triangles that looked like feathering on the shoulders, giving the Mexican team an indigenous, Aztec vibe). Those kits would go down in history for their style and their beauty; they were the kits that inspired Jesse to study typography and design. And although there was nothing Jesse could do about a sponsor's ugly branding on the front of the shirt (although the Italian sponsors did do it better), this was the part of his Lightning Designs work he loved most. He didn't love FMCG or fashion packaging. He was only hoping to get into children's books for the sake of his dad. To fulfil a promise.

'It's not work – it's a research trip,' he said. 'Sketching at Paris Zoo, but I sort of need to go tomorrow. Deadline,' he half lied.

Jesse was the boss, he didn't need to justify his movements.

'Oh Remy! How's he coming along?'

Jesse looked guilty.

'He isn't really. The agent is expecting drafts before the school holidays, so I'm running out of time.'

Jesse always felt a bit bad talking about the rhythm of his life in respect of term time, half terms and holidays. He had a feeling Max didn't feel comfortable when he spoke like that. He'd see her glaze over when he talked about parents' consultation evenings and soft-play parties, although Max always smiled and tried to look interested.

Jesse didn't know whether Max and Liam wanted kids, or whether parenthood sounded like the dullest prospect in the world to them. He knew Max was a loving aunt to her nieces. He also knew she was probably being pushed to the edge by Liam's drinking, his benders, his going AWOL until 2 a.m. She'd stopped the parlance of justification she had parroted in recent years. Blaming herself for being naïve; saying actually lots of people do coke. She'd started coming into the office at 6 a.m., as soon as the shared space building opened, going home via the West End to pick up a birthday present for a niece or meet a friend for mezze. She seemed to be in no man's land, and Jesse wasn't sure how to get past the superficial walls of their weekend chat any more. To see if she really was OK.

He did keep checking that he wasn't overloading Max with clients and commissions when she worked such long hours, but she'd smile serenely and say she was just finishing up, or had life admin to do.

Jesse's book agent, Maddie Feynman, on the other hand, was a mother. She spoke in that parent patois that becomes all-encompassing. So when she said she wanted Jesse's first draft drawings to her 'by summer', ready for submitting to publishers in September, Jesse knew that she meant by the third Friday in July. 'By summer' always meant by the end of the third week of July.

'Well Paris sounds like a great idea. Will you stay over?'

'No just a day trip, I need to be back here to draw all weekend.'

It had taken Jesse weeks of sleeping on the sofa before he'd confessed to Max that he was having marriage problems, that February morning Max had found him curled up in a sleeping bag in the space between their desks.

'Are you OK?' Max asked calmly when she saw him on the floor. Her first instinct was to think that he had got trashed like Liam, so she was so relieved he was sober, she wanted to cry. She almost did cry when Jesse told her that Hannah wanted to cool things off for a bit. He couldn't bring himself to tell her about the FaceTime call.

Max was kind and compassionate and asked if there was anything she could do to help, but she still didn't feel able to ask exactly what had happened. There was definitely more to this than Jesse was letting on. Nor did she feel able to tell Jesse about her marriage woes. How Liam would pace the flat all morning while he waited for the kitchen clock to whirr at midday, when the a.m. flap turned to p.m. and he got his own personal signal to start drinking again. A self-imposed rule that was both ridiculous and futile. Max was glad to be out of the flat for five of those seven days a week. The sound of the whirr at the weekend made her feel sick.

When Jesse started sleeping in his mates' spare room, and ended up staying longer than just the three weeks of housesitting he said it was, he told Max it was more serious: Hannah had had an affair. Max was horrified, she felt wretched. Still, she couldn't bring herself to tell Jesse how unhappy she was with Liam. She felt a pang of guilt; a flash and a reminder of when she hadn't stood up for him in college, when he had spoken up for her. If only she could speak up now, Jesse might not feel so alone.

Jesse played with a pot of cloud-shaped paperclips on his desk, a Paperchase relic he had pinched from Ida.

'I might be going with a friend actually,' he said vaguely.

'Oh, right?' Max replied, trying to sound just as cool.

'Yeah, an actor.' Jesse tried to avoid Max's eye. 'Has an audition in Paris tomorrow, so we're both going out on a field trip, if you will.'

Max felt a frisson of joy. The deliberate omission of a pronoun, the lack of a name, made her raise a keen eyebrow. Jesse usually spoke about his friends by name. Max knew many of them. She hoped this meant something. Max had never liked Hannah, since the first time she'd met her. She was stroppy and entitled. She had everything Max wanted and didn't appreciate any of it. And now she had been caught cheating. Right after Jesse had lost his lovely dad.

How could she?

'Well have a brilliant time, if you do go...' Max said warmly. 'And bring me back some madeleines, yeah?'

Max had a penchant for madeleines, the cheaper the supermarket brand, and usually the drier, the better. Jesse always brought a big bag back for her whenever he went to visit his mum, although he wasn't sure where the big Carrefour stores were in Paris.

'Will do.'

* * *

Max went to meet a potential new printer while Jesse spent all afternoon finishing the typography of the football club that had just been promoted from the Championship to the Premier League – a total kit redesign from the best in the business. This font meant a lot. It wasn't one that was going to sell a million shirts in Southeast Asia, but it was one that would mean the world to fans of the club. It needed to look beautiful against the sky-blue kit. Classic. Modern. Clean. No nonsense. It was due to be signed off on Friday.

Fuck.

Jesse couldn't think.

He hovered on the Eurostar tab he had open on his computer. It would be really handy if he could speak to Minnie before he booked a return ticket to Paris for tomorrow. *Was she still going? Which train was it again? Had she booked seats?*

At 6 p.m. Max texted him to say the meeting with the printer had gone well and that she was going to pop to Westfield. Jesse replied to say good luck with GrowPots. They'd talk when he was back on Friday.

It was quiet in the shared space building beyond Lightning Designs. Jesse tried to focus on his finishing touches but couldn't stop thinking about Paris. The ticket prices had gone up twice since he'd first looked at lunchtime. He clicked on his thirtieth birthday playlist to ease the silence and set it through the Bose speaker on his desk. He remembered the gathering in a pub in Tufnell Park two summers ago. Max and Liam were there. Will and his then-boyfriend Mikey. Andrew and Elena. His forever-single friend Kenji. Ida. Hannah arranged a cake. Friends from all facets of his life. His mum and dad were in London for a few days, so they popped in early but left to take Ida home and babysit. Jesse remembered being happy. His dad was alive; he didn't know about Hannah's affair. Or affairs. Was she having them then? Might her lover have been at his party? Daft Punk, Blondie, Beyoncé.

I do like Beyoncé, he thought.

It was still light outside. There was a midsummer optimism in the air as Jesse glanced out of the window above Max's desk and saw the couriers, taxis and buses hurtling down Gray's Inn Road, sunlight in drivers' eyes, people with places to go and purpose. Jesse thought of Ida and what she would be doing right now. Whether she was watching TV, and if so, with who. Daisy, Janey, or new au pair Henrike? The conversation about custody rights had been a disaster.

Don't do it to yourself.

He looked back at his desk, which was usually neat but right now covered in designs.

Focus. Work.

Jesse couldn't focus but he didn't want to go back to Andrew and Elena's yet. He was torn between working on the club shirt and his dad's book. MC Solaar came on his playlist. 'La Belle et le Bad Boy'. He remembered dancing with Max to it at his birthday party while Liam clung to the bar, drinking his way through Jesse's tab as best he could. Now he thought about it, Jesse couldn't even picture Hannah there after the cake. He couldn't remember what she wore, whether she had danced. Maybe she'd been sneaking off to make calls or have dalliances in a dark side street; maybe he had erased the memory of her being there.

Fuck it.

He clicked back on the Eurostar tab, a return to Paris, and hovered over seats for the first train out and the last train back. If Minnie had

changed her plan, he could still have a productive day. He wasn't depen-
dent on anyone else.

Standard or first?

Jesse's phone rang. A number he didn't recognise. A shrill glimmer of
hope that Minnie had tracked him down, that he could ask her if her
plan to go to Paris tomorrow was still on. Whether he was still invited, or
was she just drunk when she'd suggested it. Might she have forgotten?

'Hello?'

'It's me.'

Oh.

'Everything OK? Is Ida OK?'

'Yes she's fine – she's with Henrike.'

Henrike. The person who had been spending more time with Jesse's
daughter than Jesse had. Henrike spent more time with Ida than
Hannah did. The whole thing was ridiculous.

Jesse couldn't speak. It had gone so badly when he'd suggested last
week that he move back in; when he said it could work if he had full
custody and Hannah got a second home. Or that they move further out
of London, so they could get two flats for the value of their one. It could
work.

Hannah was furious. She said he couldn't evict her. He was bullying
her. Gaslighting her. That he had no chance of custody, especially not
when he couch-surfed at friends' houses. She realised as she said it that
her words only made him more determined. To get on an even keel and
then the courts could decide.

'She's happy with Henrike, they get on like a house on fire!'

'She'd be happier with me. She doesn't need an au pair, I'm her dad. I
can work from home. I can do everything you—'

'DON'T tell me I can't, Jesse,' Hannah shot back.

He wasn't going to say that. He was sure Hannah was capable of
anything. What he was going to say was *I can do everything you don't want
to*. But he didn't. This all seemed so unfair. How did it get to this?

* * *

Jesse paused the Spotify playlist so he could hear Hannah clearly. Perhaps she had thought his suggestion over.

Deep breath.

'I didn't recognise the number.'

'It's a new work phone.'

Jesse thought of the tracks and trails Hannah had blazed with her old work phone and what she might use this number for. Who was privy to it.

'I wanted to talk to you.'

It had been almost a week since Jesse's proposal that he move back in. Maybe Hannah had come round to it; her tone certainly sounded softer than when they'd last spoken, when Jesse had dropped an exhausted Ida home after another day milling around London, trying to avoid both West Hampstead and Kentish Town. She hadn't met his eye after his suggestion on Friday night. On Sunday night she'd told him to *go fuck himself.* After a working week of plate spinning, maybe she realised they could do this like grown-ups. Maybe Hannah could see they didn't need Henrike. Maybe the thought of the freedom she could have as a weekend parent would actually fit her life better. Jesse just had to walk the tightrope very carefully for the next few minutes. Make her see this could work, and it could work amicably.

'What's up?' he asked, as lightly as he could. 'What do you want?'

'You, Jesse. I want you.'

19

DAY FOUR

Now

Minnie stepped off the escalator onto the platform of St Pancras station and rubbed an eye with the back of her knuckle. In front of her hung a wake-up call.

I WANT MY TIME WITH YOU, read the neon-pink scrawl under the decadent white and gold railway station clock. The sun hadn't risen yet through the vast arching windows framed by industrial grey-blue wrought iron, so Tracey Emin's words glowed that bit brighter, an illumination lifting Minnie's mood, lighting her path.

She stopped going over the lines in her head, stopped walking, mesmerised by the artwork.

I want my time with you.

One sentence, six words, which were more beautiful and potent than anything Minnie had seen on the script in her hand.

She sipped her coffee and tugged on a wayward lash. It was not yet 5 a.m. and the station felt asleep, apart from the bleary early risers, the reluctant shop workers opening up, or the people getting the 06.01 first train to Paris.

Minnie started moving again, towards her carriage at the back. She wondered if Jesse was nearby. Without phones, without being able to call or message him, she craved to know whether he might join her. She wondered why he had left Alpine NW1 so abruptly and so glumly when, really, she had wanted to party with him and for the night never to end; for him to come back to her flat. Instead he had left in a hurry and she had gone home and done something else she regretted. Tony wouldn't approve – she hadn't told him that either.

As she reached the carriage matching the number on her ticket, Minnie took a slug of coffee and looked along the platform in both directions, at the other passengers getting on board. She looked backwards at the people beyond Perspex screens, still going through passport control and security. She looked over to the enormous bronze statue of a couple in a clinch under the clock. She looked to the figure of Sir John Betjeman clutching his hat in an imagined breeze. Figures in human shapes but none of them took on Jesse's reliable form.

Too vague. I was too vague.

Why would a guy she hardly knew go to Paris with her based on an offhand drunken comment she had made while she was grinding to UK garage with another man?

Fucking idiot.

She knew she shouldn't have brought up Ida that night too. It was clearly upsetting for Jesse, on a level she couldn't understand. Minnie had chastised herself a hundred times about how the Saturday before last had ended.

Minnie sighed as she felt for her passport in her skirt pocket and stepped onto the train. She felt a slight chill on her legs from the air conditioning and questioned her audition outfit. After feeling hot and confined in her waitress uniform at Queen's, she'd opted for a short flippy polka dot skirt worn over a ballerina bodysuit with a low back and a small cotton ruche between her small breasts. She'd chosen DMs over ballet flats, and oxblood red nails to give Veronica Valla more of an edge; her fitted Levi's denim jacket with a frilled collar softened her look. Minnie's legs were like her mother's – pale and elegant, yet strong – it was the confidence with which Minnie wore skirts and shorts that made them *good legs.*

Minnie walked down the carriage, found seat forty-three (by the window, facing forwards at a table) and slid in, grateful that no one else was in the carriage yet; that no one else was sitting around her. She put her phone and script on the table in front of her – she had two hours and seventeen minutes to plug in and really hone her lines.

As passengers boarded, Minnie felt a strange mixture of nervousness, excitement and disappointment, all in one knotted ball in the pit of her stomach, and she couldn't quite assign which emotion to which direction.

Sleep. Try to sleep.

As the half-empty train pulled out of the station, Minnie was relieved to have the table all to herself. She closed her eyes and thought about the cocktail class over a week and a half ago. How thoughtful it was of Jesse to arrange it. How much fun she'd had. How she'd wished she could ask more about what sort of a man Jesse's dad was. What had happened with his wife. What his daughter was like. What they had done for Father's Day. All questions she wouldn't usually hesitate to ask a person with candour and no holding back. Characters. Minnie loved characters. She loved playing them and she loved learning about them. But she often talked too much to hear as much as she wanted to.

She inhaled a deep sigh that turned into a yawn and the knot in her stomach churned as she remembered her audition – how she should be thinking about that instead of Jesse – but figured sleep would be the best preparation. The train, with its soporific rhythm and thrum, and the space around her, was conspiring to help Minnie doze off.

She closed her eyes and rested her head against a thin scarf she'd packed, in the gap between the chair and the window, knowing it would be too hot to wear later. The forecast in Paris was twenty-four degrees and sunshine. Minnie stretched her legs out in front of her and felt the train snake out of the station.

She was half asleep and halfway to Kent when she was woken by a polite voice.

'Is this seat taken?' asked a man.

Minnie opened her eyes.

'Get out!' she said in delight.

'Nice to meet you, I'm Jesse,' he said, extending a hand. Minnie resisted the urge to jump out of her seat and hug him. Instead, she laughed and shook his hand.

'Nice to meet you Jesse, I'm Minnie.'

* * *

Jesse was standing in a cream T-shirt and jeans, an apple green sweatshirt tied around his waist. He smiled and put his daypack on the shelf above them, then slid into the seat opposite Minnie. She pulled her legs back quickly then extended them out again, until they nestled between his. Comfortable. He made her feel comfortable.

'You made it!' She tried not to smile too hard.

'I nearly didn't. My tube stopped just outside of Euston, we were waiting for ages. They were just closing the gate when I shouted and they let me through.'

'That's cutting it fine.'

'I walked up and down the train and didn't see you!' Jesse blushed at how keen this made him sound, so tried to downplay it. 'Assumed I misheard you, or you weren't going any more.'

'Oh I'm going!'

He laughed. 'I can see that.'

Jesse nodded at the script in front of her, sitting next to her passport.

'How are you feeling?'

'Sick.'

'Can I help?'

'Hmmm...' She pondered the question.

Jesse looked out of the window at the sun rising over green fields, shooting through his eyes like a prism, refracting light into the space between them. Then he looked back at Minnie intently.

She tucked her hair behind her ear.

'I never know at this stage whether to go over it again or just put it to bed. There's a sweet spot, you know?'

He didn't know but nodded.

'Which I seemingly can't grasp given my last few auditions.'

Jesse picked up the script.

'You're Veronica Valla, highlighted?'

'Yup.'

'So I'll be... Johnson Stone – cool name – he's mafia, right?'

'Right, he's the muscle, but they're both about to double-cross their boss.'

'OK, shall I just start from the top?'

Minnie thought it might be useful to run the scene out loud with a male counterpart, but she was so happy and relieved to see Jesse she didn't want to do it just yet. She wanted to know what he'd been up to, how he was, whether he had broached the topic of custody with his ex.

'I wanted to message you,' Minnie said frankly.

Jesse studied the page. That wasn't in the script.

'Huh?'

He looked up at her again.

'It felt weird not being able to contact you.'

Jesse thought of Keenan's hands wrapped around Minnie's waist, the way he'd smiled when he looked down at her as they moved together.

'Oh.'

Minnie felt sick when she remembered the last time she saw Jesse. How the night had ended. Keenan had come back to her flat; they had kissed rampantly, secretively, in the kitchen while Hilde went to change into joggers and a T-shirt. Keenan had pressed himself against Minnie and lifted her onto the kitchen worktop. She had run her fingers through his hair, until she'd pulled back and said, 'No!'

'What?' Keenan had said laughing.

'Sorry, I'm just not... feeling it.'

Keenan studied Minnie's face to check whether she was joking or not, then realised she wasn't. Minnie looked so desperately disappointed, although she didn't tell Keenan why. He laughed to make light of it all.

'OK, make me a cuppa tea then at least?' he said. 'I'll skin up.'

'Fair dos...' Minnie said, relieved he was laughing it off. Relieved that Keenan and Hilde would have a smoke and dissect the night's service, while she could slink off to bed.

* * *

'I'm sure you could have looked me up if you really wanted to,' Jesse said, meeting Minnie's eye.

They both knew that Minnie did actually know his name.

Jesse Lightning. Typographer. Runs his own design agency. Lightning Designs.

Minnie felt wretched. After she had left Keenan and Hilde smoking and talking in the living room, she had gone to bed and searched him up on Google. She had seen his Instagram and a company called Lightning Designs came up, although she hadn't clicked any of the links or actually dived any deeper, so it didn't count. She hadn't scrolled any further than the top lines.

'I thought you'd come if you wanted to,' she said breezily, belying how much she cared.

They held each other's gaze for just a second too long. They both felt it: a longing it was best not to acknowledge.

'How's your week been?' Minnie asked, cutting the cord. 'Shit, it's almost been two. What did you do for Father's Day? I thought about you... you know...' She didn't have to say.

Jesse looked out of the window and put on his sunglasses, relieved for the shield.

'Oh, it was OK... I got a bonus four hours with Ida. We met my friend Will and his dog Bingley – Ida loves dogs, so we had brunch with them.'

'Sounds sweet.'

'Yeah, we just looked like a pair of gay dads.'

Not many of Jesse's friends had kids yet, and those who did had younger toddlers or babies. Everyone in their baby group – Andrew and Elena included – were older than Jesse and Hannah had been when they'd become parents. Jesse's only other single-dad friend, Johnny, had moved to Harrogate to follow his ex up there, so he could see his son.

Minnie smiled, thinking about Jesse and Will and imagining how sexy they must have looked. In her head Will was as good looking as Jesse and they made a cute couple. Another character. Who would play Will?

'How was it... for you though?' she asked.

Jesse let out a big sigh and looked back out to the countryside; the train was slowing down, ready to go into the tunnel.

'Shit. I miss him every day, not just Father's Day.'

He swallowed hard as a mother and her son walked swiftly down the carriage to find a toilet.

'But thanks. How about you? Did you see *your* dad?'

Minnie smiled. She told Jesse how her siblings and assorted partners had all convened for a big Byrne blowout at the family home in Hampstead, without actually telling him too much. She didn't want to tell him how hungover she was after the cocktail class date, and she didn't want to boast that she still had her dad. Plus it was best not to give away who her family was, in case they did manage to get through today without giving up the game.

She vaguely said, without mentioning names, that her mum had cooked her signature roast chicken with chorizo and chickpeas; her oldest sister had made their dad his favourite summer pudding, and their dad loved the bread maker Minnie had bought him. He'd got into baking bread in the past few years.

'Who didn't?' said Jesse, although his sourdough had turned out rock hard.

'So how did it go, with the custody thing? Did you suggest it?'

Jesse shook his head. 'Terribly.'

Minnie winced.

'But she might have mulled things over in the week since. We'll see...'

That sounded too cryptic and Minnie felt her throat tightening again. Jesse changed the subject and looked at her passport, sitting on the table between them like a grenade. He double tapped the cover with his forefinger. They could balance things out.

'I'll put that in a safe place, shall I?' Minnie joked, pulling it away. 'Plus my photo is hideous.'

Jesse couldn't imagine that.

* * *

The train plunged into a darkness beyond the windows and Jesse took his sunglasses off and rubbed his eyes. He had been so thrown by Hannah's phone call, so excited by what it could mean, that he couldn't sleep until 2 a.m., and then the alarm had gone off at 4.30 a.m. He looked at Minnie and wanted to switch sides, to sit next to her. To sleep leaning on her shoulder.

'So where are you meeting the mighty Wim Fischer?'

As Jesse asked the question he remembered being on a film set. It was during the trip to LA when his parents had taken him to Disneyland. The lot at Burbank. The observatory at Griffith Park. Quite the adventure for an eleven-year-old boy.

'At a hotel called Le Lapin Bleu – my French is terrible...'

Jesse was impressed; he had read about the hotel.

'I'm meeting him and Viola Rubin, the casting director. She's phenomenal. Did you see *Medusa's Mane*? She casts all his films.'

'I'm a little out of the loop to be honest. It's all been *Encanto*, *Coco* and *The Little Mermaid* for the past six years. Although I did see *Joker* at a baby friendly screening at the Odeon when Ida was really tiny... I'm pretty sure there was nothing baby friendly about it.'

Minnie laughed.

'That film is darrrrk.'

'Hopefully it didn't traumatise her. She slept through most of it!'

'That's so funny.'

'So what's *Medusa's Mane*?' he asked.

'That's the film before the one he's promoting now – *Swindler*,' she said, tapping the script. 'Oh my God it was so cool. Real kickass. He *loves* strong women...' Although she tailed off when she remembered something her parents had said.

Jesse looked at Minnie and nodded in appreciation.

'Well then, you've got this,' he said, picking up the script. 'Come on, from the top...'

20

DAY FOUR

Now

As Minnie and Jesse exited the Eurostar arrivals, into the throng of Gare du Nord and its shops: Relay, Paul and Carrefour Express, Jesse pointed to the sign for the steps down to the Metro. 'I'm going that way, M4 to M8. Porte Dorée.'

The way he said it sounded alarmingly French and made Minnie more nervous for her own pitiful efforts. She seemed to have forgotten all of her GCSE French in the past ten years and thought that she would prefer it if Jesse could stay with her. She looked at the note on her phone.

'My agent told me to get a taxi to Le Lapin Bleu.'

Jesse nodded.

'You know it then?'

'I've not stayed there, but I know it's very cool.' He narrowed his eyes to think. 'OK, so you're going to the fourth.'

'The what?'

'The fourth arrondissement. I'm going to the twelfth. Further out.'

'So where shall we meet then? And when?'

Jesse mulled it over in his mind's eye.

Minnie sighed in defeat. 'Shall I just get your number?'

Jesse seemed cautious, what about her rules? 'How long will your audition take?'

She looked at her watch. It was only 9.30 a.m.

'Well, my audition isn't until midday. And it depends how well it goes, I guess. I imagine I'll be a couple of hours, three to be safe?'

'OK, which train did you book back?'

'The last one. Just after 9 p.m. I think.'

'Same. OK, let's make a plan. I imagine I'll be done at the zoo by mid-afternoon, so I'll head to you for... four-ish?'

'Sounds good.' Although 4 p.m. felt like an awfully long time in the future to Minnie, when she had only just got her head around the joy of Jesse turning up for this playdate.

'Then why don't we grab some dinner before heading back?'

'Perfect. I don't really know Paris though.'

'That's OK.' Jesse rubbed the emergent stubble on his chin. 'Le Lapin Bleu is near Notre Dame, which is near the fifth arrondissement – so let's meet in the Latin Quarter. The Jardin du Luxembourg is nice.' Again he said it in a perfectly French accent that threw Minnie, but she under-stood the word *jardin* and understood Luxembourg. She'd remember that. 'Four o'clock yeah? There are some nice places to eat around there.'

As he said it, 4 p.m. felt like an awfully long time in the future to him too when there were so many other things to catch up on. But Minnie had her audition to focus on.

'Will I find it?'

'Easily. Just cross the river at Notre Dame and walk up Boulevard Saint Michel. Straight up. Or zigzag through the Latin Quarter. You'll find the *jardin* with your iPhone for sure. It's really pretty.'

'Nice.'

'Grab a chair in the gardens and I'll find you.'

'Fair dos,' Minnie said, not fully sure of herself. The audition nerves were really taking hold and she almost thought about sacking it off and spending the day with Jesse.

'You've got this, yeah?' Jesse said, putting a palm on the curve of each of her shoulders. She looked up at him intently as they stood facing each other in the bustling station as the morning commuters weaved around them. Neither Minnie nor Jesse wanted to break apart. Minnie wanted to bury into him. To smell his neck and bite it. Jesse wanted to tell her that she was going to be amazing and kiss her beautiful lips.

He nudged her, a friendly bump on the arm with a regimental fist. 'Good luck, yeah?' he said. Minnie nodded. She felt sick.

* * *

Minnie got into the back of the taxi waiting at the front of the rank and asked the driver to please take her to Le Lapin Bleu in English with a French accent. Damn, Jesse sounded native. She wished he were coming with her. She had a few hours to kill before her audition. But then she reminded herself, any time with him today was bonus time. And she'd be much better company after her audition anyway.

As the driver pulled out, Minnie looked back into Gare du Nord and saw Jesse disappear into the stairwell for the Metro. She put her palm to the window and felt a longing. She then felt stupid for trying to bend the rules of her own game and ask him for his number. She was in Paris, potentially for the biggest break of her career. And she wanted her time with him. It wasn't very Bechdel of her. Which reminded Minnie.

She awakened her phone to call her mother: Minnie always called her mum before an audition if she could, for a pep talk or some sage advice. But this morning, as the driver beeped his horn at a dawdling tourist, Minnie felt an overwhelming desire to call her mum and tell her that she might have accidentally fallen in love.

21

JESSE

Now

Jesse sat on a bench, sketching a giant anteater in the Amazon-Guyana biozone, eating a Mars bar and wondering whether his dad had ever actually been to Paris Zoo.

Why set the book here if he hadn't?

He tried to picture his dad, tall and strapping, tanned and lithe, silver-blond hair sticking up, chambray shirt sleeves rolled, walking the zoo's trails and paths, thinking of Ida and imagining a story just for her as he looked at the animals Jesse was now looking at.

Jesse's dad Lars was a crime writer, whose detective stories were best-sellers both sides of the Atlantic; three of them had been made into films, and Lars had taken his wife and son to visit various film sets in London, Los Angeles, Cape Town and Mysore.

Lars had been resolutely and roguishly single for most of his adult life, travelling the world and writing from chateaus in France, ramshackle hotels in Cuba and farmsteads in Australia, until he'd met Caryn and felt the strange sensation of wanting to put down some roots.

Caryn had been a young features writer, working for the *Sunday Times*, when she met Lars. She wasn't even meant to interview him that day she met him for a working lunch at Scott's. The books editor Geoffrey had food poisoning and sent Caryn, who was making a name for herself as a tenacious interviewer, not fazed by a politician's reputation or a celebrity's tetchy PR. Caryn did love a deliciously dark crime novel, and had read all of Lars Lightning's, so she had to remember not to fangirl during the two hours in which they ate fillet of cod Provençal and fell in love.

They got married when Caryn was twenty-two and Lars was forty-two; Caryn was only twenty-five when she had Jesse, and they were living between a house they had bought in Claygate in Surrey, a cottage in the Black Forest, and later, the house in the South of France, moving there permanently when Jesse went to college.

In the thirty-five years they were married, Caryn Lightning interviewed a host of celebrities for the *Sunday Times* – although never her husband again. She also helped Lars plot and plan; listened to his ideas and improved them. Read through his drafts, his proofs, his contracts and helped organise his book tours. She was, as Lars called her, his *everything*.

Jesse looked at the anteater and reflected that his father had been slowing down. Observing more and writing less. Doing less yoga. Talking less enthusiastically about wine. He used to write a book a year but the rhythm of his publishing schedule had slowed to a book every three years. After the pandemic, Lars stopped doing public appearances, preferring to Zoom from the French farmhouse than take all those ghastly internal flights across America to promote his books. Now there would be no new books. No book tours. A children's book perhaps, if Jesse's drawings were up to scratch. He felt an emptiness in his chest and a guilt coursed through him: he'd never got round to doing this while his dad was alive. Jesse had never told Lars how much he loved Remy the red panda. How touched he was that he had written a book for Ida. One he thought Jesse capable of illustrating.

He looked at the enclosure in front of him. Had his dad sat on this bench and got inspiration from the anteater and his haughty nose? Or was it purely his conversations with Ida that inspired him?

Jesse wanted to ask his mother, although that would acknowledge that he hadn't done anything with the book while his father was alive. He had to tell her soon, he imagined. It was odd not to have told her in his regular phone calls.

Did he come here? Did he sit on this bench?

Jesse looked around and remembered a conversation he had had with his father, on the release of his last book. A thriller set in Alaska. Jesse couldn't remember Lars having visited Alaska, neither in a research trip nor a family holiday, but the book felt so real, so barren, so raw. He'd asked his dad if he had been there on one of his tours. Had that inspired *The Icicle Twist*?

'Shakespeare never travelled to Verona you know,' Lars had replied with a wink.

Maybe he hadn't sat on this bench. His work had all come from his brilliant brain and his lovely heart. He had been to India though, researching *The Pondicherry Pursuit*; it was on that trip, about eight years ago, he'd brought back the Saraswati keyring and given it to Jesse. Dropping it from his curled fist into his son's palm and clutching it. 'She is the goddess of knowledge, art, wisdom and learning. Keep her close.'

'Thanks, Dad,' Jesse said, slightly bemused by his dad's dalliance with Hinduism and Jainism. Lars would often obsess about something he'd researched for a book. He learned cross-country skiing for *The Viking's Curse*. He learned how to play the didgeridoo when he was researching *The Red Centre*, and he became obsessed with Mozart while writing *Salzburg Spies*. His passion for Indian culture had lasted more than most of his obsessions though, and he had even given up eating Indian's holy cow, by his seventieth birthday. Sadly, it hadn't helped his heart.

Jesse sighed.

He wished he could get Saraswati back. He wished he could have his dad back.

He looked at the anteater, its funny face rummaging in the termite mound, and felt consumed by a grief he had packed away for six months. In the chaos of work. In the busyness of Ida's bustling life. In the distractions of Hannah's duplicity. In the heartbreaking hugs when he had to peel Ida off him when it was time to truly go. In the strength he needed to show his mother now more than ever, so as not to worry her. Every draining emotion Jesse had parked since December came flooding out and his body shook so much with sobs he could barely breathe.

22

MINNIE

Now

'Minette Byrne to see Viola Rubin and Wim Fischer,' she said as she reached the reception desk of Le Lapin Bleu. A small man with a bald head smiled daintily.

'May I see your press pass, *mademoiselle*?'

'Oh I'm not press, I'm an actor. I'm here to meet the casting director, for an audition.'

'Sorry no casting today, just press, for *Swindlers*.'

'Oh. My agent in London, Devon Smith... he's arranged a meeting, for midday, I'm a little early but—'

This wasn't helping Minnie's already frazzled nerves.

'Take a seat, *s'il vous plait*.' The man nodded to an area of sofas where people were sitting recording voice notes and filing copy on their laptops. A woman with a mic and boom across her lap chatted to her cameraman. Everyone around her seemed to be press, dressed in crisp shirts and jeans, not actors, who always looked a little rougher around the edges. Minnie wondered if the whole thing had been a terrible mistake. She'd felt foolish when the taxi dropped her at the hotel two hours early, so she went for a walk, looking around the shops in the

Marais, killing time. She should have gone into the hotel there and then and realised there might be a mix-up and no audition. She could have been spending the day with Jesse.

But she was here now. This was her shot. And hopefully Viola Rubin and Wim Fischer would realise and she would be seen any minute now.

* * *

Two hours later, Minnie's phone battery was almost wiped. She'd messaged Rosie, Lillia and Anthony for solidarity. Her dad Jeremy had messaged to ask:

> How did it go Plummers?

Minnie never knew why her dad called her Plummers. She replied to say she was still waiting to go in. Her mum Geraldine, who must have not been with Jeremy this morning, messaged soon after:

> Did you meet him? Intrigued x

Minnie was feeling agitated and trapped. If she left the hotel, she might miss her chance. If she stayed there never to be called, she might waste this one glorious chance of a day. She turned to an American journalist sitting next to her. A woman with deep-set brown eyes and glossy hair. She'd been on the phone talking to a boss or editor about her interview for the past twenty minutes, but everything sounded cryptic, as if she were talking in code. Minnie tried to listen, for a distraction and to pass the time. For a journalist, the woman didn't impart much.

When she finished another, shorter, phone call Minnie jumped in.

'You met Wim Fischer then?'

'Yah. Wim Fischer this morning, Brad Pitt this afternoon.'

Minnie gasped. 'Oh, wow.'

'Yeah. A day of two halves!' she joked. 'I'm just waiting for my car.'

Minnie looked at the journalist zipping up her laptop and Dictaphone. She yearned to be interviewed by a woman like her one day.

'Is it all press up there? Do you know if there are any actors around?'

'Oh, I don't know, I was just moved along a production line. I was only here to interview Mr Fischer. It's a circus up there. I don't even have my own camera team today, I had to use theirs – although I noticed *some* people did...' The journalist sounded wronged, and Minnie realised that whatever your discipline, things didn't always go your way.

'Oh, right.' She smiled, glad for the conversation more than anything. A reminder that she wasn't invisible. She was there. The wait had been long. She wished she'd brought a book or at least a magazine. She'd picked up *Le Monde* and lamented it; she ignored the *Wall Street Journal*. She was relieved when a man dropped *Paris Match* on the table and she could look at the gossipy photos.

'Oh, that's my car,' the woman said gratefully, as she looked at her phone screen. Minnie would be grateful to be meeting Brad Pitt this afternoon. Her dad had had a small part playing his brother in a film twenty years ago, and said he had been lovely, when all the school mums stopped to ask. The journalist stood up and smoothed out her cream trouser suit, dropping her press pass on the floor. Minnie picked it up and handed it to her. Zahara Zaman, *New York Times*. 'Thanks,' she said, taking it.

'What's he like? Wim Fischer?' Minnie asked, as Zahara Zaman was about to walk away. She stopped and looked at Minnie cautiously.

'He's an asshole.'

23

JESSE

Now

'*Papa? Pourquoi le monsieur pleure?*' a little girl asked her dad, clutching his hand, as she looked warily at Jesse.

Jesse, aware that the girl had seen him crying, did the best acting he could, turning his quiet, harrowed face into a laugh, which made him look and sound demented. The child looked even more alarmed.

'*Le fourmilier...*' Jesse said, pointing to the anteater, his eyes red. '*Il a une drôle de tête non?*' He said it not all that convincingly. The girl looked between the anteater and Jesse, unsure. The father nodded and looked at Jesse's sketchbook.

'*C'est un très bon dessin,*' he said over his shoulder, his tone sitting somewhere between awe and pity.

'*Merci.*'

Jesse slung his sketchbook and pencils into his bag and decided to move on. He needed to hone his drawings for Beryl and Meryl, the chatty scarlet macaws and seek out Felix the flamingo, one of the central characters in *The Amazing Adventures of Remy the Red Panda*, all before meeting Minnie on the other side of the city. He'd been sitting quietly at the zoo for hours but time passed quickly when he was sketching, as if he were in a vortex where time sped up. He looked at his phone screen: it was already 2 p.m.; he needed to get on if he were to sketch the macaws and the flamingos and get to the Latin Quarter for 4 p.m. He stood up from the bench and nodded to the father and daughter, who decided to take the seat and use it as a base for a snack pitstop.

'*Bonjour*,' Jesse said with a little salute, as he wandered down the path towards the birds. He looked at his phone again. The tracker app was open, giving him data on the planes coming in and out of Charles de Galle, Orly and Beauvais. None of these flights interested him today. Today he couldn't get Minnie out of his mind; he couldn't stop thinking about her, as if he were holding onto all the nerves and excitement for her audition too. It was probably over now. How had it gone? Would they be able to celebrate? What was the director like? He googled Wim Fischer and looked at the photos. He looked even more eccentric than the anteater.

24

MINNIE

Now

Minnie examined her nails and noticed white edges starting to wear through her oxblood red tips.

Shit.

It's not that she had to look perfect – Veronica Valla seemed like the type of assassin who might have chipped nails – but Minnie wanted to look slick and put together, so she could feel her most confident. As the clock kept ticking, she doubted herself more with each minute.

What's going on?

By 3 p.m., Minnie had almost stopped caring about her lines. She was furious to have wasted a day in Paris sitting on a sofa and it felt less and less likely that she was going to meet Wim Fischer or Viola Rubin today, if ever. Minnie knew this happened. Auditions were often delayed. Curveballs thrown. But never had an audition felt less like an audition and that she'd turned up to the wrong thing on the wrong day. She rubbed her legs, cold in the air con of the hotel atrium, the temperature jarring against the sunshine outside, as wealthy and well-dressed guests arrived for meetings or bookings from the side-street entrance, a floral canopy off a busy street in central Paris.

Minnie looked at her phone and sighed as obviously as she could. Her manners were waning. It was 3.04 p.m. and she had only fifty-six minutes before she was due to meet Jesse, and only 9 per cent battery. She had asked three times at the desk if anyone was coming for her, and the bald man – who had been for his lunch and come back – told her that someone would be with her soon.

She started to panic about getting to the Jardin du Luxembourg in time. Would she find it? Would Jesse wait if she were late? How would she cope alone in Paris without any charge in her phone? She had to get back to Gare du Nord by 8 p.m., with or without Jesse.

I should have got his bloody number.

Minnie typed Jesse Lightning into the search box on Google again, to see if she could message him on Instagram, and saw the battery life drop to 6 per cent.

Dammit.

She put her phone to sleep and looked up, frustrated now at the lackeys and the journalists.

This is just rude.

Everything felt very strange; everything felt a little off. She'd been to enough auditions to know she was not best placed to get this part. But then this was Wim Fischer. Enfant terrible of Hollywood. He could do what he wanted of course.

25

JESSE

Now

'You're in Paris? I didn't know you were going to Paris. Why didn't you say?'

Jesse stopped at the jaguar enclosure, dropped to his haunches so he could see in, and looked at his watch.

'Nor did I!' he said cheerily.

'What are you doing there? Another fashion brand?'

'No, actually I'm doing some research. For the book.'

Hannah was silent for a second.

'The kids' book? You're still doing that?'

'Yeah, Remy the red panda. I got an agent, I told you.'

'Yes but I thought it was just a vanity project.'

Jesse peered at a low level through the glass, so he could see the jaguar up close as it paced past. Its eyes were apricot-coloured and sad.

'A vanity project for your dad I mean.'

Jesse put his thumb and forefinger to the inner corners of his eyes and pressed. The fatigue from only two and a half hours of sleep had caught up with him now Minnie's dynamism was absent. She had a way of lifting his energy.

'It was one of his last wishes,' Jesse said wearily.

'I know,' Hannah backtracked. 'And it'll be great. Anyway, I'm just checking in between meetings. Did you think about what I said? Shall I book a table for tomorrow night?'

Jesse opened his eyes and looked back at the big cat.

'We can go to The Highlander. Your favourite.'

He exhaled a stream of air onto the glass and saw it mist up. He just didn't know what to think. He didn't know what to say.

'I've already asked Henrike to sit.'

That didn't help; Henrike only reminded him.

But.

If Jesse could get past the affair. If Hannah *was* as truly sorry as she said she was. Maybe it was a One Of Those Things they could chalk up to experience. To life not being perfect but them overcoming the odds anyway. Maybe they would laugh about it one day.

It's never going to be funny.

But Jesse could fall asleep reading Ida bedtime stories any night of the week. He could wake up feeling her little limbs and elbows digging into his back in the marital bed. He could be there for any school pick-up and drop-off he wanted. He could remember all the things that had made him fall in love with Hannah in the first place. He was the well-travelled boy who spent summers in France and Christmases in Germany. She was the smartest girl in the village – the smartest girl in Surrey it seemed. A numbers machine, who got offers from every university or job she applied for. Hannah loved that Jesse wasn't like the other boys – he was quietly confident and creative. He would take great pleasure in fashioning a box, or a wall or a sculpture. He wasn't doing what everyone else at school was doing as they applied to Leeds, Nottingham, Bristol and Brighton. Jesse was dead set on going to Reading, a city that sounded underwhelming but the Graphic Communications and Design course excited him. She liked that he was different. Creative. Handsome. He loved her brilliant, selfish, brain.

Jesse got up and walked from the jaguar enclosure to the leopards, where a sleepy big cat was flopped on a platform, its eyes catching the sun and flashing green. He thought of Minnie and wondered how she was getting on.

'Jesse?'

'Yeah, sorry. It's just a bit crazy here. I'm trying to get my head around everything. How's Ida?'

'She's fine. Henrike will be picking her up in an hour or so. Look I have to go jump on a call. You will be back by tomorrow, won't you?'

'Yeah yeah, I'm coming home tonight.'

Home.

Except it wasn't his home.

There was a nervous pause. If Jesse blocked out all the sadness and noise, maybe the pause could be like the excitement of the early days. When he'd first got Hannah's number and sent her a text.

'Well it'll be great to see you, Jesse. I'll get Tara to book us a table.'

26

MINNIE

Now

'Ms Byrne?'

Minnie had sunk so low into the lobby sofa that it became an effort to bounce up out of it. The black Lycra of her ballerina bodyvest felt a bit sticky. She needed air after three and a half hours of waiting, of holding her breath. It was a quarter past three, and she was about to give up.

'That's me!' she said as she managed to get up. 'Was me!' she joked flimsily, as she fell back into the copious velvet in what felt like slow motion. She still wasn't happy about it.

The American assistant with a headpiece curled around her ear and a tablet in her hand gave an impatient, patronising smile. She must have been around the same age as Minnie but wore her access to Wim Fischer and Viola Rubin as her currency.

Minnie got back up, grabbing her bag and stuffing her thin scarf and the copy of *Paris Match* into it and followed the woman down the corridors to a lift. The smell of Korean viburnum, sweet and succulent, came from the courtyard, and Minnie inhaled theatrically.

'Wow don't you love that smell? Reminds me of the past.' She thought about Hampstead Heath; the Byrne home in Ireland. The sweet honeysuckle smell of summer evenings.

The woman didn't answer.

Minnie had to remember not to witter. Sometimes she could be *too* friendly. Sometimes she talked so much she knew even as she was speaking that she was making a situation worse and not better. It was the point at which her power started to slide away. She hated having to remember to not be affable and open, it went against every fibre of her being.

They got in the lift and the assistant pressed a button.

'Busy day?' Minnie asked as the doors closed.

'Crazy...' the assistant said, rolling her eyes and jabbing the button at the top, not a drop of an apology for having kept Minnie waiting for hours, without even a glass of water.

'I bet. But I am so psyched to meet Viola. She's a hero!'

'Ms Rubin had to go to another meeting. She left.'

'Oh.'

Maybe the assistant did think Minnie was press.

Shit.

'Do you know I'm here for an audition?'

The woman looked at her clipboard and ran her finger down a list of names.

'Yes, that's fine. Mr Fischer is very good at this,' she said. 'His eye is *amazing.*'

The lift opened onto a light and airy room, where men and women seemed to be milling around quietly, as if trying not to wake a sleeping toddler. A young man was packing away a screen with *Swindlers* artwork on it. Two security guards were talking about Kylian Mbappé in low voices. Another woman was zhuzhing up some flowers on a coffee table and straightening a chair. The assistant gave one of the security guards a nod and opened a set of closed double doors that led to another chamber, where a woman in a pencil skirt and fuchsia pink shirt with a pussy bow collar strode through.

'Good luck,' she said, giving Minnie a penetrating smile, and headed out.

Minnie nodded.

'Sit,' the assistant said, waving a hand to the sofa in the middle of this suite. Minnie sunk into another sofa and looked around the room. How many more rooms went off this one? An elegant carriage clock on an ornate mantel said it was almost half past three. How long would it take to get to the Jardin du Luxembourg from here? Jesse said it was walkable.

Where the hell was Viola Rubin? This was Minnie's shot to meet the best in Hollywood.

Surely she didn't have a hope of being cast without a casting director there to see her audition.

I'll just having to fucking smash this.

The assistant knocked twice on the double doors the woman with the pink pussy bow had just come through and let herself in.

'Mr Fischer, I have Minette Byrne for you,' she announced, to a room beyond the capacious suite.

'I'll be just a second,' he called, as if from the bathroom. A German accent. A voice Minnie recognised from interviews and award shows on television.

How embarrassing, Minnie thought. Might she have just caught Wim Fischer having a poo between appointments? She winced to think.

'He won't be a moment,' the assistant said expeditiously. She left the room and walked back into the antechamber with the security guards, to wherever else this network of opulent tunnels led to.

Minnie felt uneasy as she listened to the noise of Paris' boulevards outside. A beep. Motorbikes. The siren of a foreign emergency vehicle. She looked around the room devoid of personal effects. Minnie had met plenty of famous people before. There was often an actor or an artist spending long weekend lunches with the Byrnes. She wasn't as fazed as most might be. Although she was hyper curious to meet Wim Fischer, and even more excited by the prospect of starring in one of his films. She really wanted this part.

Remember your lines, remember your lines.

Minnie started to mentally recite them.

Maybe she was actually going to run the scene with Wim Fischer himself. Maybe there wasn't another assistant in there. When she'd auditioned for the part in a Marvel movie the director hadn't even looked up as Minnie played the scene out with a bored casting assistant.

Minnie heard a toilet flush softly in the distance. A trickle of running water.

'Actually, Ms Byrne, why don't you come in?'

She looked cautiously towards the voice beyond the suite.

'I'm just taking a moment after one hell of a day.'

Minnie walked through what looked like a bedroom and followed the echo of his thick German accent.

This is weird.

It could only be a bathroom off that.

This is fucking weird, she thought, as she walked in and saw Wim Fischer in a bubble bath. She hoped he wasn't naked under the foam, but wondered, why wouldn't he be?

Minnie looked behind her, to see if anyone had seen her. One part of her felt like an intruder, another part felt abandoned. She reminded herself she hadn't asked for any of this. She had just wanted to audition with Viola Rubin. She had earned an audition with Viola Rubin.

Maybe it's a German thing.

Her family had stayed at a spa in Baden Baden when they went Interrailing one summer in her teens. All five children were mortified by the men slapping their naked bottoms and balls on the wooden slats of the sauna, as they spread their legs and inhaled the purifying air. Maybe Wim Fischer was that kind of guy. Maybe Minnie was being a prude. Maybe she was being too British.

Still, it felt wrong.

This was a business meeting.

'Velcome, take a seat!' he said, indicating the closed lid of the toilet. Minnie didn't want to sit on a toilet, even with the lid down, so she hovered in the doorway. Her boots felt clumpy and inappropriate against the elegant marble floor, but she wasn't going to take them off.

'Erm, hello, Mr Fischer. I'm here for the—'

'I know who you are! The youngest Byrne child! And aren't you precious?'

Minnie was uncertain. Her parents hadn't worked with Wim Fischer, she knew that. So what did he know about her?

She tried not to look at him sitting in the bath but didn't know where else to look. He was talking to her. Wim Fischer didn't look like the enfant terrible of moviemaking to her, but it had probably been twenty years since he had been called that. He was a small man with a puff of thinning curly hair and a delicate gold chain around his neck with what looked like a bar of gold bullion on the end of it.

Minnie nodded politely and pointed her thumb over her shoulder behind her.

'I can wait outside you know, no hurry.'

I've been waiting fucking hours as it is.

Except there was a hurry. She thought of Jesse and wished he were here so she could sense check this with him. She wished she could run out. She needed to be at the Jardin du Luxembourg in half an hour and this bullshit audition had already taken up too much time. Hollywood's enfant terrible looked like an old man, shrivelled as he luxuriated in a marble sunken tub.

'Sit down, sit down!' he directed, more forcefully, nodding to the toilet. Minnie looked around. Maybe this was how she was going to have to do the audition. Sitting on a toilet playing out the scene with a naked director in the bath. She thought about the scene she had gone over and over in her head. It was set in a bar after closing. A tense discussion between a hitwoman, a Mafioso and a corrupt cop. She so wanted this role.

Minnie sat, tentatively and primly, on the lid of the toilet, and crossed her legs.

'Shall I go from the top of the scene my agent shared with me?'

'Hmm, I like to improvise a little.' Wim Fischer shrugged, unapologetically. 'Why don't you get in with me, *ja*? We can do the scene together like that. Make some real eye contacts.'

Wim Fischer said this as if it were perfectly normal.

Minnie thought of the woman who had led her here. How unsisterly it was of her to put her in this situation. Did she have a clue this was happening? Worse, of course, of Wim Fischer for making her feel like this. Perhaps he invited his assistant into his bath all the time and she struggled to say, *No*. Geraldine and Jeremy hadn't known much about him, they tended to do more stage than film work, although Geraldine had been in lots of films in supporting roles. And all of the Harry Potters of course. Minnie knew they wouldn't be very happy if they saw how uncomfortable Wim Fischer was making their daughter feel right now.

'Is this a joke?' Minnie got the courage to ask, with a nervous smile.

'I beg your pardons?' Wim said, his accent almost comical. Except there was nothing funny about the situation.

'Is this a test?' Minnie asked, flabbergasted.

'A test, my dear?' Wim Fischer looked neutral, although of course it was a test, it was an audition.

Minnie dug deep to find her voice.

'Are you testing me?' She cleared her throat. 'Are you being the parody of a creepy film director, just to test me?'

Wim Fischer's face was passive. Bemused even.

'I just thought you might like to fuck me. Get some chemistry. See how we would work together. Whether we would make a great team.' He said it so matter-of-factly Minnie wondered if her entire life had been a lie. She sat on the toilet feeling revolted and repulsed. Did her mother ever have to do this? The famous Geraldine Byrne. Be put under pressure and duress; was she ever pressed upon, or worse, by the creepy Fischers and Weinsteins of the world?

She thought of her mother's face. She envisaged the outrage on it. She imagined her, shouting, voiceless, in the opposite corner of the bathroom, telling Minnie to get the hell out and run.

Minnie rose from the closed lid of the toilet seat, feeling slightly nauseous as she stood and steadied herself. She thought she might be sick but didn't want to lift the lid or stay in the room a second longer. She put her hand over her mouth, her palms shaking and lowered her shoulders, before leaning onto the door frame for support.

She looked back at Wim Fischer, still waiting for his response as he started to stroke his penis in the water.

'Why don't you go fuck yourself?' Minnie said, as she took a deep breath and walked out of the bathroom, through the bedroom, the suite, and into the lift, committing career suicide with every step.

27

DAY FOUR

Now

Jesse rushed through the lofty green gates of the Jardin du Luxembourg and wound along the sandy gravel path looking for Minnie. He was fifteen minutes later than he had said he would be – he hated being late. He hated it when people he was meeting were late. And he hated that he didn't have Minnie's phone number to text her and tell her.

Enough with the silly game now.

He couldn't see her beyond the beds of orange and yellow flowers, or the spiky dahlias; he couldn't see her by the pond, where gleeful children were setting wooden sailboats down onto the water. So he kept walking, past neat slopes of grass fenced off by trim barriers ankle height, past flowerbeds of pink and purple blooms: pansies, geraniums and petunias, walking a lap around the park under the palms and fig trees, panicking with each step, until he finally spotted her. Minnie's denim jacket was slung on the back of a sage green metal chair, the low curve of her black ballerina top revealing the grace of her spine. Her legs were curled underneath her as if she had folded herself into origami. Her short black bob was askew, revealing the most exquisite neck.

Jesse felt a surge of relief, until he noticed that there was a sadness in the rounding of Minnie's shoulders. He stopped. He didn't want to make her jump – he could sense something was wrong even before he saw her face.

'Hey,' Jesse said softly, reaching out to put his hand on her shoulder but stopping himself so sharply he almost flinched.

Minnie turned and looked up. Her smile was flat and polite. Inky trails on her cheekbones told tales of tears and weariness.

'Hey,' she replied flatly.

'What happened?' Jesse felt another stab of panic in the pit of his stomach.

Minnie's eyes were glassy as she looked back at the ornamental urn on the wall in front of her. Fuchsia pink bougainvillea tumbled from it. She uncurled her legs, planted her boots on the floor and took a deep breath.

'I am not thick-skinned enough for this,' she said.

Jesse pulled up a chair next to her, the scraping sound of metal on gravel making Minnie shudder.

'I think that's why I fought it for so long.'

He sat down.

'Fought what? What's happened?'

Minnie threw a succession of small stones at the urn as if she were trying to hit a specific target.

'Acting. Why did I come here? Why do I do it to myself?'

'What do you mean?'

'I hate putting myself out there. I hate rejection. I'm scared of it all. I'm too scared to fucking fly, how could I think I could meet people like that in the best of circumstances and "perform" for them, let alone when I'm at my worst.'

Jesse put his backpack on the gravel underneath their chairs and leaned in, his elbows on his thighs, his hands clasped together.

'Do you want to talk about it?' He waited as they watched families and their wooden toy boats, their sails painted with the flags of Belgium, Japan and Sweden. A mother applauded her daughter. A security guard in a neat navy forage cap strolled with smiling authority at passers-by. 'You don't have to—'

'I should have listened to my parents.'

'Why?' Jesse was so confused. 'I thought they supported you.'

'They didn't think he was all that. The director who "champions kickass women".' Minnie said it with a venom that threw Jesse. He hadn't seen a poisonous side to her before. 'He also tries to take advantage of them.'

'God, what happened?'

'I feel sick.'

'Shit. Do you want me to get—'

'I can barely think about it.' Minnie put her hand over her mouth.

'It's OK, you don't need to tell me, but...' Jesse looked around the park, feeling a little helpless. He looked to the handsome guard standing with his arms behind his back. 'Is there anything I can do?' There was a thickness in the still summer air. 'Are you physically OK?'

Jesse thought a thousand years into his future. Of Ida and her descendants, fighting and battling through an army of faceless men.

Minnie's stone hit the dot she was after on the urn.

'Not really.'

She looked at Jesse and saw the panic on his face.

'It's OK, he didn't touch me.'

Jesse exhaled at the sky.

'Filthy fucker was in the bath. Asked me if I'd like to get in.'

'What the fuck?! Was he naked?'

Minnie looked like she was going to be sick.

'Sorry.' Jesse let out an angry sigh. 'Fuck!'

'No, it's not your fault. And yes, he was.'

Her pallor was almost green.

'What about the casting director? Were you left on your own with him?'

'It was just him. I was kept waiting. For hours, literally hours sitting there like a fucking lemon. It didn't even look like I'd turned up on the right day, it didn't look like anyone was expecting me. Eventually I was led to his suite. And left alone there while he was in the bath.'

'*What?*'

'I'm not joking.'

'Clearly not. Nothing about this is funny. Slimy fucking c—'

'I have no idea whether it was an elaborate set-up or opportunism. Either way he's a disgusting little man and he's got it coming to him. Somehow.'

'Damn right. Shit.' Jesse shook his head in disbelief. 'How did you get out of there?'

'I told him to go fuck himself and walked out.'

Jesse sighed. 'Well done. Bloody hell, you could have been paralysed.'

Jesse watched Minnie, staring ahead. Eyes transfixed.

'Look, why don't you report—'

'No Jesse, I don't want to tell anyone yet and I don't need fixing!' she said defensively. 'I know that's how it looked when we met. The first time. Probably every time. I know I'm a total mess and I have just *blown* my fucking career, but... but I can sort it out.'

Minnie's phone went off, making her jump. It said Mama Bear on the screen. She rejected the call, switched her phone off, and put it in her bag. 'It's about to die anyway...'

Jesse wanted to touch her as much as he didn't want to touch her. They sat side by side in silence.

'JP wanted to fix me – he would throw money at "the problem", to try to get my spark back, make me the perfect arm candy, this exciting prospect. "My ingénue",' she said as she curled her nose. 'Just until the point I fell for him and then...' She moved her fingers across her throat as if she was beheading herself.

Jesse shook his head. 'Of course you don't need fixing.'

He said it so resolutely, he was almost angry. He thought she was the perfect human being: brilliant, bright, funny, beautiful – and she had walked away from someone who had just committed a ghastly abuse of power.

'I'm just wondering if we should go to the police, to make a statement?'

Minnie shook her head. 'No.'

'But what if—'

'No!' She said it more sharply this time. 'We've barely got four hours left in Paris. I do not want to spend them in a police station.'

Jesse nodded. 'OK, well, when you're ready, you can report it, you know. I'm pretty sure.'

'Report him for what? He didn't actually do anything. I don't think it's a crime for an adult to proposition an adult. No one will listen anyway.'

'No, but you need to be heard.'

Minnie looked at him in confusion. 'I see Tony every week. All I do is talk at him, at my friends, at you...'

Jesse shook his head. 'That's not what I meant.'

He pictured Minnie's family – he didn't know who they were but from what she'd said they sounded loud and chaotic and that it was hard for her to be heard among all the characters. Why had she been so happy to settle for someone as disgusting as her ex, just because he made her feel adored for ten minutes.

'What do you mean?'

Jesse couldn't put his finger on it, and she wasn't a project to fix, even if he had helped her with her therapy homework.

'I dunno. I just think you're more powerful than you know.'

Minnie looked at him, her face softening.

'I mean, you just told Hollywood's adored Wim Fischer to fuck off. That's powerful. Not many people would have had the guts.'

She smiled.

'And look at all the things you're doing to change what's made you unhappy. You got help, made inroads, you went up to a fucking idiot shouting at a kid in a coffee shop and got him to pull himself together before an interview...'

'Well I didn't quite...'

'Honestly, don't even question yourself and what you're doing. I'm sure you're an exceptional actor. Keep on keeping on.'

Minnie nudged into Jesse with her arm.

'Thank you.'

'Ha, what do I know,' he laughed.

Minnie narrowed her eyes at him. What *had* happened with his ex? What was the deal with them? Why couldn't she ask him?

Jesse took his phone out of his pocket and looked at the sky.

Why the hell did he track fucking planes?

'What's going on with you and that app?' Minnie half snapped. 'Is it your wife?' She hated the way the word *wife* clung to her lips.

Jesse smiled, almost bemused. 'When do you have to be back in London?'

Minnie mentally ran through her diary.

'I'm working at the races on Sunday, then it's Wimbledon fortnight. I've obviously got the summer season down pat...'

Jesse was already buckling up his backpack and slinging it over his shoulder.

'Why?'

'Come on, I have an idea.' Jesse stood up.

'What?'

'Let's get out of here.'

Minnie looked up at him, his form silhouetted in the late and low afternoon sun.

'What about dinner? Will we make our train?'

'Don't need it.' Jesse extended an arm and held out his hand to help Minnie up.

'I'm not going on a fucking aeroplane if that's what you think.' She took his hand and it felt comforting and it felt wonderful.

'Come on...'

28

DAY FOUR

Now

As the sun set on the zoetrope of cornfields, citadels, bridges and rivers out of the train window, Minnie looked at Jesse intently across the table. This time she was travelling backwards, racing at high speed to an unknown destination.

'Are you going to tell me where we're going?'

They hadn't gone for dinner and they hadn't gone back to Gare du Nord. Instead, Jesse had navigated them to a different train station, gone to a kiosk and bought tickets in French so fast and so fluently, Minnie didn't pick up a single word.

'We're going to run in a field.'

'What?'

'Isn't that what your therapist – what Tony – suggested? Be joyful. Go running with gay abandon through a field?'

Minnie laughed, half in terror, half in awe. Jesse had listened.

'Fuck Wim Fischer and fuck your ex.' Jesse said it so bitingly, Minnie could see a flicker of irritation in his jaw. 'We're going to run all that shit away.'

'In a field?'

'In a field.'

'This is a long way to go to find a field.'

'Yeah there aren't many in Paris.'

Minnie and Jesse looked out of the picture window in comfortable silence as their legs kicked out in front of them, Minnie's slotted between Jesse's but not touching, like the opposite sides of a backgammon board.

'He called me actually,' Minnie confided after some quiet. 'JP.'

'Oh really?' Jesse's cheeks flushed. 'What did he say?'

'He said, "Congratulations, darlin', I saw your programme was gonna be on the telly..."' For an actor, Minnie did a poor impression of an Essex accent. Jesse felt heat run through his face. He wanted to ask what she had said in reply, but didn't. He didn't want to talk about JP.

'Well fuck 'em all. You need space and you need air and you need to run in a field.'

'Now you're making me sound like Theresa May.'

'Trust me, you're not Theresa May.'

Minnie looked at her watch.

'Well we're not going to make our train back to London.' She laughed. It was the first time Jesse had seen her truly relax since the horror of her audition.

'Doesn't matter.' Jesse shrugged with a carefree look.

29

DAY FOUR

Now

'Darling! Oh my goodness! What are you doing here?'

A tanned woman with short golden-blonde hair and half-moon reading glasses looked up at her son in adoration before wrapping her arms around him, almost in relief. Hugging him seemed to be medicinal, judging from the replenished look on her face. 'Where's Ida? Is everything all right? Come in, come in!'

She smiled and beckoned Jesse and Minnie through the front doors of the stone farmhouse with ivy creeping over its exterior. Even in the dark, Minnie could tell the stone was cream, the shutters were blue and the ambience was tranquil.

'Ida's fine, she's at home, everything's fine.' Jesse's mother threw him a loaded look – she didn't buy his calm candour. He squeezed her shoulder as if to say *really*. 'Mum, this is Minnie – Minnie this is Caryn, my mum.'

'Wonderful to meet you, Minnie, do come in.' Caryn smiled in warm confusion as she put her arms on Minnie's and kissed her once on each cheek.

'Lovely to meet you too. Wow, this is gorgeous!' Minnie said as she walked in and looked around the entrance, where one wall was rugged and stone, another smooth, plastered and painted cream. A large table with a mixture of chairs around it dominated the space.

Jesse slung his backpack on the table and stretched like a cat.

'Come on through. You'll have dinner? I've a stew on the Aga.' Caryn couldn't contain her excitement as she led them to a kitchen with yellow cupboards, terracotta tiles and a hotchpotch of different style artworks, tea towels and utensils. Copper pans sat proudly next to plastic colanders. The room felt rustic, garbled, and smelled of red wine, red meat and comfort.

'We were in Paris today for... for work, weren't we?' Jesse turned to Minnie, who was too busy looking around and smiling to concur. 'And we decided to jump on a train here.'

'Goodness, well aren't I lucky? What a lovely surprise! Can I get you a drink? Beer? Wine? Lemonade?'

'Actually I am parched,' Minnie said, holding her neck. 'A lemonade would be perfect! Thank you.'

Caryn opened an old looking fridge and took out a jug of lemonade Minnie assumed was homemade, it smelled so zingy.

'I'll have one too thanks, and a beer. I'll get them...' Jesse said, taking the jug out of his mother's hands. Caryn didn't know what to do with herself; she seemed happy and flustered.

'The stew is probably still warm...'

Jesse looked at Minnie to see if she was hungry. They'd grabbed a baguette as they'd ran through Gare de Lyon but hadn't eaten since then. 'It's beef,' she added, giving Jesse a contrite look. Caryn had stopped eating beef when Lars turned seventy and decided to become vegetarian, but it had gradually made its way back on the menu since he died. The house smelled cosy for it.

'That would be amazing,' Minnie said, clutching her stomach. 'It smells incredible.'

'Yeah I'll go for some too thanks, Mum.'

Jesse put ice cubes into three glasses and poured the lemonade over them from its jug with a stirrer, a satisfying chink and crunch sound that helped Minnie shelve her stress.

Jesse and Minnie had taken the last train from Paris to Avignon and were lucky to get the one taxi at Avignon station when they stepped off the train to balmy air and cicada song. Minnie couldn't see much in the dark save for the odd stone house lit dramatically behind palms, cypress trees and bushes, as they travelled for almost an hour until they reached the village of Gordes. The taxi stopped at the end of a short stone path lit by stick lights to guide them on foot to a rustic cream and grey stone house with blue shutters, another chirrup of cicada song announcing their arrival to the unsuspecting lady of the house.

It was gone 10 p.m. and both Minnie and Jesse felt as hungry as they were tired.

'There's plenty – I haven't really got used to cooking for one,' Caryn said cheerily, although her heart broke with every step she took towards the much-used Le Creuset dish on top of the Aga. 'I'll stick some bread in the oven just to warm it up. It's this morning's.'

Jesse handed Minnie her drink then followed his mother around the kitchen, getting plates and cutlery, his heart beating almost to the floor. Apart from the sound of toads and cicadas in the bushes outside, there was an eerie quiet without his dad's effervescent presence lifting the home with his talk into the late evening. This house hadn't felt right since his dad died. Nowhere felt right since his dad died.

It was only the third time Jesse had been home since. He'd spent two weeks here in December with Ida, drinking coffee, clearing rooms and sitting, utterly baffled and shocked while he and Caryn arranged a small funeral in France, while they planned a memorial service for wider friends and family, plus the UK literati, back in London, at a church on Hanover Square five days before Christmas.

Jesse brought Ida again for a week in the Easter holidays, to escape from the stalemate with Hannah, and stay somewhere they could just *be*, rather than hanging out at Andrew and Elena's or traipsing around museums. It was Easter Sunday when Jesse finally told his mother about Hannah's affair. He hadn't wanted her to know, lest they work through it, but when his mother asked him what the hell was going on and why he still seemed to be sleeping at a friend's house rather than at home, he couldn't lie. Caryn sobbed, for her grief and for Jesse's, while

Jesse assured her that everything was going to be all right. It was just a blip.

* * *

While Caryn fussed over bread and wine glasses, and Jesse reassured her that really, everything was fine back in London, Minnie walked through to the eclectic living room and looked at the pictures on the walls, the mismatched rugs on the stone floor, and the endless shelves of books, looking like they could tumble out. Art books, dictionaries, biographies, books on writing. An old encyclopedia set that looked like it had been bought in the 1980s. Or the 1880s possibly.

On one smaller side wall, every shelf was bursting with books that had similar spines, with writing in similar fonts, shouting out their titles and authors in capital letters. James Patterson. Jonathan Kellerman. Patricia Cornwell. Lars Lightning. Then the penny dropped. That's where she knew the name.

Minnie pulled out a Lars Lightning book at random, turned it over, and looked at the headshot on the inside back cover. The author had familiar muddy blue eyes and light hair, although this man's hair was more white than dirty blond, still messy and thick in the same ruffled style.

Shit.

Minnie had read some of these books. They sat on the shelves of her parents' home in Hampstead. She had enjoyed them too. Her dark side loved a crime thriller. She always marvelled that she could never predict whodunnit.

Jesse stepped into the living room, lowering his head at a familiar point on the low wooden door frame.

'Plot twist!' Minnie said, holding up a hardback of *The Pondicherry Pursuit*.

Jesse smiled wanly.

'So this is why Remy is a departure! Your dad is Lars Lightning.'

'Rumbled,' Jesse confessed. Minnie's game of no frills, no fancy, and knowing nothing about each other was fast unravelling.

'I love his books! *The Viking's Curse* was sooo good. It inspired me to go to Scotland a few winters ago. My sister Lillia and I – we tried to see the Northern Lights from there because they'd sounded so epic in the book and well...'

She trailed off as she ran her finger over a shelf entirely dedicated to Lars Lightning: hardbacks, paperbacks and foreign editions. 'I didn't realise.'

Jesse smiled. Equal parts proud and heartbroken.

30

DAY FOUR

Now

'So what were you kids doing working in Paris?' Caryn asked, as she replenished three deep glasses of red. She watched Jesse and Minnie eat as if they were tucking into a midnight feast, which it almost was.

Minnie told Caryn about her audition for Wim Fischer's as-yet-untitled next big film, and how it had gone terribly. Caryn had written a profile piece on Wim Fischer when his debut came out twenty years ago and said she didn't realise how awful he was, otherwise she wouldn't have been quite so favourable. At the time he was the toast of Hollywood.

'How terrifying. Poor you! Have you told the police?'

Jesse shook his head gently.

'No, I just ran. Out of the room, out of the hotel, out of the street, to meet Jesse.'

Caryn looked at Jesse with concern.

'I'd been at the zoo,' he said. 'For Remy,' Jesse confessed. 'Although, did you know, there isn't a red panda at Paris Zoo either?'

Caryn looked startled, by Minnie's ordeal mostly, but also by Jesse's progress.

'I don't even think a crime was committed,' Minnie said, stabbing a plump butter bean with her fork. 'He propositioned me and I said no.'

'But it's a terrible abuse of power!' Caryn said, horrified.

Minnie nodded. 'I know. I'll talk to my parents when we get back to London. They'll know what to do.'

Caryn raised an eyebrow and watched Minnie's features as she ate voraciously.

'I'm just gutted about the movie. I wanted to meet Viola Rubin and I wanted that part. So much.'

'Well if he's like that at a meeting, imagine how ghastly he would be to work with!' said Caryn. 'Lucky escape, I am certain of it.'

Minnie acquiesced.

'You'll be fine,' Caryn said sagely. 'I can see it.'

Minnie had only been in her house for an hour and already Caryn was completely charmed. It was a charm Caryn assumed would take Minnie far, even if the girl didn't believe it herself.

Minnie and Jesse ate quickly, to power through their fatigue, and at midnight, having got Minnie a phone charger and some summer pyjamas, Caryn announced she was going turn in. It was a cold reminder for Jesse that his dad wasn't asleep upstairs, or at a yoga class, or away on a book tour. He was gone.

'Shall I make up the spare room?' Caryn asked, as neutrally as she could. She hadn't had a chance to talk to Jesse on his own about who this disarming woman was and what she meant to him. He might even have reconciled with Hannah; they hadn't spoken for a couple of weeks, which was a long time in their relationship.

'Yes please,' Minnie and Jesse both replied firmly.

'Here, I'll help.' Jesse followed his mother through the house to the laundry cupboard and held out his arms to make a shelf.

'I'll clear the table,' Minnie called cheerfully.

'Oh, no need to do that!' Caryn shouted back, but Minnie carried on, trying to make herself useful.

While Caryn and Jesse made up the bed and Jesse told his mother he had got a children's agent for Remy – that he was finally making progress with it – Minnie washed up the dinner plates and glasses in the kitchen.

As she stood at the butler sink and looked out of the window onto darkness, she became aware of her mobile phone bouncing back into life on the kitchen counter. She glanced at it – still no signal. It had died just south of Paris and she didn't know any numbers by heart to text anyone on Jesse's phone. She hadn't texted her parents to say how it went, or that she had left Paris, but not for London. She hadn't texted Hilde to say she wouldn't be back tonight. She hadn't texted Devon to say how horrific the audition was.

As she plunged her hand into the suds and circled a cloth around patterned plates, she thought about Wim Fischer, a shrivelled little man in an enormous bath tub. How repulsive the whole scene was. What a waste of her time. She wanted to cry but the anger inside her countered it. How was she letting men, and their appraisal of her, shape her life? After *everything* her parents taught her.

Jesse walked into the kitchen.

'Mum's gone to bed,' he said with a smile.

'Your mum is awesome,' Minnie replied, her anger softening.

'I think she thinks you're pretty awesome too. Although less so for doing the washing up. You didn't have to you know.'

Minnie knew.

'Is she OK?'

Jesse nodded.

'I think so,' he said, picking up a tea towel. 'It's just weird... Anyway, are *you* OK?' He looked at her. Feet bare on the cool stone floor in her short skirt and ballerina top, and remembered how the day had started, as if there had been a hundred hours in this day.

Minnie flicked the suds off her hands as she finished the last side plate. She turned around and leaned back against the sink, folding her arms.

'Yeah I'm all right. Trying to convince myself the film will be shit anyway.'

'A rotten tomato!' Jesse said triumphantly.

'My parents predicted the script wouldn't pass the Bechdel test. *Medusa's Mane* didn't. So... you know... they had their concerns.'

Jesse didn't know.

'What's the Bechdel test?'

'Jesse, you have a daughter. You should know what the Bechdel test is.'

Jesse started drying up the plates and cutlery on the side, waiting for an explanation.

'My parents always judge a work of fiction – a movie, a book or TV programme – on whether it passes the Bechdel test, regardless of whether they enjoyed the film or not. And if it doesn't meet the criteria, they like it a little less.'

'So what's the criteria?'

'Well the work of fiction has to have at least two female characters in it, and they should be named.'

'Right.'

'Who talk to each other.'

'OK...'

'About something other than a man.'

Jesse stopped drying the plate, dumbfounded.

'Surely every work of fiction passes this test?'

'Jesse, you have no idea.'

He was baffled as he tried not to drop his mother's floral plate onto the floor.

'Loads of things don't pass the test. Although if I'm right... I think your dad's books do – otherwise my parents wouldn't have loved him.'

'That's a relief.'

'We were discouraged from watching or reading things that didn't meet our parents' barometer of equality when we were kids. Then it was given a name: a cartoonist in America – Alison Bechdel – actually made it A Thing, but my parents had already followed it as a life rule.'

Jesse shook his head.

'I can't believe stories don't pass it today.'

'Oh please! Half the films that have won Best Picture at the Oscars fail the Bechdel test. It's so commonplace, people don't even notice. *Avatar*: fail. *Cocaine Bear*: a surprising pass. Although I doubt that won any Oscars...'

Jesse thought about all the cartoons Ida consumed. *Encanto* and

Frozen passed of course, although he wasn't sure about *The Little Mermaid*, given Ariel's motivation for becoming a human was to be with a man.

'What about *My Little Pony*?' He winced.

Minnie's face lit up.

'*My Little Pony* has exceptional girl power: sisterly ponies working together to solve problems in the community. No man troubles.'

'Thank fuck for that.'

'*Shrek* on the other hand... the first movie fails dismally, but they redressed it in the sequels.'

'So the movie you just went to audition for, was Veronica Valla not a kickass woman?'

'I hadn't seen the whole script – you never see a whole script at this stage, unless you're an A-lister. She might have been the *only* woman in it for all I know, and then it's a fail. Maybe not, but my parents had concerns after they streamed *Medusa's Mane* the other night.'

Jesse thought Minnie's parents sounded amazing.

'And you know what pisses me off most?' Minnie ran her fingers through her hair in exasperation.

'What?'

'I am totally failing in the Bechdel test of my own life.'

Jesse looked puzzled.

'What do you mean?' He threaded the damp tea towel through the oven handle. It would be dry in no time on this warm night.

'When I'm talking with my girlfriends, or when I'm talking to Tony, it's invariably about JP and how he dumped me. Or I'm talking about—'

Minnie stopped herself and took a sharp intake of breath. She looked briefly at Jesse and away with a scowl.

'Hey, are you OK?'

Minnie picked up her phone. 'Dammit. I still can't get reception.'

'It's hopeless here. Do you want to use Mum's landline? She still has one.'

Minnie looked at the clock on the kitchen wall and sighed.

'No, it's OK, it's late. I'm wiped out. They'll be all right.'

She rubbed a despairing hand up through her short fringe. She looked tired and defeated. Jesse pondered her.

'I put pyjamas and towels on your bed – and some shorts and a vest Mum dug out. She figured you're about the same size. The spare room is up the stairs and left, at the end of the corridor.'

Minnie felt bad for snapping.

'Thanks, Jesse.'

'Hey. That's OK.'

'I don't know what I'd have done if I wasn't with you in Paris today. I have no clue where anything is, I couldn't think, I can't speak French…'

'I'm sure you would have been fine.'

And, thankfully, they both knew that much was true.

* * *

As they whispered on the landing of the farmhouse, and Jesse assured Minnie she could help herself to anything she needed, Minnie felt compelled to stand on her tiptoes and give Jesse a wholehearted hug.

'Thank you, really.'

Jesse was taken aback, but hugged Minnie in return, his arms not fully wrapped around her.

'I mean, I don't have any clean pants and you've made it even bloody harder to get home, but thank you.' She pressed her cheek into his chest and tried to ignore the rhythm of his beating heart. 'This is a lovely home. And I am going to sleep for days. Well, not literally days, we don't have time…'

I want my time with you.

Jesse smiled.

'Thanks for letting me tag along,' he countered, and Minnie released herself, smiled and opened her bedroom door quietly.

Jesse walked a little way down the corridor, glanced out of the open hallway window at the sparkling sky and stopped on the threshold of his room.

'Hey, did you see them?'

'See what?'

'The Northern Lights, in Scotland?'

'No. Next time.'

Jesse looked at her cynically.

'I will see them without flying, Jesse Lightning!' Minnie assured him as she pointed a finger. And there, she realised she had said it. His name out loud.

31

DAY FIVE

Now

Minnie woke to the thrum of bees on the lavender under her open window. A hum so soporific it almost pulled her back to sleep, were it not for the fresh scents of the plant, the countryside and coffee wafting up from the ground floor. It was the most beautiful, calming alarm call Minnie had ever experienced, and it assuaged her momentary panic when she first remembered how far she was from home.

She rubbed her eyes, got out of bed in Caryn's summer pyjamas and opened the rickety wooden door, looking down the hall to see Jesse's door was closed.

Minnie walked down the corridor and paused, raising a fist to knock for Jesse, then deciding not to. She wanted to see him, to see his sleeping face and know more about him, but she carried on quietly, downstairs, hoping not to disturb anyone.

Coffee. She could smell coffee coming from the kitchen; perhaps Jesse was already up. Minnie didn't make it as far as the bright kitchen. As she walked through the expansive open living room she saw Caryn on the terrace at the back of the house. She was leaning over a wall, facing the view of the Luberon valley: a patchwork of green and brown fields stretching out ahead of her.

'Morning!' Minnie said croakily.

Caryn turned around, clutching some weeds she was pulling from the cracks between the stones.

'Morning, love. Sleep well? I didn't wake you, did I?'

Minnie smiled hazily. 'I slept blissfully, thank you.'

Caryn looked relieved.

'It was so nice to wake to my natural body clock. And the bees and the lavender!'

Part of the terrace was shaded by a canopy with a grapevine whose roots were so thick it was hard to see the structure it had entwined. Minnie stood, her own feet rooted in the sunshine, inhaled and reached her arms out wide as her stretch morphed into a yawn. The air smelled fresher and sweeter than anywhere she'd been.

'That's what Jesse likes most about it here. Waking up naturally. No sirens or traffic noises. Although I doubt he's woken naturally since Ida.'

Minnie smiled.

Caryn half smiled back, not knowing how well Minnie knew Ida, but landed on not very, given she hadn't said anything about her.

'There's coffee in the pot; I'm about to head out to the market.'

Minnie looked unsurely at her phone.

'Actually, can I come with you?' she asked, making a shield for her eyes against the climbing sun. 'Get a few supplies and check my messages.'

'Of course!' Caryn replied. 'That'll be fun.'

'Great. I just need to get dressed, although this...' She looked down at the stripy pyjama shorts and vest she was wearing.

'You wear it well!' Caryn admired.

'Great, I'll just grab my boots and wallet...'

'If you want flipflops there are some in the flower room, on the other side of the stairs. We're about the same size.'

'That would be amazing, thank you.' Minnie went inside.

'Wonderful, I'll write Jesse a note.'

Minnie found the room on the opposite end of the house, with the same proportions and dimensions as the kitchen. 'Flower room' sounded intriguing, and it looked like a very elegant utility room, with a washing machine, another butler sink, and gardening shoes by the back door. In the middle was a butcher's table, distressed in blue and white wood, with low oval baskets filled with dried flowers on the top. Some baskets had just lavender in them, some were mixed wildflowers. This room, she mused, that was probably an afterthought, was the most stunning in the house. Minnie loved it and leaned her head into a basket to inhale the scents, before taking a pair of flipflops from a rack by the door.

When Minnie returned, Caryn was leaving a note for Jesse on the dining room table where they'd eaten late last night. Jesse's backpack was open, its contents spilling out, his sketchbook and drawings on large sheets of paper pulled from the sketchbook as if he had been dwelling on them in the middle of the night.

Minnie stopped and gently moved paper around to reveal other sheets underneath. His drawings were magical. Soft. Painterly. Beautiful skies overlooking earnest animal friends.

'Wow,' Minnie said softly. 'I didn't imagine...' She stopped talking and looked. Drinking them in. 'They're gorgeous!'

Caryn glanced up over half-moon spectacles, a sparkle of pride in her eyes. It was the first time she had seen them too.

'Exquisite, aren't they? I was just looking.' She sighed. 'I don't know where he gets it from; his father and I both deal in words not images. As you can tell from the farmhouse, we don't have a very good eye for... style.'

Minnie loved the ramshackle décor. She would happily make that flower room her bedroom and sleep a lifetime of blissful nights in it.

'But ever since Jesse was tiny, he's drawn and designed. His eye is stunning. Always has been.'

Minnie leafed through a few more of his drawings. Preparatory pencil sketches. Early watercolours. Remy the red panda tentatively dipping a toe in the penguin enclosure water. Remy sliding down an elephant's trunk with a joyful look on his face. Remy riding on the back of an ostrich. They were enchanting.

'His teacher at nursery in England called Lars and I in once, aston-ished. He'd made a net of a box. He was only three. She thought, *No it can't be*, but at the end of the nursery day she folded his lines and bent the paper, and – hey presto – a perfect cubed paper box.'

'So clever.'

Caryn put the lid on her pen and left the piece of paper with her note on it in plain view next to his sketchbook.

'Come on, we have to get to the market before the best bread has all gone.'

* * *

Caryn handed Minnie a spare helmet and packed string bags in her panniers. Minnie hadn't realised they were going by moped.

'Hop on!' Caryn said gamely, grateful for some company.

Minnie swung her leg over and sat on the back, the sun already warming the seat against her thighs. She gripped the little steel side handles at the back of the seat. It felt too intimate to hug someone else's mother when her own might be worried sick, but she thought sitting as she was would suit Caryn's warm yet perfunctory style.

On the drive they wound past olive groves and lavender fields, past pink and ochre farmhouses and an ancient windmill. Minnie wanted to stop at every turn but was mindful about getting the best bread. She could already taste it, smeared in creamy salty butter.

In Gordes, Caryn parked a few metres away from the castle wall and propped the moped on its stand.

'Just leave your helmet on the handle, no one will take them.'

At the foot of the castle, in the village's centre, artisans sold fabrics and linens, billowing in lively prints; soaps, shampoos and tonics made of lavender and lemon. Food sellers sold their homegrown olive oil, honey, cheeses and bread. Caryn bought her favourite five-seed sour-dough while Minnie paced around in awe, as if she was in heaven, mindful of how small the panniers on Caryn's bike were, or her bag strewn across her body.

At a fruit and vegetable stall bursting with cherries, tomatoes and apricots, Caryn picked up a lemon so big and bright that Minnie thought it must be a prop.

'Give it a smell,' she commanded, wafting it under Minnie's nose.

'Unreal!'

She closed her eyes and inhaled, a moment of pure calm, curtailed when she remembered why she was here in the village; what she needed to do. She looked at her phone. She had a signal and messages were beeping in. Mostly from her parents, sisters, brother and Hilde. One from JP.

Proud of you Kiddo x

'Sorry, I just need to check in...' Minnie said, waving her phone.

'Of course! I'll do some errands and then...' Caryn narrowed her eyes and pointed to a cafe tucked in a shady corner of the square with Chez Lucille written on an awning. 'See you over there in a short while? It does the best hot chocolate and pastries.'

* * *

Minnie walked around the village aimlessly as she called Hilde first, then her mother. Telling them both what a Grade-A creep Wim Fischer had been, how she was safe, and how she had ended up in Provence, wandering around a village wearing a kindly stranger's pyjamas and no bra. They had responded differently. Hilde was more worried than Geraldine, who thought it sounded magical and wanted to transport herself there immediately.

Both asked when she would be home and she told them she had to get back for a waitressing job at the races on Sunday. It was Friday morning and she realised she didn't care too much about getting back, it was so beautiful where she was.

'I'm gonna troll him on Instagram so everyone knows what a mother-fucker he is,' Hilde declared.

'I will talk to your father – there has to be some repercussion for this, it is wholly unacceptable,' Geraldine said more diplomatically.

When Minnie hung up she texted her sisters something friendly but opaque, then retraced her steps back to the square, mindful now to look up at the white stone buildings that had turned dusty pink, perched on top of each other in this sentinel village that felt so removed from her hideous experience in Paris; from her heartache in London. She felt her shoulders lower in relief. *It too will pass.*

* * *

Minnie rounded back through a cobblestone street onto the market square and saw Caryn in the far corner, sitting at a metal table for two, reading the paper.

'Ahh, there you are! All fine at home?'

Minnie tucked her phone away.

'All fine.'

'I ordered you a *chocolat*. This village has the best hot chocolate in all the world, and this cafe has the best in the village.'

'Then I am in luck, thank you.'

Minnie pulled the metal chair out and sat down, crossing her legs. The sunshine on her shoulders felt restorative.

'How did you end up here? It's incredible.'

'Lars came on a writing retreat; he must have been on deadline.' Caryn looked like she was thinking. Tracing through timelines and dates and books and heartache. 'Must have been around 2002 because we bought the house in 2003. And... well, there was no looking back really, we loved it here so much.'

'It's beautiful.'

Minnie licked the hot chocolate foam from her top lip.

'When did you move permanently?'

'Well Jesse was ten when we bought the property. We did think about moving then and him going to international school here, but he was about to go to secondary school, and he had a nice life in Claygate. A good bunch of friends. So we'd come for the holidays. Long summers. That kind of thing. Jesse soon made lots of friends here too. And because we have a pool, all the kids would come to us.'

'You have a pool?'

'Yes, at the side of the house.'

Suddenly the image of the lonely only-child boy with a terribly old dad that Minnie had conjured didn't seem to fit.

'And Jesse being a summer born meant he always had his birthday parties here.'

Minnie felt bad that she didn't know when his birthday was. But why would she? He didn't know hers.

'Wow.'

'Yes, yes, it must have been 2002 because *Nick of Time* was out in 2003, and – well, lots changed with that book.'

Minnie nodded. She had read it and seen the film.

'We moved permanently in 2011. I remember being a bit homesick around 2012 – London Olympics and all that – but it was one very short blip. We never looked back. Well, until...'

Sadness set its veil over her soft eyes.

How heartbreaking to be in this dream place, a place she had discovered with the love of her life, and not be able to share it with him any more. Minnie looked at Caryn and felt terrible for her.

'How did you two meet?'

Caryn was startled by the question, as a waiter set down two glasses of water and a plate of pastries.

'*Merci*,' she said. Minnie emulated her.

Caryn didn't think Hannah had ever asked her the question, but Minnie had an endearing curiosity about her. An inquisitive face that Caryn couldn't help furnishing with details. Plus, talking about Lars kept him close. She was so terrified he would drift away.

'Well, as I said last night, I was a journalist, I still am, although I haven't written much lately.'

'What sort of journalism do you do?'

'Magazines and newspapers. I did a lot of cover interviews and profile pieces. Big celebrities and the like. Whenever such and such was promoting a book or a film or a beauty brand, I managed to talk my way into interviewing them.'

'Sounds really interesting.'

'Oh it was, and it fitted around Lars' novel writing after we got together.'

'And his novel writing must have fit around your work too...' Minnie said cannily.

Caryn gave her a look as if to say *clever girl.*

'I was young when I met him.' She looked almost bashful, as if it could have been a lifetime ago, a youth misspent; a gratitude in her gaze made it obvious it wasn't.

'He was a bit of a playboy back then. A "serial monogamist" they started calling it in the nineties. I was dispatched to interview him and... well, we fell in love.'

'Oh wow. It sounds magical.'

'Yes, as a journalist you do always hope to ask the questions that will get to the core of someone, really find out what makes them tick. I suppose I hit the target with Lars.'

'You made him tick.'

Caryn smiled warmly. *Who was this girl?* She had an inkling.

'My parents weren't so happy. He was twenty years older than me. But it was easy to fall for him and they soon did.'

Minnie tore a piece of almond croissant from its curled horn.

'What was he like?'

Characters. Minnie wanted to know about this character. Caryn looked choked.

'Gosh. It's hard describing him to people who don't know him. How do you sum up a man of his brilliance, his imagination – how do you describe love in just a few words?'

Caryn took a sip of coffee to compose herself. 'He was the source. The source of everything. Laughter, warmth, compassion. He was a wonderful father. He and Jesse were just...' She shook her head. 'My parents worried about me getting together with an older man for all the wrong reasons: that he would cheat or stray or not settle down. What they should have been worried about is that we wouldn't have enough time.'

Minnie thought of Jesse back at the farmhouse. Was he still asleep? What did his sleeping face look like?

I want my time with you.

'But there you go,' Caryn said blithely. 'I'd do it all again.'

'I'm sure you would. It's inspirational really.'

'Oh I don't know about that...' Caryn looked mournful. 'It's just incredibly sad.'

Her eyes looked vacant and Minnie felt terrible that Caryn was sitting at this table with her when she should have been sitting here with Lars.

'I was seeing an older guy,' Minnie said quietly, as she finished her croissant. Caryn's brow raised with interest. 'He was double my age. My parents only met him once, at a dinner at one of his restaurants, but they didn't warm to him. They never said, but I could tell.'

Caryn looked apologetic, and wondered what Minnie's situation was now. Was she just a friend to her son?

'I think I might know who your parents are,' Caryn said with a knowing smile.

'You do?'

'You are the spit of your mother. Your eyes. I interviewed her once, you know?'

* * *

As they ate they talked about Caryn's love of dried flowers, how maintaining the farmhouse was a full-time job in itself. How she would get back to writing one day, if she could only take the jobs she would love. After breakfast, Minnie perused the market and bought cherries, two pairs of fifties looking knickers, a sundress and a pair of gold espadrilles – plus a toothbrush from the pharmacy, then they both felt a pull to get back to Jesse at the house. To see what he was up to.

On the journey back, Caryn pointed out Marc Chagall's former home and studio, and told Minnie about his exile from the Nazis, forcing him to flee persecution in Paris and escape to the Luberon valley. 'His daughter Ida then took the house over.'

'Ida?' Minnie shouted from the back of the moped.

'Yes. Jesse and Hannah loved the name. I do too of course.'

When they got back Minnie walked into the farmhouse clutching her wares.

'We have bread!' she declared, to no one, as she entered the kitchen to the smell of sweet fried food.

Caryn put the string bags down on the kitchen counter and they looked at the empty frying pan on the stove.

'He might be by the pool,' she said, stopping to listen to a distant splash. 'He does love a pancake by the pool. You go, I'll unpack these. That end,' she said, pointing to the other side of the house.

Minnie walked cautiously through the cool interior to the flower room and out of the side door with the shoe rack next to it, to the garden. Along the side of the house ran a wood and tiled awning and underneath it, a long outdoor dining table with orange and white metal chairs. As Minnie walked by it, she heard echoes of dinner parties past.

Jesse was doing lengths of a long rectangular swimming pool, turquoise against the verdant trees around it. She watched his tanned arms raise in triangle formations, his elbows in perfect rhythm powering him through the pool. Minnie stood dumbfounded.

As Jesse stopped to tap the far end of the pool and turn around, he saw her, face transfixed, skin pale.

'Oh, you're back.'

'Morning!'

He stopped and wiped the water off his face with both palms, his arms glistening.

'How was it?' He smiled.

This was such a different vision to the harangued man Minnie had met in Bondiga's Books six weeks ago, she couldn't quite believe it. This Jesse was golden, relaxed. So sexy she wanted to dive-bomb in, there and then, and wrap her legs around his waist.

Jesse and Hannah.

Ringing in her ear, she could hear the way Caryn said those names. Hannah was Caryn's family, not Minnie.

'Success?' he asked with a smile as he rose out of the pool and plonked his athletic frame onto the side. Minnie hadn't imagined Jesse would be such a specimen.

She had to remember her words.

'Success,' she repeated succinctly. 'I have clothes, cherries, espadrilles – oh and a toothbrush, so no more stinky-breath Jeff for me.'

Minnie was barefoot, still standing in Caryn's striped shorts and vest. She so wanted to jump in and swim to him, but something stopped her. Perhaps it was the espadrilles in her hand.

'I made pancakes. Wasn't sure if you were going to eat at the market?'

Jesse nodded to a stack oozing with the purple juice of cooked blueberries, under a mesh cloche with bees stitched onto it, sitting on a little table under a parasol at the far end of the pool. The table was set for three, as Jesse was accustomed to.

Minnie had already had an almond croissant and sampled cheeses and charcuterie at the market, but her stomach grumbled.

'That would be lovely,' she said, as she walked to the table and sat herself down.

Jesse pulled a stripy towel from a metal chair and dried himself off.

'This is unreal, Jesse.'

He smiled proudly as he sat down.

'Totally not what I imagined for you.'

'What did you imagine for me? Grumpy old mancave?'

She really wanted to tell him about her family. How she had grown up with a famous father – and mother – how she would understand certain things about Jesse that most people couldn't. But she'd already crossed enough lines in this game, so she stopped herself.

'No, I just pictured a quieter life for you.'

'It doesn't get quieter than this,' Jesse said, puzzled. 'Did you call your parents? Hilde?'

'All good. I told them a grumpy stranger has kidnapped me and it's quite the ordeal.' They locked eyes and Jesse cleared his throat. 'Did you tell them about...?'

Minnie cut him off with a raised hand.

'Yes. I did, but I do not want to talk about that today.'

I want my time with you.

Jesse nodded. Noted.

He passed her the pancake stack and she took the one from the top with a fork.

'Oh my God, Jesse, these look like the best pancakes I've ever seen.'

'Bon appétit!' he said, taking one for himself. 'So what did you want to do today? Head back to Paris? Go home?'

Minnie looked around her. A dragonfly darted skittishly over the pool.

'Can we stay for a bit?' she asked, almost guiltily, tucking in. Jesse dug in.

'Of course. I don't need to be back in London for a few days.'

Jesse wasn't due to have Ida this weekend.

'Can we stay forever?' Minnie blurted, holding Jesse's gaze. His chest inflated with a half gasp, droplets of water trickling down the contours of his body.

Minnie had crossed a line, but she could make it back.

'Just kidding, fair dos, we both have work...'

She tried to sound blasé.

'Well I do need to show you around first.'

'Your mum gave me a bit of a tour—'

'There's somewhere I need to take you.' He stood up, water dripping from his hair to his nose, the morning sunshine making his wet skin sparkle. The smell of light chlorine and roses.

Minnie was mesmerised, by how cool and composed he now was compared with the man she had met. He played this game well.

Jesse paused, almost waiting for Minnie to say something.

'Do you want to swim first?'

Minnie looked down at herself.

'I don't have a...' She gestured to her body. No bikini, no costume, and she didn't want to borrow his mum's. 'I could use a shower though.'

'Cool, you go first and I'll go after you.'

Minnie looked at him, flushed – she wanted him to go in with her – and couldn't speak.

'Then I'll take you on a road trip.'

32

DAY FIVE

Now

Showered, fresh and wearing her new white and blue striped sundress, Minnie bypassed Caryn on a phone call to someone in English, in the living room, and went to look around the gardens while she waited for Jesse. The view from the edge of the orchard was even more spectacular than the view from the terrace: wider, more expansive. Cypresses, sunflower fields, lavender tones, all in one mythical landscape. She inhaled so many vibrant scents all at once it was hard to differentiate them. Combined and bottled, they would smell of summer, like the perfumes across the province in Grasse. A scent of tomatoes started to permeate, and Minnie followed her nose to the greenhouse, where jewelled red orbs peeped out from behind abundant leaves. She went inside the elegant glass structure and touched a tomato so ripe it came off in her hand.

She sniffed it.

'Incredible.'

If Minnie were to conjure the perfect tomato, this is what it would look, feel and smell like.

'Ah, you're here!' Jesse said as he saw Minnie, black bob slicked back and damp, her new sundress swinging above golden espadrilles, large tomato at her nose. 'Mum sent me to get some figs... the high ones. Want to help me before we go?'

Minnie's face was almost obscured by the giant red fruit.

'This is insane!'

'I know right. I'm always saying, they should sell their fruit at the market too. But they give most of it away, at the end of the driveway. What they can't fit in pies or salads anyway.'

They.

It hung in the still air between them.

'Come on, grab a basket,' he said, nodding to a stack on the floor at the edge of the greenhouse.

In the orchard stood three strong and fecund fig trees, ready to release their bounty from beneath frilled leaves. Jesse picked those he could reach from standing while Minnie held the basket, then he got a ladder from the greenhouse.

'You want to summit or do you prefer to keep your feet on the ground?'

Minnie looked down at her dress.

'I'd better be the base...' she said, as she put a solid foot on the bottom step and made way for Jesse to go up. As he climbed she watched his muscular, tanned calves tighten and tilt with each step. A perfect specimen. She wanted to touch his skin with her fingertips, to loop her arms around him and anchor herself to him. She shook her head and looked up.

'I love figs, in all forms,' he said as he reached out to pick one. 'Salads, jam, tarts... my mum makes the most amazing fig tart.'

'I bet.'

'Do you know how my dad liked to eat them best though?' Jesse said, looking down at Minnie, who shielded her eyes from the sun.

'How?'

'Fig fucking rolls. You know those biscuits, packaged up like little parcels. Dry as.'

'Hahaha, fair dos, they are good.'

'He always got me to bring him a pack of fig rolls from England when I came over. When he had this!'

'Crazy.'

Jesse stretched his strong arms to the sky while he grabbed each treasure, putting some in the basket on the top step, carefully handing others down to Minnie to put in hers, their fingers brushing each time.

'I think that's it,' he said as he started to step back down. Jesse sighed, balancing the weight of the basket with the precariousness of his footing. He turned too fast, his head started spinning, from the sunshine and the height, and he sat suddenly halfway down the ladder.

'You OK?' Minnie asked, startled by Jesse's sudden lack of balance and his abrupt stop.

She took his basket and placed it on the floor next to hers.

'Jesse?' She went up a few steps and put a hand on each side of the ladder, on either side of him. 'Are you OK?'

He blinked rapidly for a few seconds and shook his head. He looked dizzy.

'Jesse?' Minnie asked with more alarm.

He nodded, his eyes still closed.

'Yeah, weird, just started spinning out.'

'It's pretty hot already.'

He looked at the greenhouse as he tried to gather himself. He blinked rapidly as he glanced out at the valley, as if he were trying to focus.

'We don't have to go sightseeing you know, we can hang here. I think I'd be happy hanging here.'

'No, no it's cool,' Jesse said, looking back to Minnie. He hadn't realised how close she was to him, standing between his legs. One hand now on his shoulder, the other on his bare knee. He hadn't noticed the concern in her eyes. 'Honestly, totally fine. I just... I don't know...'

Minnie was astute enough to know.

'It's OK, Jesse, it's OK.'

He shook his head as if trying to shake off any trace of a tear that might come. He felt embarrassed.

'You're OK.'

She looked at him intently, reassuringly.

'It's just... it happened there. In the greenhouse. I don't think I've been in there since... until today. It just hit me.'

'It's OK.'

'It's not OK,' he said with a half-smile.

She stroked his leg and squeezed it.

'Fig fucking rolls...' he said to himself with a wry smile. 'Come on, let's get going.'

* * *

Caryn was off the phone and reading a newspaper by the time Jesse handed her the basket. Her eyes lit up with the possibilities of the harvest.

'Thank you, darling,' she said, 'I'll put them in the kitchen.'

'I can do it...' Jesse said, heading back inside.

'Are we going on the moped?' Minnie asked, following him. 'Shall I change?'

'Do you want to take my car,' Caryn called, over her half-moon glasses. She and Minnie waited for answers as Jesse came back out.

'We'll go by car, if you're sure?'

Caryn nodded.

'Great,' Minnie said, shaking her now-dry hair.

'Want to come, Mum?'

'No, you know what, I'm going to send some emails. Pitch some features ideas to old editors.' She looked at Minnie, almost as if Minnie had suggested it.

'Oh, brilliant.'

Minnie saw a flash of relief flit across Jesse's face. Some normality might be creeping back into his mother's life.

'Got everything?' he asked.

Minnie opened her arms and palms out as if to say *take me as you see me*.

'Well I don't really have anything else, so yes!'

33

DAY FIVE

Now

Jesse walked Minnie to the passenger side of the beaten-up Fiat 500 on the driveway and opened the door.

'Thanks!'

Minnie thought the car had been decorative when they'd arrived in last night's twilight; it looked old and dusty, but it started with a chug, and Jesse deftly turned it around as if he had a thousand times, and drove down the gravel track to the road.

She put on her cat-eye sunglasses and stretched her arms, letting one reach out of the open window towards the sky. This was the life. Morning sunshine. Fresh air. A new dress. A chi-chi car. She leaned on her arms on the ledge of the open window and looked at her reflection in the wing mirror; her hair was now shaggy in the wind. She narrowed her eyes and imagined she were the star of a 1950s film, going on an adventure with a beautiful guide. Her dress even looked the part.

Jesse and Minnie headed south until a citadel emerged from a sea of cherry orchards and vineyards, with a village perched below them, that looked down onto more villages below that.

A picture-book outline of a medieval enclave emerged: a church, grey stone rooftops tinged pink and peach, the colour of unpainted plaster.

'This is beautiful!' Minnie gasped, feeling rejuvenated. She looked to Jesse, and then to his hand changing gear. She yearned to wrap her fingers around his.

Jesse wound into Ménerbes village and put on his own sunglasses as he pulled up outside a smooth cream house with shutters the same vivid verdant shade of the cypress tree that leaned languidly against one wall.

'What's this?'

'A house I love. I think you'll love it too.'

Minnie already knew she would.

'Shall we have a look?'

'I'd love to.'

They got out of the car and walked towards stone steps to an open terrace, leading to the grand cream house. It was stunning. Minnie spun around as she walked and imagined she were playing another role. That this was *their* house; that they had Ida and their own children running through it in a future sphere. That he went to harvest fruit and paint the view, and no one broke each other's hearts or died suddenly.

Get a grip.

They walked through a little courtyard. A small fountain emitted a comfortable trickle.

He's married.

Jesse ran his fingers under one of the jets.

This is just a game.

'Who lives here?' Minnie worried they were intruding on another family.

'Oh, it's a museum now, but it belonged to Dora Maar.'

'Who?'

'She was a filmmaker, an artist, a photographer. She was part of Picasso's scene – she was his lover.'

Hairs tingled on the back of Minnie's neck as Jesse said *lover* and she put her palm across it, in the hope he wouldn't notice.

'Picasso bought her this house.'

'Interesting,' Minnie said as she raised her chin. Her family had had a robust discussion about Picasso during their Father's Day dinner, after her brother Anthony had brought their dad a print and Lillia had said he was a cultural appropriator and a misogynist. Picasso, not Anthony.

Was he a misogynist? Would his paintings pass the Bechdel test were there a measure for art? Minnie raised the issue quietly as they walked in and Jesse stopped to ponder it. He too had read the recent tide of change, although his thoughts were interrupted by a friendly woman in a black dress and red lipstick, whose face lit up when she saw Jesse.

'Ahhh, Jesse, tu es de retour! Salut! Comment vas-tu? Tout va bien?'

'Oui oui, Hélène, ça me fait plaisir de te voir. C'est une de mes amies de Londres, Minnie. Est ce qu'on peut regarder un peu la maison?'

The woman smiled at Minnie.

'Bien sûr! Nous avons une conférence qui commence dans une heure, vous pourriez peut-être rester pour ça?'

'Ahhh merci, mais on ne peut pas rester longtemps, on part vers Arles, mais merci.'

The woman looked at Minnie again and nodded.

'OK, on se retrouve bientôt pour boire un verre, oui?'

Jesse said yes and they hugged each other fondly, while the woman went to greet a man who was arriving to give a lecture.

'She was nice.'

'Yeah, she manages the place.'

'And we're just allowed to walk around?' Minnie asked.

'It's a museum, but they also run lectures and artist workshops. They used to let me come here and sketch when I was young. Not that we didn't have a beautiful view up in Gordes, but... it was just nice to meet some like-minded people. Share some inspiration. Most tended to be painters and I moved more into design, but... Hélène's always been cool. We used to hang out.'

'It's lovely. I think I might find a lot of inspiration here...' Minnie said appreciatively as she peered into a drawing room and all the characters on its walls.

In one study an older man greeted Jesse in French and they talked for a few minutes while Minnie concentrated on a letter Dora Maar had written to a lover. As she tried to read the notes next to the letter, as she tried to decipher what was being said, she listened to the men gliding between French and English so seamlessly, it was as if neither noticed which language they were speaking. It sounded sexy. Jesse was sexy, and Minnie felt completely thrown by how all-encompassing this felt. Only weeks ago she had been crying over JP in Tony's office. Was she that shallow?

The man clearly knew Jesse's family, and when Jesse thanked him for letting them look in this room today when they had an event on, he said, 'No problem!' and for Jesse to pass on his wishes to his mother.

After half an hour they had seen all the rooms, as well as prints of Picasso's portraits of Dora Maar, and they needed to get out of the way, so Jesse led them back to the car.

'God that was stunning!' Minnie declared, as they took one last look at the house basking in the sun. 'Definitely the sort of place I'm going to get when I buy...' Minnie said with a wink.

'Definitely the kind of place I'll move into when I'm not crashing at my mate's house,' Jesse replied, in self-deprecation, as if he thought he was the world's biggest loser.

Minnie wondered why her parents had never bought a holiday home in France or Europe. They had the means, but they had everything they ever wanted in the house by the Heath. Objects to fascinate them and love in abundance.

* * *

Jesse got them back on the road, winding down the valley to the sun-baked city of Arles, the landscape in front of Minnie turning from greens to browns but looking strikingly familiar, although she couldn't put her finger on why.

They saw a Roman amphitheatre come into view, dusty and timeless. The Rhone sparkling under the early afternoon sun. Minnie rubbed suncream onto her pale shoulders, careful not to get any on her sundress.

'This is gorgeous, Jesse, and so different to where we've just come from.'

'Lovely isn't it? It's been a hub since Roman times. My dad loved coming for dinner and getting engrossed in the history here. "Heart of the cultural conversation my son," he'd say to me after one pastis too many. With a sparkle in his eye.'

Minnie smiled; it was the first time Jesse had seemed relaxed talking about his dad. She nodded and looked out of the window.

'Van Gogh lived and painted here...'

Minnie sat up. 'Oh really?'

'Yeah more than two hundred works.'

'Perhaps that's why it looks familiar; I've already seen this place in the National Gallery,' Minnie mused.

'Maybe. Gauguin and Gucci blew through here too.'

'Gucci?'

Jesse nodded.

'Gucci took over the city with a Cruise show in 2019. I did some typography for the show notes.'

'Oh wow.'

She glanced across at Jesse's shoes on the pedals of the tiny car. They were battered Birkenstocks not Gucci loafers, and she loved him all the more for it.

Minnie's phone beeped five times, chiming with incoming messages, one after the other.

'Ahh, and I have signal again.'

'Come on, let's park up.'

As Jesse paid for the parking, Minnie got out and glanced at her messages, replying to her mum and to Hilde, but not to JP, who had messaged again, to ask how the audition had gone in Paris. The thought of where to begin in fashioning a reply made her feel slightly nauseous, on several levels.

Jesse's phone chimed too, and he looked at it, and at a plane overhead, before pocketing his car key and leading Minnie towards the direction of town. It would have been the most natural thing for him to hold out his hand and lead her, but he couldn't.

Get a grip.

She's still in love with a slimy man.

* * *

They ambled through shady medieval backstreets and sun-drenched squares, all a thousand hues of cream, stone and rust, grey buildings with blue shutters peppered throughout.

'So where are the Van Goghs?' Minnie asked. 'Is there a museum?'

'There is... but it doesn't have any Van Gogh canvases...' Jesse laughed.

'What?'

'You will genuinely have seen more in the National Gallery.'

Minnie pouted.

'But walk along this street in a few hours and it will look very familiar under the stars.'

Minnie stopped and looked back and forth. The ochre street cafe with a blue doorway. The balcony above the awning. It looked like a corner from *Café Terrace at Night*, except the sun was capturing it.

'No way!'

She looked around and noticed tourists taking photos.

'It is.' Jesse smiled. 'Just picture swirls of stars above and you're there.'

'Can we come back later?'

'We can do whatever you want.' Their eyes locked again.

She was desperate to take his hand.

Don't be silly.

* * *

Minnie and Jesse walked the city at a sleepy summer pace, stopping for crepes on a pretty square, ambling along the river, visiting the Musée Réattu, where they saw some Picassos and a letter Van Gogh had written to Gauguin, lamenting his psychological state in the months before he cut off his ear and handed it to a prostitute during a psychotic episode.

It was everything Minnie had hoped for, for her afternoon in Paris, only now she was in a southern cultural hub. Which seemed more... Jesse. Golden. Laconic. Creative.

'My dad loved this city,' Jesse said, as they walked around the Amphitheatre. 'He said it had three golden ages: the Roman era. The art boom of the late 1800s. And today.'

By the time they collapsed at a small wooden table in the Hotel Nord-Pinus, both Jesse and Minnie had the feeling that *today* was special, that they were on the cusp of something new and exciting.

'So, esteemed tour guide, what are we doing here?'

'Pastis,' Jesse declared. 'It's a little Provence tradition. A pre-dinner pastis. Have you ever tried it?'

Minnie thought of the array of bottles behind the counter on the wall at Alpine NW1 and all the lock-ins she had enjoyed there, but pastis seemed out of reach from her drunken memories.

Jesse ordered in French and they waited, Minnie looking around the room in awe, Jesse sitting in proud contentment, until the waiter came back with two pretty glasses.

He poured yellow liquid straight from the bottle and added what looked like water – but it could have been another spirit for all Minnie knew – with unassumed flair.

Minnie's eyes widened. 'Fair dos. They do drink in style.'

'If this place is good enough for Picasso and Hemingway...'

'Hemingway? No way.' Minnie told Jesse she had played Maria in an adaptation of *For Whom the Bell Tolls* at Mountview and Jesse raised his glass and said '*Santé!*' to that.

Minnie took a sip.

'Hmmm, that's actually good.'

'It's called a *Mauresque* around here. Pastis, water and orgeat syrup.'

'What the hell is orgeat syrup?'

'Almond, sugar and rosewater or orange blossom – I think this one has orange in it.'

Minnie sipped and concurred.

'So why did you keep this so close to your chest at cocktail school? You could have taught Thomas a thing or two.'

'He'd have strung me up for trying to steal his thunder.'

They laughed, took another sip and locked eyes. This was not part of the game. Their raised hands touched, and then their little fingers, and then they put down their glasses and entwined all the fingers of their right hands, pulling their chairs into the table with their left. They slipped in together so naturally, they both knew the game was over. Their faces drew together, dreamy contemplation unwavering. Lips tentatively urging closer. Until a text went off on Jesse's phone, tucked away in his shorts, and he jumped.

'Shit! Sorry, I have to check it... in case... Ida...'

'Of course!'

They released each other's fingers and Minnie looked around the bar. It was filling with the buzzy and the beautiful. Vibrant locals starting their weekend in style on a Friday afternoon.

Jesse looked at his phone and his face dropped. He put a palm to shield his eyes.

'What is it?'

He let out a sigh and whispered a quiet *fuck* at his screen.

'What's the matter?'

'Hannah.'

Minnie's heart sank.

'I had a weird call from her on Wednesday night.'

Minnie frowned, and wondered why Jesse hadn't mentioned it on the train when she had told him about her call from JP. But then, what right did she have to know? She didn't even know what the hell was going on with his marriage.

'What's up?'

'I'm meant to be having dinner with her in London... in about four hours.'

'Oh.'

Minnie's eyes prickled and she didn't want to acknowledge why.

'So what are you going to do?'

34

DAY FIVE

Now

Jesse and Minnie whizzed around country bends, past ancient citadels, as the sun started to lower, lighting the lavender fields of the Luberon valley the deepest purple Minnie had ever seen. Minnie felt tipsy after a second pastis that Jesse had to abstain from so he could drive, and her senses felt alive, her vision richer, as she drank in the shades and scents of Provence in the golden hour.

'Look at that!' she said, at nothing in particular and everything that was spectacular, her hand out of the window, daring her fingers to kiss the bushes and hedgerows as they wound through the countryside.

After forty-five minutes, Jesse pulled up at a gravelly inlet at the side of the road on the edge of rolls and rolls of lavender fields. A humidity and thickness had filled the air. He turned off the engine and they sat in silence, ears sharp as they tuned into the sounds of sunset, chirruping, buzzing and breeze.

'How did those cicadas not keep me awake last night?' Minnie whispered.

'They stop when the temperature goes below twenty-two degrees. Some August nights can be *pretty* noisy.'

'I bet.'

'What's the birdsong?' she asked.

Jesse held his hand up and concentrated.

'Common whitethroat, and turtle doves... can you hear the coo?'

'Yes.'

Then a rumble hit the distance. Or was it a combine harvester?

'A storm?' asked Minnie.

'Hmmm, not likely, but it does feel muggy. Come on, just in case...'

* * *

As they walked towards field after field of lavender bushes, Minnie gasped in awe.

'The colour! It's so vibrant!'

Jesse's hands were now in his pockets as he ambled thoughtfully.

'That's what I love most about these fields. The way the colour of the lavender changes throughout the day.'

'How so?'

'At dawn it's pale and misty. Tinged grey. In the midday sun, surrounded by bees, it looks almost white tipped. In the evening, it glows this deep rich purple. I've tried to find the colours and replicate them, but there is no Pantone reference for any of them...'

Minnie laughed.

'My dad describes it best though, in *Riviera Runaway* probably. I'll have to dig it out.'

Another ominous sound rumbled in the distance.

'What's it like when it rains?'

Jesse looked back over his shoulder as Minnie followed the path he'd cut.

'Beautiful.'

She gasped quietly. The sun was still shining despite the noise in the sky, glistening off the spire of a church in the distance. If a storm was coming it was rising inside of her.

They held each other's gaze just a fraction too long again. Jesse broke it.

'Come on,' he said as they approached a stile. 'We don't have long.'

They climbed over and into an arched glade where the sun glittered through a tunnel of trees. The hum of the bees was getting louder – or maybe it was thunder getting nearer. The smell of lavender was certainly stronger, as the small wood opened out to the largest and most beautiful lavender field Minnie had ever seen. Neat rows of dark, rich purple led up to a pale grey stone abbey on a hill.

'Oh my goodness,' Minnie said. 'It's stunning.'

'Here you go!' Jesse declared. 'Here's your field.'

'What?'

'Tony said you should run carefree through a field. There isn't a more beautiful one in the world.'

'Oh my God.'

It was the most thoughtful thing anyone had ever done for her.

Minnie welled up before putting her fingers over her closed eyes, inhaling, and opening them again. The field really was that purple, tips of the lavender fronds glittering gold under the angle of the low dipping sun. 'I have never been anywhere so stunning in all my life.'

'It's yours.'

Minnie swallowed hard and looked at the building in the distance.

'Who lives there?'

'It's an abbey.' Jesse looked at his watch. 'But it's closed now. The tourists will have gone. You can run like a banshee, if that's your will.'

Minnie grabbed Jesse's hand like it was the most natural thing in the world and threaded her fingers through each of his. She looked at him, her eyes glimmering as she led them, walking towards the abbey determinedly. As her pace quickened, she let go of his hand. Jesse followed her golden espadrilles, flashing as they trod their path. Minnie broke into a run, laughter bursting from her chest, her eyes closed and the brush and bristles of the lavender bushes kissing her shins as she passed.

Jesse had to start running too, to keep up, his heart brimming to see that Minnie loved this place as much as he did.

'This is unreal!' Minnie shouted, as she ran, becoming more out of breath with each step, as the field started to incline towards the abbey. A roll of thunder rumbled nearer now, making Minnie scream, a scream that turned into a laugh; bees darted away. The foreboding in the sky hit Minnie with a fear and a sense of dread, and suddenly she felt as if a dark cloud was looming low, above her shoulders. She was so utterly happy it made her feel so dreadfully vulnerable. Her panting and laughter turned to panic, shallow breaths and tears, as she stopped abruptly, turning around to face Jesse. Her face suddenly serious. He stopped, alarmed.

'What?'

Minnie rushed back to him and placed a palm on each of Jesse's cheeks.

'Don't go back to her,' she said. As if she had seen what was coming.

'What?' Jesse said, dumbfounded.

'Don't go back to her. I want my time with you,' Minnie whispered, breathlessly, as she looked up at him and kissed him decidedly. She drew back, startled by how startled Jesse looked. Then he lifted her, her legs wrapping around his waist as he cradled her, as she clung on, kissing feverishly as they both willed the sun not to set.

* * *

Minnie sat on top of Jesse as the heavens opened, as if out of nowhere, and the rain clouds released their burden on the lavender fields. Her white dress was soaked and stuck to her at the bodice as she hitched it up, until they locked together, rocking and moving to the sounds of their breaths and the rolls of thunder. The bees and birdsong had stopped, and they felt entirely alone, as if they were the only two people in the village, the province, the world, until she fell onto his chest, his T-shirt wet through, the storm passing.

They lay side by side on their backs for a few blissful minutes, dents in the neat rows of lavender around them.

When Minnie propped herself up and emerged, the world looked completely different. The temperature had dropped; the cicadas had stopped singing; goosebumps fizzled on her arms.

She sighed.

'Well Tony was sort of right. Make new friends, try new things...' She said it with a sharp irony. 'I feel great.'

They both suspected Tony would *not* approve.

Jesse propped himself up on one elbow, digging into soil where the ground had become wet, and circled Minnie's face with his other forefinger as if she were a treasure he had just found.

'Thank you,' he said, more formally than he meant to.

'You're welcome,' Minnie laughed. 'Thank you.'

The air lifted, a freshness rolled over on the scents of lavender and rain, and the storm clouds that had come from out of nowhere started to break. A sunbeam, nature's only straight line, powered through a crack in the clouds that seemed to be fast shifting shape.

'Well my new dress is a little ruined,' Minnie said, unsticking the top of it from her chest, trying to avoid the hem touching the earth.

'My mum's always got towels in the boot for her flowers, I'm sure we can salvage it.'

'I don't care.'

She lay back down, resting her hand on Jesse's T-shirt, shocked by how the day had turned. Jesse looked up at the sky, aware of the scratches on his forearms and the scrapes on his calves, which were starting to sting. Through a widening gap in the clouds they could see blue again, and a plane's fuselage sparkled in the last glimmer of sunlight, leaving a performative vapour trail in its wake. If the plane had a banner on the back of it, it would have said, 'You broke the rules BIG TIME!'

Jesse took his phone out of his pocket.

'Nouvelair, Paris Orly to Oujda... which I think is... Morocco. Yep, it's Morocco.'

Minnie pulled away and sat up.

'Look, what is your deal with planes? Is it her?'

'No!'

'Are you as scared as me?'

'Of planes? No.' He looked across to Minnie. 'Of falling for you? Terrified.'

Minnie smiled, then leaned over to give him a reassuring kiss.

'So what's the deal?'

Jesse sat up and rested his arms on his knees. He watched a shiny petrol blue beetle crawl over his forearm, scurrying for shelter, and let it be.

'Last November I went to Nigeria, on a research trip.'

Minnie listened.

'I'd been asked to design for the next Africa Cup of Nations which is always the coolest job. I get to go and really look at designs. Street art. Typography that's typical of the region. Create a font. It's fascinating stuff.'

Minnie's eyes widened. She'd never been to Africa. She couldn't believe Jesse just hopped on a plane for research.

'How long did you go for?'

'Maybe five days – I never like going away for long.'

Ida.

'I lost something really important on that trip.'

'What was it?'

Jesse lifted the beetle from his arm hair and nestled it into a lavender bush.

'Whenever I went away, or whatever I was doing really, I always carried this silly trinket with me. My dad's keyring.'

He pictured the serene deity, her haunting beauty.

'I had it all trip, with me in my pocket. Got home and – boom – disappeared.'

Minnie's brow creased.

'It was just a silly thing, but I called the hotels, tracked down the taxi driver, called every cafe and diner I had stopped in during that trip, trying to locate her.'

'Who?'

'It was a little Indian goddess statue. Her name was Saraswati. Just some tourist tat I suppose. There wasn't even a key on the keyring.'

'Sounds special if it was your dad's.'

'It was. My dad was on a research trip to India with my mum, ages ago, and he bought it for me. He was really taken with it. He gave it to me when he got home, said she was a good luck charm for my new business.

She would be in my pocket in those early make-or-break meetings. I clutched her when Ida was born. I asked her to give me the wisdom to be a dad myself. Took her everywhere with me, always in my pocket. A month after I lost her, my dad died.'

'Well that's not your fault, you know.'

Jesse looked like he wasn't so sure.

Minnie wondered how the hell she could find a keyring like that short of going to India herself, but she already knew it wouldn't be the same.

'I'm so sorry.'

'I was such a mess when my dad died... then everything with Hannah. It took me a while to remember... having to empty my pockets at airport security in Lagos, I had to put her in the tray when I went through the X-ray machine. So I'd been on a wild goose chase for nothing.'

It still didn't explain the flight tracking. Was he looking for a flight to Lagos?

'Did you leave her at the airport?'

Jesse remembered the tension of Andrew and Elena's wedding back in February. The distance between him and Hannah in their finery. Their shoulders not touching. Her bag falling on the floor, the clank of its metal strap clinging to his chair.

'Months later I remembered, I did have her going through security on my way home. I did! So I'm pretty sure I dropped her on the plane, and she must have clung to the metal under the seat – sometimes she would cling to a radiator or the fridge. She must have been magnetic.'

Minnie pushed a strand of Jesse's hair back up off his forehead.

'I dropped some stuff at one point during the flight. Felt around, picked everything up. Or so I thought. But I didn't realise until I got home she was gone. And I only realised a few months later that that's where she must be. Or where I think she is. It's the only explanation. I wasn't pickpocketed. No one would have stolen it if I was.'

'So what's with that?' Minnie looked up to the sky.

'I follow her. I looked up the flight records and found out the registration of the plane that day from Lagos to London.'

'Like the flight number?'

'The tail number – that actual aircraft – now I like to know where in the sky she is.'

'You think your dad's keyring is still there? A cleaner didn't pick it up? Or someone else dropped *their* things, scrambled around for them, and found her?'

Jesse narrowed his eyes and looked up. Did he sound mad and grief-stricken? Probably.

'I think she's still up there.' He put a hand to the sky. 'Going about her adventures under seat 23C.'

Minnie laced her fingers through Jesse's, on his hand reaching out. They kissed again.

The clouds had almost entirely dispersed now. As fast and as thick as the air and the storm had come, it had cleared, although the light was fading.

'What are we going to do, Jesse?'

He looked at her, half broken, half galvanised.

'Come on,' he said, jumping to his feet and pulling Minnie up. 'Let's dry off. We can get dinner in the village. We're close to home.'

Home.

Minnie felt the pull of that home, the pull of the clock ticking on a day she didn't want to end.

* * *

At dinner, their clothes and eyelashes all dry, Jesse and Minnie hardly let go of each other. Talking intently, listening close. Stealing kisses between bites of veal and ratatouille; lamb and rosemary. Jesse switched his phone off after the fourth angry text from Hannah. They shared the best chocolate fondant Minnie had ever eaten.

Along with Aperol and red wine with ice.

The air felt fresh and warm again by the time they pulled up outside the house, although the cicadas were still silenced.

Caryn was asleep but she'd left another note on the dining table, to say there was a frangipane tart on the oven and she was going to bed.

'Shhhh...' Minnie said, putting her fingers to Jesse's lips. She took his hand and led him through the farmhouse, to the flower room and out to the pool, where she stripped off, swam one tantalising, teasing, silent length naked, and waited for Jesse to get in and follow. They made love as quietly as they could against the deep end, before going up to Minnie's room together and drifting off in each other's arms. The last thought Minnie had as she fell asleep, was of Jesse's wife, and a question of whether it was really over.

35

MINNIE AND JESSE

Now

The bees hummed under the window again, but it was the sound of a moped starting in the distance, and Caryn going off to the Saturday market in Pernes, that woke Minnie. Sunshine streamed through the blue shutters and Jesse watched her eyelashes flicker.

Minnie was half asleep, the warmth of the morning making her pale skin look luminescent. Jesse stroked her cheek with his thumb. Marvelling at the sweep of her thick black lashes.

She stirred.

He waited.

'Hmmm.' She stretched. She rolled over towards Jesse's chest and put her hand on it, comforted by the touch of his skin, by the feel of his arms around her, the scents rolling in through the open window.

Her eyes flickered open and Jesse was startled by the alarming beauty of her pale green irises as the colour crept out and her pupils shrank. He wanted to tell her that he loved her but he feared that Minnie's was a face that might break his heart. Within the hour, she would.

'Good morning,' Jesse said, placing a tender kiss on her forehead.

'Morning.' She smiled into another stretch, self-consciously covering her yawn.

Minnie's features settled again and Jesse ran his thumb across her eyebrow.

'I have never seen anyone so beautiful in my life,' he whispered in quiet awe.

Minnie wrinkled her nose. 'My morning face leaves a lot to be desired.'

'It's beautiful.' Jesse proved his vehemence by dotting kisses on her forehead, cheeks and chin, as though he were rooting himself to the four points of a compass.

'And my crying face...' Minnie said, totally crumpling her features. 'My crying face is definitely not anything to behold.'

'Your crying face is *stunningly* beautiful,' Jesse said, unwavering.

Minnie opened her eyes properly and looked up at Jesse until he came into focus. A sudden flinch washed over him, which made her jar. She sat up and wrapped the sheet under her armpits as if it were a dress, creating a curtain, a divide, between them.

'How do you know what my crying face looks like?' The question had an undertone of accusation.

Minnie thought back to the Jardin du Luxembourg and whether she had been sobbing when Jesse arrived. She definitely hadn't been crying. She had been angry and despondent, but she hadn't shed a tear over Wim Fischer in front of Jesse.

Jesse looked flummoxed and sat up against the wrought iron bedstead, his forearms flexing as he rubbed the back of his hair.

Suddenly everything felt as jagged as the Dora Maar painting they had seen in the house in Ménerbes. The energy changed in such a quick stroke. Minnie felt like she'd been punched in the stomach.

'Er...'

She thought through a mental scroll of her showreels, her Instagram posts, any work Jesse might have found on YouTube.

'Hang on,' she said. 'You cheated. You looked me up!' Minnie didn't know whether to be outraged or flattered. 'You broke the rules!'

'I didn't, I promise. I didn't know your name – I *don't* know your name – this is crazy!' Minnie was startled by how flustered he suddenly seemed. He looked as frazzled as he had when she'd first seen him in Bondiga's Books all those weeks ago. Not like the relaxed man she had fallen for in France.

'So... when did you see me cry?'

And suddenly Jesse's face looked much graver than she could ever have imagined.

36

JESSE

Three Months Ago – March

It was something benign that Andrew had said the week before that slowly made Jesse bristle.

'*He was three sheets to the wind...*'

Andrew was making an offhand comment about a colleague at an office party but it made Jesse baulk. Hannah was the only person he knew who said *three sheets to the wind*. It made him think. It made him dwell. In the office that day, when Jesse was working on a sleeve badge for a top-flight Turkish Süper Lig club, he kept thinking of that very English phrase. *Three sheets to the wind.*

The paranoia set in over the following few days. A bleak weekend when he didn't have Ida. A throwaway remark Elena made about Andrew smelling like green juice when he came back from a walk.

'What?' Andrew had said defensively.

'You smell of green juice. I wondered if you were sneaking off to the pub, but it smells like you've been sneaking off to Whole Foods,' Elena joked.

Andrew shook his head and said he was given a sample of *something or other* the other day in John Lewis.

And then the penny dropped. Jesse could smell it too. It was one of Hannah's rotation of fragrances. Lime, Basil & Mandarin. Had Andrew started wearing it, or had it rubbed off on him?

That Monday morning at breakfast, Andrew casually mentioned to Elena he had a work dinner in Mayfair. Elena chastised him for not putting it in the calendar and he apologised. Said he was a *naughty boy*.

Jesse remembered Hannah calling her lover a naughty boy during sex. He felt sick.

On top of that, Jesse and Hannah had had an argument the night before – she had a work dinner in Mayfair tomorrow and Leonor would be babysitting, on trial as a potential nanny. Jesse didn't want Ida to have a nanny, he wanted to spend the evening with his daughter, but Hannah doubled down and said Leonor would sit. It turned into their worst row so far.

Over breakfast, Jesse hatched a plan.

They weren't getting anywhere. Hannah had shown no remorse or accountability for her part in the breakdown of their relationship; she still hadn't told Jesse who her lover was.

'What time will you be back?' Elena asked Andrew, as she hurried with the twins out of the door with their backpacks.

Andrew shot Jesse a sheepish look.

'Erm, nine or ten?' he said.

Elena and the twins went to school. Andrew downed his coffee, said, 'Bye, buddy,' and went to work. Jesse came close to smashing up the kitchen – or rummaging through Andrew's bedside table drawers, he felt such a righteous rage. Instead he headed to work where he made small talk with Max and thought all morning about how he could catch them out.

'Are you OK, Jesse?' Max had asked when she realised he wasn't listening to a word she was saying about the cat food packaging she was working on called Tippytoes.

'Yeah – yeah!' he said, unconvincingly. He couldn't stop connecting the dots. The night walks. Andrew's subdued anger about Hannah's treatment of him. It lacked the fervour of Elena's indignation.

Three sheets to the wind.

You smell of green juice.
Dinner in Mayfair.
Naughty boy.

* * *

Jesse didn't know as much about Andrew's job in the City as he did about Hannah's in Waterloo, so at 4 p.m. he made his excuses to Max and left Lightning Designs for the offices of chartered accountants Bartholomew Hynes, Hannah's employer, on Waterloo Road. He waited at the Pret A Manger opposite, pretending to work but watching the doors of Hannah's building like a man possessed. He tried to write emails to agents, to see if he could set up a meeting with one – an illustrator friend had said Maddie Feynman was shit hot in children's publishing – but he just couldn't think. He caught his grimace in the reflection of the window, hair sticking up, stubble thick, jaw clenched, just at the time Hannah came out of her building and hailed a taxi.

'Shit,' he whispered to himself, scraping his laptop into his bag and grabbing his (third) coffee from the table. No wonder he looked terrible.

He saw Hannah get in and hailed the first taxi he could, grateful the traffic was slow in pursuit at rush hour.

'Mayfair please, mate,' he said. 'But follow that taxi two cars ahead. They know where we're going.'

Jesse tried to sound as neutral and as normal as he could, despite the unhinged reality that he was following his wife like a depraved stalker. He felt sick and disgusted at himself. For lowering himself to this, for being so needy as to want her, after she had had another man inside her.

Cheating scum. The pair of them.

Then he remembered how Andrew had suggested he get therapy recently. It hadn't landed well because Hannah had suggested it only a few days before.

'Why don't you see someone? Help you through this... this time?'

After a tense cat and mouse at a distance, Jesse's taxi pulled up behind Hannah's at a side entrance off Hyde Park Corner that led to a grand yet discreet hotel. An expensive place to have their trysts, Jesse thought. But then they couldn't do it in either of their homes.

'That's £18.70 please, mate,' the driver said. Jesse fumbled and ducked down as he pretended to find his card, while in his peripheral vision he saw Hannah skip into the prim hotel entrance and look left and right, before opening her arms to greet someone.

Jesse paid, got out of the taxi, then tentatively followed, smiling through his revulsion as the man on the door nodded at him and doffed his top hat. Then he saw Hannah. In an embrace. A kiss on the lips. A squeeze of her arse, while she and the man went off to the lifts and their room, giggling conspiratorially. Excited by what was to come.

Jesse felt nauseous. But at least it wasn't Andrew.

Rain started to mix with the traffic noises on Knightsbridge and Jesse went to the bar off the flower-filled lobby to have a drink. Something strong. What had become of him? He thought of a faceless foreign girl looking after his daughter while his wife was getting fucked by a man who grabbed her arse like a letch. A sickness rose inside him, bile in his throat. Jesse had another gin and tonic to quash it.

An hour later, Jesse saw him, in the reflection of the glass behind the bar. The man who Hannah had gone off with on his own in the lobby, settling a bill. Hannah didn't seem to be with him, so Jesse left a twenty-pound note on the counter and walked into the reception area.

Will he know who I am?

Jesse watched the man thank the receptionist and head out to a waiting car.

He wanted to call after him.

'*Mate! You just fucked my wife! And all the while I've been wondering if we can make it work...*'

But the man got into the car, black shirt, black trousers, white trainers, without a care in the world.

The concierge held the door open for Jesse.

'Umbrella, sir?'

'Are any of these taxis, mate?' Jesse asked.

A waiting driver heard him.

'Where are you going?'

'Where that car is going – I forgot to get the postcode from him.'

'Jump in.'

The spying and subterfuge got worse as Jesse's new taxi followed the car in front, onto Hyde Park Corner and up towards Marble Arch, then north onto Gloucester Place.

'He's not going to Glasgow is he?' the driver joked.

'Nahhh!' Jesse said, trying to take the edge off his voice. The man in front was on the phone. Jesse pictured Hannah showering back in the plush hotel room, washing away the guilt. Or was there not any?

Jesse's taxi followed the car towards Edgware, then right past Baker Street and Madame Tussaud's, slowing as they passed through Regent's Park towards Albany Street in the rain.

Where the fuck are we going? Jesse thought, equal parts repulsed by the man on the phone but relieved that he wasn't Andrew. The windscreen wipers got more frantic and the muggy March rain pummelled the roof. The car in front crawled through Camden Town, to a quiet side street between the station and the lock, and Jesse sighed in exasperation. What was he going to do – rugby tackle the guy to the floor in a rainy gutter?

'Here you go, mate,' the cab driver said, as the car in front put on his hazard lights and pulled in, and the man in black got out.

37

MINNIE

Three Months Ago – March

'Listen, babe. I'd like to say it's not you it's me, but you've definitely changed.'

Minnie's shoulders slumped and she looked into her lap, trying to banish the prickle in her eyes. She played with her fingers while she waited for this awful crushing moment to end. 'You know it.' He tried to say it as kindly as he could, but JP was a businessman, and sometimes in business you just had to be honest. No point beating around the bush. If something wasn't working, change it.

'These last few weeks, the fun, the spark, the joy... it's sort of...'

Minnie looked up and JP pushed his fat fingers together and then opened them out like a funeral lily in full bloom.

Gone.

A barista with green hair placed a coffee and an iced coffee on the little round table in the middle of the cafe. *Minnie's cafe.*

Her brow creased. She'd had a sick feeling all day. She had been waiting for an update from Devon. On why *Summer of Siena* had been placed on hold after all the money that had been spent on it; she was waiting for feedback on an audition for an ITV drama she hadn't heard

anything for, which was never a good sign. And she still hadn't heard
back about the Marvel film, but had long assumed it was a no. Devon
hadn't returned her call for three days, adding to her feeling of despera-
tion. And the waitressing gigs had dried up: Christmas and summer
season were busiest; Minnie had turned down the few spring gigs she
was offered, so she could be available to JP. Being a waitress didn't really
fit with being his arm candy.

Minnie half expected the fuselage of an Airbus A380 to fall onto
Bondiga's right there and then, crushing her and JP. The March storm
raging against the large glass windows, rain and rush hour, certainly
added to the possibility of a plane being struck by lightning over
London.

Minnie took a deep breath. She knew what was coming; she wanted
to vomit. She tried to fight it.

'But it's just a blip. I've been a bit worried about my career lately,
that's all. If *Summer of Siena* isn't broadcast, I've pretty much wasted a
year and am back to square one.'

'Oh, babe...' JP said, as if he were comforting a child.

'I'll sort it out, I'll get my mojo back. I'll get back in the game.'

'Yeah well there's nuffing I can do about the game, babe, we roll with
the punches and we keep our sparkle, otherwise we're gonna bring
down the people around us, ain't we?'

'I'm sorry.'

Minnie looked like a remorseful child, trying not to burst into tears.
She bit her lip and briefly looked around, embarrassed that Kip might
have worked out what was going on before she had. This was Minnie's
cafe, *her* spot, her place to read books she didn't have much intention of
paying for. She didn't want to have to flee and find a new local, but as she
sat there, rejection and remorse searing through her, she just wanted to
disappear into a puddle, and into the drain outside.

'It's all right, don't be sorry,' JP said, trying to ease her guilt. 'When
something ain't working, we switch things up.'

Minnie looked at JP playing with a sachet of sweetener as he looked
intensely at her, studying her, just to check she was still not worth it. She
kept her gaze firmly on the pink sachet and then looked him in the eye.

'But I love you, what will I do without you?'

JP gently tapped the end of Minnie's nose.

'You'll be fine. Look at you! You'll dust yourself off and pick yourself up. You've got time on your side, babe, more than I have!' He gave a chuckle to himself, laughing at his little joke. He put a hand on Minnie's knee and squeezed it. Proud of himself for his kindness. For stepping up at fifty. He used to get his PA to do this for him.

Minnie started to cry, as quietly as she could repress it. JP shuffled in his chair. He didn't really want the coffee she'd bounced up and got him as soon as he walked in. He was tired and spent and wanted to go back to his apartment, call some mates, maybe play a bit of poker.

'Babe, come on, you know my style. I was never a forever guy, was I?'

Kip walked past proprietorially, pretending to look for empties, outraged by what was playing out.

Minnie's cries got more unabashed, her face withered. This was so public and so humiliating. Between breaths she managed to muster together the words that hung at the back of her throat.

'Are you seeing someone else?'

JP looked at her as if to say *are you serious?* As kindly as he could.

'Of course I am, babe!'

'What?'

'Behind every good man is a few good women.'

Minnie shook her head, her mouth wriggling; a tear fell into it.

'How many women?'

'Oh come on, babe. You wasn't born yesterday.'

'How many?' she snapped now. Kip looked over. Other customers looked up.

JP did some mental maths.

'Four, five maybe.'

Minnie gasped.

'Including me?'

'*Not* including you.'

You have to be cruel to be kind, JP thought.

He squeezed her knee one last time and handed her a napkin someone had left on the table. It looked unused.

'Look after yourself, kiddo.'

And with that JP got up, leaving his coffee untouched. Minnie's body shook and her face completely crumpled, with grief and rejection.

* * *

Outside Bondiga's Books, in the pouring rain, Jesse put his palm to the window as he watched his wife's lover – his thick neck and pink hands that had been touching Hannah's naked body only an hour earlier – break someone else's heart. The beautiful woman with black hair and green eyes, sitting in the chair opposite him, broke down and sobbed.

38

MINNIE AND JESSE

Now

'That day in the cafe. Before my meeting with my agent.'

'What?'

'When *fucking Orson* bounced his ball in my hot coffee.' Jesse tried to play it for laughs.

'What about it?' Minnie's face was already set to do battle.

'It... it wasn't the first time I'd seen you.'

'What's that?'

Jesse got up and threw on some well-worn jeans from the spare wardrobe, before sitting on the upcycled chair next to the bed, his elbows on his thighs.

'I haven't told you what happened with my marriage because I was too embarrassed. But Hannah had an affair.'

'Shit, Jesse.'

'I caught her in January. By March I suspected it was still going on – it *was* still going on. I followed her. Not stalker like, I just knew she was still seeing her lover and I started to get paranoid. I started thinking she was sleeping with our friend. I had a really dark week, I thought I was going mad.'

Minnie was utterly confused. 'I don't...'

'I followed Hannah to a hotel where she met up with... him. They went off to a room, had sex – I assume.'

'Was it your friend?'

'No.'

'So what's going on? I don't understand. Is that why you were so stressed out that day I met you? You knew she was still sleeping with him?'

'No, this was about a month before you and I started talking, six weeks maybe. After they were done, I followed Hannah's lover...'

'Right...'

'And the day I followed my wife's lover was the day my wife's lover broke up with you.'

'I don't understand.'

'It was JP I followed to the cafe. To Bondiga's.'

Minnie looked aghast.

'That's where I saw your crying face.'

Minnie held her hand to her mouth, the way she had that day in the cafe, as if she might be sick, as it all fell into place.

That's why Jesse and his wife had split. That's why Jesse had looked at her in shock and recognition when Orson bounced the ball into his coffee. He hadn't recognised her from her work. He had spied on her when she was at her most vulnerable, when she was at her lowest ebb.

'JP was shagging *your* wife?'

Jesse nodded solemnly.

'And you knew this all along?'

'Well not exactly...'

'But...'

'But yes, I did know this when we first spoke.'

'I thought your scorn for him, your compassion, was in support of me.'

'It was.'

'But you were just spying on me!'

'I wasn't! I promise.'

Minnie clutched the sheet closer to her chest.

'I went back to the cafe a couple of times, only because I wanted to confront the sleazebag. Find out who he was. I wish I'd done it that day as he left.'

'What, while he was dumping me?' Minnie put her head in her hands; she felt mortified. The public dumping, her biggest humiliation, had happened in front of Jesse too. And he never told her.

'When I managed to get a meeting with Maddie Feynman, I realised Bondiga's was around the corner. It was another chance to go back and look for him. Not that I should have gone back that day.'

Minnie looked at him, startled, even more hurt.

'No – no – I mean, I shouldn't have been thinking about him at all that day, I should have been focusing on my work, my dad's book.'

'That's why you were spoiling for a fight with a kid.'

'But then I met *you*.'

Jesse pressed his fingers together. Minnie shook her head and stood up, sheet still clutched to her body like a savage bride.

'Why didn't you tell me?'

She looked for her sundress, bra and knickers, picked up from the poolside and strewn on the back of the chair behind Jesse. He stood up, flustered.

'There just wasn't a good—'

'I feel awful! This is awful!'

She tangled with her bra then threw it angrily on the bed.

'You were standing outside in the rain, spying on me?'

'No! It really wasn't like that!'

'Then why didn't you say?' she spat.

Jesse looked dumbfounded.

'You knew *all* along who I was. Even when I was writing down the rules at your table, like a fucking mug.'

'I didn't. I *still* don't know you, your name. All I knew was this awful thing that linked us.'

'You did! You cheated!'

Jesse slumped on the edge of the bed, exasperated. 'Hey this was your stupid game!'

Minnie looked at him, hurt again, and threw her arms up in the air and her sundress over them. She zipped it up furiously.

'Well you had ample opportunity to tell me how fucked up it was.'

Minnie gathered her things wildly and started cramming them into her bag.

'What are you doing?'

'I'm going home. I don't know what's going on any more.'

'Please, Minnie, it's not what you think.'

Jesse put his hands on her waist and tried to pull her into the gap between his legs.

'Why wouldn't you tell me something so massive? My boyfriend was fucking your wife! He might still be! You watched me get dumped! And you never thought to tell me? All this time we've spent together, and you never thought to tell me! I feel like such an idiot, Jesse. Let me go!'

PART II

TWO MONTHS LATER

PART II

TWO MONTHS LATER

39

JESSE

Now

'Jesse, I'd like you to meet Burgess Hastings,' Maddie Feynman said, indicating to the old man who was sitting in an armchair in her office. 'I wanted to get you both in for a powwow because, as much as I would like to say this came from submission and I'm really earning my 15 per cent, Burgess contacted me when he got wind of Remy.'

The old man stood up gingerly.

'Oh.' Jesse was puzzled. He'd only submitted the final draft to Maddie in late July, and wasn't expecting to hear an update until after September, when *The Amazing Adventures of Remy the Red Panda* would be going out on submission to publishers. But Jesse knew from his dad's relationship with his agent, a powerhouse called Bill Linkletter, that if your agent called a meeting, you went.

Jesse shook the man's hand effusively, but carefully. He was older than Jesse imagined people in children's publishing looked – he didn't really seem like a *children's* kind of guy, he looked about one hundred and four. They both sat down in the armchairs opposite Maddie, and Jesse tried to feel a sense of hope and optimism; he tried to push aside the memory of the last time he was in this room. The coffee stain. His fluster. *Her.*

'Biggest regret of my life was turning down Lars Lightning. You know I was sent a manuscript of *The President's Play* in 1979?'

'No, I didn't...' Jesse still wasn't sure who this guy was.

'I thought, this right-wing clown character of a president will never resonate. People won't buy it! And then Reagan took forty-four states and I realised I was the clown because *The President's Play* was already a *Sunday Times* and *New York Times* bestseller – and not one of mine.'

Jesse smiled, appreciatively. The man was being kind.

'But I want to make that right.'

Maddie explained that Burgess wasn't active in publishing any more, but he was on the board of Talisman, the second largest publisher in the UK. Jesse had heard of Talisman of course, but not Burgess. He looked like he might have retired in 1900.

'We would have been the biggest publisher in the UK if I'd have bought your father...' he lamented, as if he were a dying man at solemn peace with his regret.

'But what about children's books? Do you publish picture books?'

'Oh,' interjected Maddie. 'Their children's imprint *is* the largest in the UK. Tyger. They're headed up by Kathy Carnegie at their office in Farringdon.'

Burgess explained that Kathy was on holiday with her family in Greece right now, but wild horses wouldn't have stopped him going along for a chat anyway. Striking while the iron was hot. Before other publishers got wind.

'We'd love Remy. We'd love Lars *and* Jesse Lightning. I spoke to Kathy from her holiday yesterday and she can see a series, a TV spin-off, merchandise, the whole shaboodle. She's *very* excited.'

Maddie nodded encouragingly.

'Has she even seen my drawings? Has she seen my dad's manuscript?'

Jesse looked between Maddie and Burgess.

'She has now. From a photograph thingy Madeleine did with her phone. And this was even before *I* saw your drawings in the flesh, young man...'

Jesse laughed to himself. He didn't feel particularly young. And unless Burgess had been living under a rock for the past ten years he would have seen Jesse's drawings, his designs, his typefaces, he just wouldn't know it. 'I had a feeling about this project. And now Maddie has shown them to me – well I will speak to Kathy and we will make you an offer we hope you might consider...'

Maddie looked between the two men excitedly.

Jesse rubbed his golden stubble. He thought of his dad. He thought of his little rental apartment in a Brutalist block of flats between King's Cross and Bloomsbury. How the rent was insane but he wanted to buy the two-bedroom apartment for sale next door which was on the market for £750,000. It would be perfect for Jesse and Ida. A manageable walk to school. Near his office, near the Eurostar to see his mum. A weighty advance could help him cobble together a deposit without having to take a loan out against Lightning Designs.

'This sounds wonderful, thank you,' Jesse said, humbly.

'I can't let lightning *not* strike in the same place twice,' Burgess said with a twinkle.

OK, that was a bit cheesy, Jesse thought, but the old guy was really sweet.

'Please do consider it, dear boy. Kathy will contact Madeleine, and I will get our exceptional contracts team to come up with something...'

Maddie nodded. Kathy Carnegie was clearly someone she knew and thought highly of. They could talk later over the fine print.

'Thank you,' Jesse said, looking at Maddie for assurance. A flash in her eye and a gentle smile gave him 100 per cent confidence. 'Thank you very much.'

Maddie's assistant got them all tea and macarons and they made chit-chat for half an hour before Burgess stood and picked up his Panama hat from the stand by the door and said his goodbyes.

They all shook hands, then Burgess paused in the doorway. He had the look of a man who was once immense. His summer shirt and cream chinos now too big for him.

'Your father,' he said thoughtfully. 'I met him at many events, book fairs, dinners, what have you...'

Jesse waited on tenterhooks.

'He was a scholar and a gentleman. An exceptional storyteller.'

Jesse wanted to cry.

'His body of work is prolific of course, but it's wonderful that his legacy will continue through you.'

'Thank you,' Jesse said, pressing his palms together, just as his father did.

* * *

As Jesse left Fox & Feynman's Camden office and stepped out onto a blistering hot pavement, he put his right hand in his pocket. Where was she? Where was Saraswati? He wanted to tell his dad that he had done it, he had got them a children's deal. *The Amazing Adventures of Remy the Red Panda* hadn't been a neglected afterthought on a big pile of things to do.

He wanted to tell Minnie. He wanted to know how she was. He still didn't quite believe she had gone.

* * *

Jesse had held Minnie's hands in the bedroom of his parents' farmhouse and begged her to wait. He promised to make her pancakes or French toast, and that he would book their seats back from Avignon to Paris and Paris to London. He kissed her on the lips and she stayed still, leaving him shocked by the extremity of her reaction.

Minnie showered while Jesse got on with breakfast; then he showered and told her to start eating while it was hot. By the time he got out of the bathroom, Minnie had gone, her breakfast untouched.

Caryn came back from the market minutes later to see Jesse sitting alone at the bistro table by the pool, swearing she had just seen a girl who looked like Minnie, in Monsieur Delep's van heading towards Avignon. She realised straight away, from Jesse's despondent face, that it was Minnie in Monsieur Delep's van. She had gone without him and without saying goodbye.

'Oh darling, what's happened?' Caryn asked, as she slumped onto the metal chair opposite him, swatting a wasp away from the table. The pancakes looked a little despondent too. 'Everything seemed so adorable between you two!' She studied her son. 'I didn't want to ask... but I had high hopes.'

Jesse shook his head.

'I've really fucked up.'

'How?'

Jesse told his mother how he had seen Minnie in a bookshop cafe back in March being dumped by Hannah's lover; about Minnie approaching Jesse when he was back in the bookshop in May, before his meeting with Maddie Feynman around the corner. About Minnie's proposition; about her game. About how they weren't meant to know too much about each other; how they weren't meant to fall in love. He looked nervously at his mother as if he might already have done.

'Well what are you waiting for, Jesse?' Caryn admonished.

He looked up, surprised.

'What about Hannah?' he asked.

'After the way she's treated you? Fuck Hannah!'

Jesse was shocked. He had never heard his mother speak so vehemently and bitterly about anyone.

'If your father knew what she had done to you...' Caryn's voice cracked and she took a sip of Jesse's water. 'If he knew... at the moment when she was most meant to support you...' Her eyes filled up, her finger jabbed. Jesse saw the heartache his mother carried for him laid bare. She couldn't finish her sentence. She swatted another creature, a small fluttering dragonfly this time, as Jesse remembered the text message he'd received last night, while he and Minnie were in the pool.

Thanks for making an effort Jesse. Nice touch.

Then the five messages Hannah had sent him straight after. Calling him a headfuck. Asking why he said he wanted to be a family.

Jesse hadn't wanted to be a family. He couldn't bear the thought of it since he'd seen JP grab Hannah's arse in the lobby of The Berkeley. Since he saw her complete and utter lack of remorse at the situation, while he was sleeping in their mates' spare room and she was having sex in fancy hotel rooms. All he had wanted was to be a dad to Ida.

Caryn took another desperate glug of water.

'You need to go and find her, darling, it's so obvious.' She levelled him with a look of instruction. A mother telling her son what he must do. 'Nothing much has felt right in the past six months, not until you two walked in together the other night.'

Jesse smiled, defeated.

'There's a problem.'

'What?'

'I don't have her number. I don't know her address. I don't even know her name.'

'Don't be ridiculous!'

'What?'

'You don't know her name?' Caryn asked, in despair.

Jesse shook his head.

'It was part of her rules. Her game, her idea.'

'It's so obvious!' Caryn almost snapped.

'What is?'

'She's Geraldine and Jeremy Byrne's daughter for God's sake!'

'What?'

'Yes! So I'm pretty sure that makes her last name...'

'Fuck...'

'Byrne,' they said in unison.

Caryn levelled him again.

'You're welcome.'

'How did you know? Did she tell you?'

Caryn shook her head, exasperated by her beautiful boy as if he were seven again, taking so long to make his ice cream look pretty, licking it into a perfect shape on top of his cone, it melted all over his nice new ECCO shoes. She shooed him away.

'Go! She'll be halfway to Paris by now.'

* * *

Minnie had gone. She wasn't at the ticket hall in Avignon. She wasn't on the first train to Paris that Jesse could get. He walked up and down the entire twelve carriages to check, four times. He couldn't see her at Gare de Lyon and he scoured Gare du Nord for faces, but none of the women he ran to with black hair and pale skin were Minnie.

Jesse had to accept she didn't want to know him any more. Perhaps it was a bit creepy. Sleeping with your wife's lover's spurned lover. Did it look like revenge? It certainly hadn't been. He'd tried to resist her game; he'd tried to resist falling for her.

In a moment of self-pity around the middle of July, Jesse remembered Minnie said her agent was called Devon, so he googled acting agents called Devon in London. Devon Smith came up who worked for a talent agency called McFadden Higgs. Devon was a beautiful man who looked like an actor himself. Jesse knew instinctively that he was Minnie's Devon. He clicked on Devon's list of clients and saw Minnie's mesmerising headshot.

It would be one way of trying to reach her. But Jesse didn't try. He felt too predatory. He couldn't forget how he'd pressed his hand against the bookshop window as he'd watched Minnie being dumped. It was an awful thing not to tell her. He should have told her at the zoo.

As school broke up in July, Jesse submitted his pages to Maddie and moved out of Andrew and Elena's house, into the Brutalist block near King's Cross. The thought of spending a long hot summer with the twins was too much, especially while he and Hannah were still at loggerheads over Ida and how custody would play out. Hannah had been furious at Jesse, for the way he had given her hope in June; for the way he had stood her up.

Jesse looked up to the blistering city sky outside Fox & Feynman Literary

Agency, looked at his phone and searched the familiar tail number on his plane tracker app.

Wow, Auckland.

That was the furthest Saraswati had been since he'd started tracking her. If she were even on the plane. Maybe Minnie was right. A cleaner or another passenger might have found her. He screwed up his hand in his empty pocket and had an idea. Coffee. Bondiga's Books was two streets away. Minnie might even be there.

40

JESSE

Now

The entrance to Bondiga's Books opened into the book section, the middle third of Alistair Bondiga's cultural empire. Records were to the left, cafe to the right, a cornucopia of books were piled in front of him. Jesse picked up a copy of *Yellowface* from a table by the till so it would look like he had something to read, whether Minnie was or wasn't there. It was a lovely bookshop. He wondered if his father knew it. Lars had done the circuit of all the slick indies in London: Goldsboro, Daunt's, Libreria, Word on the Water, plus he'd always draw a crowd at Foyles and Waterstones when he did signings or talks. Jesse wanted so desperately to talk to his dad right now. Tell him about Remy. Ask him about Bondiga's. Something significant had happened to him in this bookshop. Could lightning strike a third time?

He'd been back once since the day Minnie fled France. He met his friend Kenji there before they went to a gig at Camden Stables. He said there was a cool bookshop cafe where they sold craft beers and didn't tell Kenji about the subtext. That he'd hoped to bump into Minnie again. Kenji was so charming and affable, Jesse thought that if they did see

Minnie, he would be a good buffer. She wasn't there that day, and he didn't recognise any of the staff. Today, as he walked through to the right, to the open coffee shop with the large windows looking out onto the street, he did recognise the barista with the green hair. Minnie had spoken to him the day they'd met, used his name perhaps, although Jesse couldn't remember it.

Jesse went up to the counter, book and phone in hand – ready to order a coffee but realising it was 4 p.m. and he should be celebrating.

'A can of Neck Oil please, mate,' Jesse said, nodding to the fridge behind the counter.

The guy served him politely and efficiently, asked him if there was anything else he wanted, but clearly had no idea how life changing today was for Jesse; how life changing that day had been in May. *Fucking Orson.*

Jesse paid and was just about to take his beer and book to a window seat – the one Minnie had been sitting in the day she'd approached him – when he paused and turned back.

'Hey, mate, Kip isn't it?'

Kip smiled. 'Yes?'

'You haven't seen Minnie in here lately have you? Minnie... Byrne?'

He saw a softness wash over Kip's neat features.

'Ahhh Minnie.' He said her name like it were a blessing.

Jesse looked at him eagerly. Kip shook himself into action and swiftly picked up some cups.

'Not for ages,' he replied, slightly offhand, as if he might not tell Jesse even if he had. Kip checked himself and softened. 'I think she's been busy; she's in a new TV show or something.'

'Yeah I know. Starting next month. Or something...'

There was a pause.

'So she's not been in then?'

'No,' Kip said. 'But Steph, who works here, Steph saw her in the West End the other day. Back with that creep she was seeing.'

'What?'

'Yeah sausage fingers, the one who dumped her in here. During my fucking shift.' Kip gritted his teeth.

Jesse shook his head, totally dejected, marvelling at how JP had done it.

'Sorry, dude – she got to you too?' Kip gave a rueful look. 'At least you got to have a coffee with her.'

41

JESSE

Now

Jesse walked into Lightning Designs, his shoulder nudging the glass door open as was customary, only this morning he wasn't carrying two KeepCups of coffee. In his right hand was a bottle of Veuve Clicquot and two champagne flutes, in his left was a bag of madeleines he'd picked up from the monthly continental food market outside King's Cross station.

'Morning!' he said, as cheerily as he could muster. As predicted, Max was already there. Judging from the empty cup on her desk and the fresh aroma of coffee, she'd already had her brew.

'Oh hi, Jesse,' Max said calmly, eyeing the bottle. 'Big bank holiday? Or are you starting the weekend early?' She half winced as she said it.

It was only the Tuesday after the long weekend, the last long weekend of summer, which Jesse had spent painting Ida's bedroom in his rental flat, even though on Friday he'd had the news that he would be able to put a deposit down to buy the flat next door. Bigger, nicer, brighter. And he could paint it whatever the fuck colour he wanted, not just the vanilla one the landlord approved. Ida deserved big and bold. Not beige.

Late Friday afternoon Maddie had phoned Jesse to confirm an

'exceptional and highly tempting' offer that publisher Tyger had put together. Six figures. Merchandise tie-ins. A meeting was already lined up with the studio who had made the biggest British animations of the past twenty years. 'We could take it to auction, but my gut says not to, Jesse...' Maddie advised, as Jesse was dipping a roller brush into a paint tray. 'Tyger's offer, experience and enthusiasm will make Remy a household name. Your father's estate, and you, could make money from this for decades. It's quite a legacy, not that your father doesn't already have one...' she quickly added.

It was fine, Jesse thought. People didn't need to be precious talking about Lars around him. He was so proud of his dad already; he knew his dad had been proud of him. But this could be Jesse's legacy. A love letter to Ida. Income for a flat and savings for her if she wanted to go to university one day. The chance for him to say, 'I didn't forget, Dad. I did the drawings you asked.' Even if he was saying it in his head.

* * *

'Remy has a home!' Jesse said with a smile.

'That's wonderful!' Max said. She stood up and hugged him awkwardly, Jesse careful not to drop the bottle, bag or glasses. Max wasn't really a hugger, but this was a special occasion. And if she leaned over Jesse's shoulder, he might not see her cry.

Except he felt it. Jesse felt the sadness in Max's ribcage and her bones. He felt her almost melt through his arms and onto the floor.

'Hey... are you OK?'

Max stepped back and put her hand to her chest. 'Not really, but it doesn't matter now... this isn't about me. Honestly, I'm chuffed to bits for you.'

Jesse put the champagne, glasses and madeleines on Max's desk.

'Heyyyy...' he said, seeing tears were on the brink of tumbling from her placid eyes. 'What's going on?'

Max shielded her face, her brown skin flushing. 'It's fine, really. I just...' Her voice cracked. 'It's OK.'

Jesse studied her sympathetically.

'I just can't go on any more.'

'What?'

She shook her head and Jesse watched her sit back down.

'I can't go on. Liam – he's just...'

Jesse looked up to the ceiling and exhaled.

'He's the fucking pits.'

Jesse wasn't expecting something so stern. He perched back on Max's desk and extended a hand to her shoulder.

'Are you OK?'

'I am now. Now I've decided I'm not going through another bank holiday, Christmas, birthday, Easter or just any run-of-the-mill day like that again.'

'What happened? Want to talk about it?'

'Not really.'

Jesse nodded and glanced through the Crittall doors at the other arrivals into the big shared building. The interior designers. The freelance writers. The coders.

'Actually yes, I do,' Max said, defiantly. As if saying it out loud would help her stick to her guns.

Jesse slid his backpack off, put it between his feet, and listened.

'I'm tired... so tired. Of his drinking, his fagging. The coke. Of going out with him and him disappearing. Of pretending we're this happily newly married couple who "like to party" when he's too old to be scraped up off the floor at the end of the night. He's almost forty!'

Jesse had forgotten Liam was older than them. His lifestyle certainly didn't sit with that.

'He looks another ten years older than that. This... this *life* makes him so craggy. So dysfunctional.'

Jesse nodded.

'I don't want to go out. I want to grow up. I want to stay in. I want to cook Sunday lunches for Nadine, Jim and the girls. I want to go for walks and not worry that he might puke in the bushes, or be looking at his watch craving when he can start. I'm sick of going to people's weddings and him drinking the bar dry. It's embarrassing. He doesn't care about me. He doesn't care that I'm often on my own, a bystander, while he gets shitfaced. And I'm the one to pick up the pieces...'

'Oh Max. I knew it wasn't great but—'

'I want kids,' she blurted, as she cried into her sleeve.

Jesse put his palms on the table's edge.

'Alice and Annabel were over yesterday. Nice summer lunch on the terrace. I'd cooked. Jim likes his food. Nadine and I were chatting. Liam was antisocial. Couldn't be bothered to engage in conversation. Sat on his own on the sofa, getting himself beers and no one else.'

Jesse winced.

'Alice came running out with what looked like porridge on her hand from the toybox – we have a little toybox, for when they come over. She said, "Errrr, Aunty Max! It stinks!" Her hand was covered.'

Jesse put his hands to his face to shield his eyes from what he guessed was to come.

'Liam puked in there days – maybe weeks ago – just used it as a toilet. Didn't clear it up or think. Probably didn't even remember. All over my nieces' toys.'

'Man, that's gross. I'm so sorry.'

'Alice shoved her hand in when she went to get a toy.'

'Shit, that's not cool.'

'It's never cool. Nadine can't stand him anyway, but she lost her shit yesterday, and I totally get why.'

Jesse sighed. 'So what are you going to do?'

'It's over. I'm done. I'm so tired.'

'Have you told him?'

Max nodded.

'I told him he needs to be out by the time I get home from work.'

'Today?'

'Yes.'

'How did he take it?'

'He was weirdly belligerent. Said I can't do that to him. Well, guess what? I can. I bought that flat. The mortgage is in my name. He's never really contributed, before we were married or since. He hasn't kept a job for more than a few months. Blames everyone except himself. Blames me, resents me for loving what I do.'

A tiny fragment of Jesse felt happy in this sad scene. That Lightning Designs had afforded Max happiness, a sanctuary. It was often hard to tell with her, she was so measured.

'Do you think he'll move out? Today?'

Jesse studied her face while she pondered.

'It's not like he doesn't have places. He can go to his brother's. Or his druggy mates'.'

'That's not your problem. I imagine he's had enough warning...?'

'Yeah, he has.'

'Want me to go with you at home time and check?'

'I'll see if he's left on the Ring doorbell. Otherwise, maybe, thanks.'

'No problem.'

Jesse stood and picked up the champagne and put it in the small fridge behind the door, that only ever housed booze or Max's breakfast Bircher.

'Sorry about the champagne...' Max said.

'God no, let's save it. For a better day.' He knelt down as he laid the bottle flat on the shelf of the small fridge. He turned back around. Max was drying her eyes on the tissue she'd had stuffed up her sleeve.

'Look at us, eh?' he said, thinking of Minnie, back with JP. 'Sorry bunch. But you know what, we're only thirty-two... me only just,' he said with a wink, as if that made him younger than he was.

Jesse had celebrated his birthday at the beginning of August by a day out in Antibes with Ida and Caryn, going to the beach and eating Acacia honey ice cream on the terrace of the Hotel Belles Rives. 'If you think about it, we've not yet hit our prime. Look at what you've got in front of you. Cutting loose now, you can have everything you want and deserve.'

Max smiled gently. Uncertain, but for the first time in years, she could feel an inkling of hope.

'Starting with breakfast!' He nodded to the madeleines on the desk, and Max let out a rare and relieved laugh.

42

JESSE

Now

'First day of Year 4 – you're such a big girl!'

Jesse and Ida held hands as they walked in the September sunshine to school. New backpack and pencil case primed. 'What do you think Mrs Peacock will be like?' Jesse asked effusively.

'She was very nice when we visited her classroom on transition day. She's held a koala.'

'Oh great! Has she been to Australia?'

'She's *from* Australia!' Ida said, as if it were the biggest hoot.

'Oh wow, that's so cool.'

'She's from the place where the quokkas are... near the island.'

'Well,' Jesse said theatrically. 'You two are going to get on like a house on fire!'

'A house on fire! That's silly!' Ida said as she looked up at her dad and laughed.

There was a spring in both their steps as they walked up Pancras Road towards Ida's school. When they arrived at the gates at the bottom of Camden, Hannah was waiting outside, not making eye contact with Jesse, but smiling adoringly at her daughter. Both parents were grateful for the distraction. Ida was their focus, Ida was their everything, Ida would get them through this.

'Good morning, Ida!' Hannah said, as she unfolded her arms from across her body and opened them wide. Ida ran into her mother's embrace as Hannah kissed her cheek, squeezed her tight, then ran a hand along her messy plait, trying not to inspect it. Hannah bit her tongue. Jesse had been plaiting Ida's hair most of Ida's life, and still it looked messy. Messier than when she did it anyway. Her unruly, golden-brown waves were not easy to plait, she could give Jesse that.

'Morning.' Hannah smiled to Jesse, briskly, optimistically, keeping things civil.

'Morning,' Jesse replied.

'Are we all ready for Year 4?' Hannah asked the collective.

'I think Year 4 is going to be your best year yet!' Jesse declared, although he felt a punch in the stomach as he said it, as he let the darkness in at this most inappropriate moment and thought about all that Ida had shouldered in Year 3. Loss. Grief. Separation. 'Mrs Peacock is Australian!' Jesse enthused.

'You didn't say Mrs Peacock was Australian!' Hannah shot back, flummoxed.

'She only just told me,' he said, pointing his thumb casually at their daughter, smile forced, jaw tense.

Let's not do this now.

Hannah took a deep breath.

'Shall we?' she said as she took Ida's hand and led them through the gate into the playground.

Ida took Jesse's hand with her free one and insisted Mummy and Daddy swing her across the playground as they went. To other parents they looked like the perfect family. Same golden shades of hair, same skin, bronzed from summer, Ida swinging with glee, although a few closer friends knew that it was tricky to arrange playdates with Ida; which parent was she with that weekend? What had happened in their family for their lives to be so different to last year on the first day of school? Luckily, everyone focused on their own kids and they got to the classroom door, where Ida stopped swinging and Jesse moved her backpack from his shoulder onto hers. Hannah resisted the urge to redo Ida's plait but she fussed and smoothed her hair down all the same.

Ida kissed Daddy first, then Mummy, then she went skipping off to her friend Evie, who was already waiting with Mrs Peacock by the door.

'Bye sweetpea, love you!' Jesse said, saluting her.

'Bye!' Hannah called. 'Henrike will get you from Cookie Club!'

The parents smiled as Ida looked back over her shoulder with wide, tentative eyes.

'You'll be great,' Jesse mouthed. Ida disappeared through the door, to a little pat on the head from the teacher, and Jesse handed Ida's overnight bag to Hannah from his other shoulder.

Hannah's smile dropped. Jesse waited for the barb.

It's the hair, isn't it?

Their handovers and exchanges over the summer were terse and transactional. Hannah felt spurned by Jesse and his failure to show up for dinner when she was trying to make it work, even though deep down, she hadn't really wanted to. Marriage had bored her to tears for much of it.

In late July, Jesse had taken Ida back to France for a fortnight, where Ida splashed with grandma in the pool, ran through the sunflower and lavender fields (not *that* field, Jesse couldn't face it) and Jesse broke Caryn's heart with the words: *no news*.

'Why don't you just message her on social media, darling?' Caryn asked during Jesse's birthday lunch, as Ida went to play with a cat under a nearby table. 'That's what people do nowadays, isn't it?'

Jesse shook his head as if to say, *No, Mum, I blew it.*

In mid-August Jesse had returned to work and Hannah took Ida to an all-inclusive in Ibiza for a week, where she read around the pool while Ida made friends at the kids' club and they watched movies in the evening. Hannah had longed for company and attention and almost hooked up with a hot Spanish kids' club leader, before reminding herself that logistically it would be difficult: she couldn't exactly bring him back to her room and she suspected he still lived with his parents.

At each handover during the summer holidays, Jesse and Hannah had been cordial enough for Ida's sake but just cold enough to not become *invested*, to let the other know that they were still pissed off and hurting.

'Got time for a coffee?' Hannah said, as a child ran through the gate and got in by the skin of his teeth. Her smile was hopeful and conciliatory. Jesse didn't expect that.

He looked at his watch. He and Max were meeting a client on Lamb's Conduit Street at 11 a.m.

'Yeah sure. A quick one.'

Jesse and Hannah walked to a Turkish coffee shop around the corner from Ida's school and each ordered an Americano. Jesse fiddled with the baklava the waiter had put down with the coffees, rearranging neat squares into a neater line.

He waited for a hand grenade. Hannah was so good at releasing the pin and just throwing them.

'I've been thinking,' she said, as she tapped her palm with her teaspoon. She had her business meeting face on. Jesse waited for the blow.

'How about one week on, one week off?'

Jesse hadn't expected that either.

'It's simpler, it's doable, Henrike is willing to work like that – she found a job as a teaching assistant to support her income – not Ida's school, a special school near Archway, she doesn't mind only nannying every other week.'

That's good of her.

Jesse sipped his coffee to shield his face for a second. Let it sink in. This wasn't the way he wanted to do it, but it was a solution. He would get to live with his daughter half the time and take her to school and plait her hair and embrace her meltdowns and do all the things that he felt like he was put on the planet to do – to raise her well – and it could work like that. And a week on and a week off seemed less disruptive than hauling her things around North London every couple of days.

Just because Hannah used Henrike didn't mean Jesse had to. Just because Hannah used Henrike didn't mean he *didn't* have to; Ida clearly liked her. Especially since Henrike had brought Ida a cuddly ibex back from Germany after the summer break.

Jesse considered it. It could work.

'What about holidays? What if half term lands on your week or mine, when it's not meant to?'

'Maybe we split half terms, make exceptions those weeks. And alternate Christmas and New Year week. But I really think it could work, Jesse, with some canny diarising.'

Hannah was very good at canny diarising.

Jesse nodded. This was easier than a fight. No need for mediation or lawyers. Hannah could reason. He picked up a square of baklava and threw it in his mouth.

'Yeah, I think that would work.' He tried not to look grateful, but the immense relief he felt made him want to hug Hannah's brittle shoulders. He didn't. She had started all of this. He let out a big sigh.

'How are you?' she asked.

Floored twice in one conversation. This wasn't Hannah's style.

'Sorry?'

'How are you doing? How's your mum?'

Even when Jesse had returned Ida from France in August, Hannah hadn't asked after Caryn, widowed, heartbroken and mostly on her own in the South of France.

'Yeah, Mum's OK. Well, she's not, but she's busy. She's writing again. She's coming to London next month.'

Hannah gave a sheepish look, as if to say *best I avoid her*. Perhaps she did feel some guilt after all, some accountability. Jesse wanted to concur, to tell Hannah that she was the last person his mum wanted to see, but he felt optimism in the new cordial tone, and he didn't want to blow it.

'I'll give her your best.'

Hannah smiled and looked at her watch.

'I'd better get going, client meeting.'

'Me too,' Jesse said. 'So what do we do, get something drawn up? Written down? When do we start?'

Hannah looked at the diary in her phone.

'And what should the changeover day be?' Jesse asked.

'From next week? And shall we do Sunday handovers?'

Jesse shook his head. Sunday evenings always felt too bleak; he hated the countdown to them. The feeling of being on borrowed time. 'What about Friday to Friday? So weekends are filled with optimism and not dread?'

Hannah pondered it. That wasn't what she'd had in mind.

'I can't do bleak Sunday afternoons any more, waiting to hand her back to you. If we did Fridays after school, we'd have the optimism of the weekend together, or the distraction of a weekend with friends if we're handing back. School pick-up on the Friday can be the changeover.'

Hannah looked like such things had never occurred to her.

'OK, I suppose that could work. Except I have a mad crazy busy week this week, so do you want to pick her up after school today and keep her until Friday?'

Hannah finished the dregs of her coffee and handed back the little backpack Jesse had given her at the school gates.

This felt like a massive bonus. Jesse had just spent the first weekend in September – the last of the summer holidays – with Ida in her freshly painted bedroom, and now he could pick her up after school today and have her for a few more days. He mentally rearranged his meetings and his diary.

'Great, actually that works for me. I'm scheduled to go to LA on Saturday.'

'Oh.' Hannah looked a little put out, and Jesse remembered he hadn't actually answered her question. *How are you?*

43

JESSE

Now

Jesse closed his eyes as the engines roared. He'd never been scared of flying before. Never questioned it. He had always enjoyed the little rituals of getting onto the plane and settling into his seat; dinner, movie, sleep. But something made him nervous today as the captain said, 'Cabin crew seats for take-off.' It gave Jesse a slight daredevil thrill. As if today, he might be chancing death.

Minnie had got in his head. He closed his eyes and thought of her. Her wide-eyed smile. Her genuine ability to see the good in people, her heart-wrenching disappointment when people let her down. As the plane taxied onto the runway and the roar of the jets built, Jesse closed his eyes and acknowledged the familiar sensations: the chill of the air conditioning; the smells of processed and tightly packaged food; the sounds of the people around him; his comrades for the next twelve hours. He looked to the woman in the seat next to him and her son, who was around Ida's age, gazing out of the window from his seat. He glanced across the aisle at businessmen and backpackers; a retired couple who looked like they were heading on a hiking holiday to the lochs, not Los Angeles.

Who will grate on me?

Minnie wouldn't think like that. Minnie would think about all the people she could talk to, all the friends she might make on this flight. Were it not for her crippling fear of flying.

He thought about her, how last week he had finally done what he had been putting off since he'd got back from France in June, armed with her name. He googled Minnie Byrne.

Born 31 October 1996. Playing age 18–31. Highly skilled in American, estuary English, Irish-Southern, West Country and Yorkshire accents. Voiceover work. Acting work. Modelling work. Roles she'd played. Campaigns she'd done. Accomplished horse-rider. Jesse saw photos of Minnie on red carpets with an assortment of siblings, as a child with their famous parents, as a baby at a Bruce Springsteen concert. He looked at Minnie's Instagram – her pictures were arty and beautiful. A dish at Alpine NW1. A painting of a street urchin in a gallery. A pretty doorway in France he recognised from their day in Arles. That one didn't have a caption. There were head shots and some promo shoots she had been doing for *Summer of Siena*. In one photo she looked incredible in a huge tulle dress and DMs, standing on top of a rooftop in Soho. There was no sign of JP on her social media, but perhaps she was keeping him off grid. JP wouldn't be very good for her image.

Jesse followed Minnie. There was no follow back, so he felt a little grubby, like a lurker, but couldn't help himself. And he'd lurked a few times since. Last Friday she'd posted a cover of the glossy magazine that comes with the *London Evening Standard* newspaper, heralding her as the reluctant rising star of the Byrne dynasty. He'd seen that photo on the street too, as he'd walked past a pile of magazines stacked outside King's Cross, stopped and gasped. He commented on her post: 'Incredible, congratulations!' She hadn't replied.

Jesse had lurked again in the Starbucks queue while he was waiting in the departures lounge. He had seen an Instagram story of Minnie boarding a flight. 'LAX I'm coming for you! #bracebrace' read the text over her face, as she stood making a peace sign, with a huge Virgin plane on the tarmac behind her. Jesse rubbed the hair at his temples and shook his head. He couldn't quite believe it.

* * *

As the plane gathered speed on the runway and Jesse felt ensconced in a sense of peril, he felt a lump in his throat. He was parched. He took a slug from his Evian bottle and realised he couldn't wait any longer. He leaned his arm down so he could feel under his seat. The woman and the boy by the window weren't paying attention to his scrabbling around, and he was grateful. Take-off was a good time, he reasoned. Cabin crew wouldn't wonder what the man rummaging around the plane was doing. He felt a nervous anticipation; he wondered if the plane might career into a wall and never get off the ground. Would there be another plane on the runway and the two craft would evaporate in a ball of flames, like the KLM and the Pan Am?

I am not scared of flying.

Jesse's hand moved around, unguided underneath him. He couldn't feel anything, just a cage with a life vest rolled into it he thought he'd better not pull apart right now. He looked up above him.

Seat 23C.

He had booked this seat specifically. He had checked his old boarding pass. It was definitely 23C.

Where the fuck...?

Jesse was too tall to curl under his seat, during take-off of all times. So he switched from his right arm to his left and tried not to lean into the woman next to him as he reached one more time as the plane roared up the runway. His back arched, his stomach sick with hope. And then he felt it. The dangling loop of the ring. He threaded his finger through and pulled at it, using a little force to remove it from its metallic grip.

She's here!

Saraswati was back in Jesse's palm. Her wisdom. Her power. What it meant to him. He looked at her serene face and felt a flush of relief as he squeezed the bronze deity tight. He wanted to ask her about all the journeys she had been on while Jesse had been on one of his own, but he realised he would look a little mad to anyone who might notice, so he closed his eyes and held her.

What adventures you've had!

She *had* been there all along. Every time he looked up. It had seemed so unlikely, even before Minnie suggested it.

Jesse gripped her again, he wanted so desperately to tell his father that *The Adventures of Remy the Red Panda*, by Lars and Jesse Lightning, would be coming out next spring. He was just so sorry it had taken him so long. He squeezed Saraswati in his palm and the plane soared.

44

JESSE

Now

Despite the fact Jesse had spent much of the year in a stagnant state of grief, shock and heartache, he was a productive person at heart. Stagnant didn't suit him. And if his brief friendship and fling with Minnie had taught him anything, it was to take action – Minnie would take action.

He woke up earlier than he would have liked on Sunday morning, both cursing and saluting the sun that blasted through the long windows of his hotel at the end of Hollywood Boulevard, with a determination to get out of his funk and bring back some joy in his life. He had Saraswati back. He had a custody solution. His work was going brilliantly. Max had kicked Liam out and there was a happy calm in the office. The only fly in the ointment was that Minnie was back with that sleazeball, but Jesse had to accept it. He was thirty-two; he had his life ahead of him. Minnie's catastrophic positivity had rubbed off on him.

Los Angeles was a long way to travel just to get a trinket back, however treasured, so Jesse made a plan to be as productive and dynamic as he could for the next four days. He would put his time there to good use before picking Ida up from school on Friday.

A World Cup was coming to the United States, Canada and Mexico, and Jesse already knew he would get commissions for it. So he got out of bed, showered and went down to the dining room of the W hotel, surprised by how many other people were up for breakfast early on a Sunday morning. He picked up a newspaper he wouldn't get round to reading and ate pancakes with maple syrup and bacon while he looked at his phone and planned his art gallery itinerary. City art galleries were often closed on Mondays, so today would be an arty day, he decided. A chance to get ahead.

Jesse always found inspiration in a local gallery, whether it was in an artwork itself, the style and fonts on the menu in the cafe, or the journey to the museum: travelling by subway, bus or taxi would always throw up some unexpected inspiration.

After breakfast, Jesse headed in a taxi from his hotel in Hollywood to the Getty in Brentwood, where he weaved among paintings by Rembrandt, Turner, Manet and Monet. When Jesse got to Van Gogh's *Irises* he stopped, stared, drank them in and then closed his eyes. In a flash he was transported to Arles with Minnie. He could taste pastis on his tongue and smell the lavender entwined in her legs. He could hear the cicadas, he could see fireflies around the pool of his family home.

When Jesse opened his eyes his vision came into sharp focus on the pale green leaves and stems of Vincent's irises and he connected the dots. That's where he had seen that colour before.

In the afternoon, Jesse went Downtown to The Broad for some modern art to counter the abundance of history at the Getty. Within the cool air-conditioned curves of the white modernist building, he drank in paintings by Warhol, Walker, Haring and Lichtenstein, wondering what Minnie was doing right now. What had her first flying experience felt like? The plane hadn't crashed, he was relieved to assume. Was she having a good time in Los Angeles?

When Jesse had seen the Instagram story of Minnie boarding a plane, it had said it was posted sixteen hours ago. She had travelled to Los Angeles almost one whole day ahead of him.

Is she still here?

In Yayoi Kusama's Infinity Mirror Room, Jesse marvelled about how much Ida would love the sparkling galaxy of flashing LED lights, and how they felt like the closest he might ever get to space. He longed to show her as much of the world as he could, soon realising it was well after lunchtime and his hunger was also down to a need for food.

While he ate a Cubano sandwich in the restaurant next to The Broad – a hulking modern building that looked both raw and refined – Jesse called his friend Will from London, who was in LA visiting his new boyfriend Lloyd. Lloyd was a Hollywood lighting assistant and they had met on a dating app when Lloyd was in London shooting at the start of the year. They hadn't looked back.

'You still on for this evening?' Jesse asked.

'Yeah, brother,' Will replied, an American affectation in his tone. His relationship was obviously still going well.

* * *

That evening, Jesse met Will and Lloyd at an Italian restaurant in the Arts District where they ate spaghetti in a sea urchin sauce and Jesse was relieved to find Lloyd was even lovelier than Will had described. Lloyd had a hangdog handsomeness about him, with his bushy beard and red and black checked shirt hugging a soft stomach. He was instantly warm, welcoming and full of tips for Jesse on where to eat and go over the next few days. As Lloyd gave advice, Will fussed over Bingley the Border terrier, back home on FaceTime via his dogsitter, Beth, and her phone. Will was in LA for the whole month, and he missed Bingley terribly, but was seeking solace on FaceTime, his camera roll, and the Bingley The Border Terrier Instagram page, which had almost 100,000 followers.

'The black smoky burger at Mr T is the bomb. I think it's a chain – started in Paris, right?' Lloyd looked to Will who nodded knowingly. *Paris.* Which reminded Will of the last time he saw Jesse, on Father's Day, their brunch with Bingley and Ida. It had been Jesse's first Father's Day without his dad; he had mentioned in passing that he was contemplating a trip to Paris.

'Did you ever make it over to Paris, buddy?' Will asked as he half looked at his phone.

Jesse nodded. 'Yeah I did...'

'Wasn't there a girl?' They hadn't really been able to talk in front of Ida, but Jesse had alluded to *something*. A friend.

Lloyd raised an intrigued eyebrow. Will had told Lloyd about Jesse's unfortunate year, but he hadn't mentioned a girl. Lloyd listened eagerly. He had the face of a guy who rooted for an underdog. Lloyd looked like a bit of an underdog himself, although he and Will had certainly hit the jackpot with each other.

'Yeah with the girl.'

Jesse looked both sheepish and heartbroken.

'Shit, what happened?' Will asked, finally flipping his phone over and giving Jesse his full attention.

Jesse skipped some of the detail: he told Will and Lloyd how Minnie was an actor and had an audition for a film in Paris; how they went to his mum's for a couple of nights afterwards. That they had hooked up in Provence and why she had fled. All because of a silly game.

'Not just a silly game – I omitted to tell her when we met, that I knew her boyfriend and my wife had been sleeping together behind our backs.'

Will gasped. 'Fuck!'

'Oh no!' Lloyd looked like he might cry.

A stunned silence fell over the table.

'It's not like that's your fault though? Fucking Hannah...' Will shook his head. Jesse had protected her, he hadn't told Will why they had separated.

'It's OK. I should have just told Minnie up front. She's right, it was a bit weird.'

He told the boys how Minnie was now in Los Angeles promoting *Summer of Siena*.

'*Summer of Siena*?' Lloyd said. 'That's like, everywhere right now, that's pretty cool.'

Jesse nodded. He was so happy for Minnie, he was just desperate to tell her so.

'Is that why you came?' Will asked. 'To LA?'

'No, mate, I didn't know until I got to the airport that she was here too. Pure coincidence.'

Will gave a doubtful look.

'I had to get the plane I was getting because I left something on it. My keyring. If the plane was scheduled to go to Lahore on Saturday, I'd be in Lahore right now.'

'That's an expensive key chain,' Lloyd muttered to himself.

Jesse took it out of his right pocket and put it on the table.

'My dad gave it to me...'

Will recognised it. The three men went quiet for a moment while they looked at Saraswati, who almost glowed under the pendant light over their table.

'Look, man,' Lloyd said, wiping his mouth and placing his napkin down. 'I only just met you, but I gotta say: she's here, you're here. Seems a bit fuckin' opportune...'

Will nodded. 'There's no real reason she doesn't speak to you, is there?'

'I was deliberately dishonest.'

'You didn't lie!' Will interjected.

Jesse shrugged.

They continued to eat copious amounts of pasta and focaccia and Lloyd ordered a third bottle of Chianti while Jesse contemplated it.

'She's here with work, she's really busy. I'm just a stalker loser guy. I wouldn't know where to begin anyway.'

'You could start with her agent?' Lloyd suggested helpfully.

'She's back with her creep ex.'

'The one who Hannah...?' Will stopped himself.

Jesse nodded in defeat.

Lloyd put a rounded hand on Jesse's arm. 'Sorry, buddy.'

'Ah look what Beth sent!' Will said deftly. 'She's trying to bath Bingley, the fool!'

Lloyd twirled spaghetti on his fork, not as interested in his boyfriend's dog as he maybe ought to be.

'What harm would a conversation do at least? Call her agent! I can find out who reps her if you need me to...'

45

JESSE

Now

Jesse walked through his hotel lobby, its black and gold sofas and ostentatious palm fronds glistening in a way that made him wish he'd booked somewhere a little more boutique. He saw a copy of *Variety* on a coffee table. Minnie caught his eye, a knowing look in hers as she smouldered at him, draped on the shoulder of her male co-star, Dexter Maclay, and two other actors Jesse didn't recognise. It was on a big wrap advert around the outside of the magazine. '*Summer of Siena*! Coming to Prime this fall'.

Full of carbs and Chianti, Jesse felt aglow to see her unexpectedly, even if she were on the cover of a magazine.

Is she still in town?

Jesse looked at his watch: it was midnight in LA, 8 a.m. Monday in London. He got in the lift, unwittingly ruining the selfies of the young women who were already in there, and whizzed up to his room, tired after adhering to the advice of his dad in his head, well versed in the ways to combat jet lag: 'Adapt immediately. Live in the time you're in.' He felt as if he'd been up all night and was exhausted from a busy day of sightseeing, of catching up with Will and meeting Lloyd.

As Jesse stepped out of the lift on the seventh floor he sensed the women all raise their phones as the elevator doors closed behind him. He imagined the photos they would post.

#elevatorchic

#goingup

#takemetothepenthouse

#takemehigher

And he chuckled quietly to himself.

Back in his room, buoyed by friendship and wine, Jesse thought fuck it.

Live in the time you're in.

He looked at Minnie's Instagram again. She hadn't posted any stories since taking off on Friday, but it did say in her bio that she was 'rep'd by Devon Smith at McFadden Higgs'.

Devon.

Of course.

Jesse googled him again and found the number for offices in London, which he called, not expecting an answer after one ring. An efficient British voice spoke. Jesse was flustered. And quite pissed.

'Hi, er, can I speak to Devon Smith about Minnie Byrne please?' Jesse said, wondering why his heart raced.

The receptionist said Devon was in a meeting. Jesse looked at his watch.

Already?

'I can leave him a message.'

'No, it's OK thanks,' Jesse said, and he hung up, showered, put on the TV and fell into a weary red-wine slumber while a chat show played on the screen.

46

JESSE

Now

On Monday morning Jesse woke to the sun streaming in through the window he'd forgotten to close the curtains on, again, and decided to try calling Devon Smith, again. He had three days in LA ahead of him before flying back late Wednesday night, and he knew Lloyd was right. It was too much of a coincidence, too serendipitous, that he and Minnie were both in the same city on the other side of the world. *If* she was still in the city.

He knew he had to act on it, so he got up, rubbed his eyes, paced the room, and called the last dialled number as he flipped Saraswati in his left hand.

'McFadden Higgs, good afternoon.' The same voice.

It must have been late afternoon in London. Jesse imagined Henrike making Ida fish fingers and chips.

'It's Jesse Lightning for Devon Smith?'

The reply was swift.

'Devon can't talk right now, can I take a message?'

'Yeah, I'm in LA, and I need to get hold of him...'

'Oh, I'll put you through now.'

'Oh.'

That was easy, Jesse thought.

''Ello?' said a bouncy voice.

'Hi, er, is that Devon?'

'Speaking. Who's this?'

'It's Jesse Lightning, I'm a designer, I'm in LA, and I'm trying to get hold of Minnie Byrne, I think she's out here...'

'If it's a wardrobe matter you need to call her stylist.'

'No, I'm not that kind of designer... I was hoping to get hold of her... to speak to her.'

'Yeah, mate, she's very busy, packed schedule out here.'

'Out here, you're with her?'

'Who is this again?'

'A friend. I'm a friend of Minnie's.'

'Everyone's a friend of Minnie's right now. What did you say your name was?'

'Jesse Lightning.'

'Jesse Lightning,' the man repeated, guardedly. 'I'll see if I can get hold of her.' There was a muffled sound and then the line went silent as Jesse realised he'd been muted. Ten seconds later, Devon unmuted the call.

'Can I take a message, mate?'

'If you could just tell Minnie I'm in LA too.' Jesse scratched his head as he turned circles and looked around his hotel room, trying to find a solution, a glimmer. He looked out of the window. He could see the Hollywood sign from his suite. He remembered their conversation at the cocktail-making class. *La La Land*. Their heads drawing together, what felt a lifetime ago. 'I know she's busy but, erm, I'll be at Griffith Observatory, in Griffith Park, for the next few days. Say... 6 p.m.? But I fly back Wednesday night.'

'Sweet, mate, we have a packed schedule.'

'Of course. But if you could just pass the message on, it would be much appreciated.'

'Will do, cheers!' Devon said a bit too quickly as he hung up and Jesse threw his phone down on the bed in defeat.

47

MINNIE

Now

In a car travelling down Melrose, Devon turned to Minnie, sitting next to him along the back seat. They were heading to Wilshire Boulevard in the morning sunshine, to William Morris for a breakfast meeting with her American agent to discuss some very exciting prospects that had landed on their desks. Minnie stared straight through the front windscreen and shook her head in astonishment.

48

JESSE

Now

Jesse spent the morning seeking out sporting iconography and LA life for inspiration for future works. His first stop was the Los Angeles Memorial Coliseum, home of the 1932 and the 1984 Olympics, and already revamped for the 2028 games. On the tour through the impressive, open amphitheatre, a guide called Trent told Jesse that the Coliseum had been visited by American presidents, MLK, the Dalai Lama, Nelson Mandela, Pelé and even Evel Knievel. Jesse wandered around, drinking in the fonts and the history, while wondering whether Minnie might show up later. After Trent referred to the Coliseum as 'the greatest stadium in the world' for the fourth time, Jesse smiled quietly and peeled away from the tour to visit some other pertinent parts of the city.

He got an Uber to South LA so he could visit Mexican neighbourhoods and work out how he could tie Mexican iconography into his World Cup designs. An official World Cup logo had been unveiled last year, a rather underwhelming one, Jesse thought. But when he went to google it again, to remind him of its flatness, he was flabbergasted to see that the unveiling ceremony had happened at Griffith Observatory of all places.

Over lunch at El Mercado Paloma, a market rich with food stalls and piñatas in all shapes, sizes and bright colours, Jesse sat at a counter, ate a chicken tinga torta and drank hibiscus flower water while imagining how his designs might be better than FIFA's own. As he sketched with a biro on a napkin, he remembered some great work he'd done with Artie Donner, an American designer he'd met in London, with whom he'd later collaborated on an MLS kit.

Artie was from LA and Jesse had a thought. He fired off a text to see if they could get together. Artie replied:

> Great to hear from you! I can do drinks tonight or tomorrow?

Neither was ideal, but Jesse said he'd be back in touch when he knew how his evening was panning out.

> Great, short notice always suits me!

After lunch, Jesse took the Metro to Mariachi Plaza in Boyle Heights to see musicians for hire in another Latin neighbourhood that might influence his designs. Men in sharp silk and brocade *charro* suits played trumpets, guitarróns and violins, while Jesse walked among them, tucking dollars into their baskets and wondering how different LA might look through Minnie's lens. He wanted to bring her here, break her from the press tour, tell her he thought he might love her.

At 3 p.m. Jesse got an Uber to Sunset Boulevard, where he bought an ice cream and began his long walk to Griffith Park, making mental notes and iPhone notes about everything he had seen in the galleries, the Mercado and the square that he didn't want to forget. How he could incorporate them into a beautiful new typeface the world had never seen before for his football designs. How the fonts for *Remy* could be tweaked a little before printing. He thought about his mother in France. How September brought a new light to the fields now empty of lavender. How lonely she might be, her first autumn and winter in France as a widow; how he knew it was the right place for her because Lars' books and laughter lined the walls of the farmhouse. It was there that his imprint was greatest felt.

For almost two hours Jesse hiked, through trails, steps and brush, past locals and other tourists, up the East Griffith Observatory Trail, until he reached the vast park, a hidden gem atop a congested car-filled city.

Relief.

He stopped to drink water and take in the view, before continuing towards the grand white Greek-style building of the observatory, its three domes, one larger in the middle, shining in the golden hour like giant onions. He strolled past a sundial and neat lawns, until he stopped at an obelisk-like structure with a bronze armillary sphere on top and sat at its foot. Smooth serene statues of astronomers looking like Greek gods stood guard around the obelisk: Galileo, Hipparchus, Copernicus, Kepler, Newton and Herschel. Jesse sat, withered at their feet and took another lug of water from a bottle he'd bought from a vendor on the trail. He looked at his watch: 5.55 p.m.

Perfect.

He didn't look at his phone – what use was his phone now – as he scanned the faces of all who walked around him. Couples, families, hikers. A school group followed a harangued teacher thrusting an umbrella high in the air, back to the car park and their coach. An Indian couple kissed as they took a selfie. No one looked like Minnie.

Jesse briefly closed his eyes and tried to imagine his father standing protectively behind him, Jesse as an eleven-year-old boy. But he couldn't conjure Lars now. He worried he had forgotten his father's voice. He felt for Saraswati but his throat tightened.

For an hour Jesse people-watched, giving in to his solitude and becoming accepting of his situation. He watched the sun disappear beyond the haze of red smog over Downtown. He watched the illuminations of the city and its arteries start to sparkle, as if a light show were slowly turning on for him.

By 7 p.m., Jesse conceded that Minnie wouldn't be turning up and his ridiculous, romantic notion was just that. A notion. He texted Artie to say he was up at Griffith Park. 'I could be on the Strip in an hour?'

'Meet me in Los Feliz in forty-five minutes. Café Figaro,' Artie replied.

Jesse had to get a move on down the Boy Scout Trail to the Glendower steps, and was soon on the leafy palm-lined boulevard of North Vermont Avenue.

The elegant trees gave way to low-rise buildings, boxy trees and the odd 7-Eleven, until Jesse saw an unassuming restaurant with a pale blue awning that looked like it had been plucked right out of Paris. The Café Figaro font looked like something from the *fin de siècle* and wood-and-wicker chairs all faced out onto the street so diners could watch the world (and the traffic... this was LA) go by.

Artie was already waiting for him at a table.

'Jesse!' she gasped, standing and extending two hands, which she took his in, and kissed him robustly on each cheek. She smelled of cigarette and tuberose.

'Hey...' he said, suddenly flustered.

She flicked her deep red hair over her shoulder.

'I thought a little piece of France would suit you, sir,' Artie said with a dazzling smile, the freckles on her face sparkling in the last of the day's light. 'Plus, it's right around the corner from my condo...'

49

JESSE

Now

'So what brings Jesse Lightning to LA?'

'Research trip,' Jesse said, explaining where he'd been for the past two days.

Artie said she'd seen an incredible Keith Haring exhibition at The Broad last year and Jesse lamented having missed it, as the waiter came and Artie ordered them a Grey Goose and tonic, plus an absinthe each. Jesse felt a niggle. Paris on an LA pavement didn't feel quite right, but he suddenly needed a drink.

'I'll have an IPA as well, please.' He looked around at the tables next to him. 'Monkey Fist looks great, thanks.'

'Very good, *monsieur*,' the woman said, authentically French at least.

Artie watched the waitress walk away and then lit a cigarette.

'You're thirsty!' she said, with a twinkle in her eye. He couldn't work out if the comment was a flirtation or a dig, but he took it with a smile.

'Yeah, I just hiked up to Griffith Park and back down.'

Artie rolled her eyes in jest, as if to say *such a tourist*, then offered Jesse a cigarette from her carton.

He shook his head.

'So how's life? How's the missus?'

Jesse was taken aback. Weren't they even going to talk about work first? That thing they had in common? In a sphere dominated by men, Artie Donner was a rare gem. She had recently set up a design agency, in an industry where 0.1 per cent of creative agencies were founded by women, and deliberately employed female designers from under-represented communities. Jesse thought she was amazing and wanted to know how her business was going.

He scratched his temple awkwardly.

'Well to be honest, I don't know...'

Artie gasped again.

'You don't?'

Jesse looked sheepish, as if he were confessing a wrongdoing. 'We've separated. Split up.'

'Shut up!' Artie said, knitting her auburn brows into a pretty bow. 'Oh I'm sorry, are you OK?'

'Yeah, yeah, it was for the best. Shit timing but... when is a good time, huh?' Jesse tried to keep it vague. He didn't want to bring up his dad, and he would be mortified having to explain how his marriage had unravelled. Especially to Artie. She was probably too cool to ever contemplate an archaic institution such as marriage.

'True,' Artie said, philosophically, as she exhaled a ribbon of smoke towards the pavement.

'We're sharing custody of our daughter.'

'Oh yeah right, your girl!' Artie said, as if she'd forgotten. 'How's she doing?'

'Yeah she's great, she's seven now. She'll be fine – kids are more resilient than us, right?'

Artie nodded wholeheartedly as a different waiter brought their drinks and placed them down on the small circular table.

'Wow, break my heart,' Artie sighed blithely as the waiter left.

'What?'

'If I had this intel five years ago...' She raised her eyebrows.

'What do you mean?'

She inhaled another elegant puff and blew the smoke away from Jesse, out of the corner of her mouth.

'I wanted to fuck you so bad when we were working on MLS.'

Jesse, taking a sip of his IPA, almost choked with laughter.

'Really?' He looked at Artie as if she were pranking him.

'Yeah man! Totally. You didn't get those vibes?'

'Erm... no!'

Truth be told, Jesse had thought Artie was beautiful, sexy, glamorous, American. *So* LA. He knew about the rock stars she dated and the parties she went to. He would never have considered she would want to fuck him. Besides, he was married. It was moot.

'Really?' Artie was just as shocked.

'That's totally news to me, I thought we worked in the strictest, most professional of partnerships...' he said, now a hint of flirtation in his voice.

'Are you ready to order, *mademoiselle*?' asked the first waitress, returning with an iPad.

Jesse and Artie both ordered the *moules frites* and a basket of oven-fresh bread and the waiter left them. Artie stubbed out her cigarette and put the ashtray on the pavement under her chair.

'You know, Donner and Lightning. We made a great team.'

'We did. That kit was fucking amazing. It made football – soccer – and fashion finally align in the US.'

'Yeah I think that was more down to Ibrahimovic, Beckham and Messi, but whatever...' Artie said. 'My point is, Donner...' She jabbed a finger towards her breastbone.

'Donner?' Jesse was lost.

'Donner!' Artie smiled. Her teeth were spectacular. 'Donner means "thunder" in German you doofus! Thunder and fucking Lightning. Go figure!'

Artie downed her absinthe shot and held Jesse's eye. Her amber eyes were beautiful.

50

JESSE

Now

On Tuesday morning, Jesse woke up with a sore skull, lamenting having mixed his vodka with his absinthe with his IPA, and decided he needed to see the ocean and clear his head with sea air. He got an Uber to Venice Beach where the sensory overload of skaters, smells of skunk and psychedelic colours woke him up and he walked past impressive murals and even more impressive muscles at Muscle Beach. He wandered past a skatepark whose concrete curves were as beautiful as the athletes rolling them.

He walked for an hour along Venice Beach to Marina del Rey, watching surfers gliding towards the vast expanse of dirty blonde sand. At the peninsula in the distance he wondered whether, if he walked that far, he would be able to see Mexico. It certainly felt as if he were on a map's edge, watching himself moving as if he were able to look down over the scene. He decided to check in with Max and FaceTime her on the walk back to Venice Beach, while she might still be at work, and was heartened to see she had left the office and was out in the early evening sunshine.

'Where are you?' Jesse asked. 'Looks ace!' Max was lit by a London sunset, standing in front of a peach and navy wall, with 'BIENVENUE AU PARADIS' written across it, in a bold and brazen font Jesse loved the look of and wished was one of his. He could see The London Eye glistening down the river over her shoulder.

'A rooftop bar in Waterloo. I bumped into Kenji...' She had a rare and wicked twinkle in her eye.

Kenji came into view, his arm slung around Max's shoulder. He peered into the camera.

'Hey, buddy, what's up? How's LA?'

Kenji had a sparkle about him too. Or perhaps that was the golden hour making them glow. Jesse exhaled to the sky, a lightbulb moment. A *how wonderful; why didn't I think of that* moment, which sent his heart soaring into the California sky.

He tried not to make a big deal of it, tried not to get carried away, so he told them about his art odyssey and how he had caught up with Will and Lloyd, but something urged him to get off the phone and leave them to it.

'Just wanted to check in, see everything was OK.'

'Yeah, it's great!' Max said, looking as delightfully surprised as Jesse was.

* * *

Back at Venice Beach Jesse decided to walk to the end of the pier, remembering one of his favourite films shot there: *Falling Down*, and the protagonist, Michael Douglas' character, who met his not-so-happy ending off the end of it. Jesse loved that film. It came out the year Jesse was born and when he was fourteen, Lars told Jesse about it; that the central character had inspired the famous Dash Draxler, a cop on the edge, who was the star of five of Lars' bestselling books.

'I owe a lot to Joel Schumacher, to D-Fens...' Lars said, as he'd enlightened Jesse one Friday family film night. Caryn didn't enjoy it, she found it too stressful, but Jesse had marvelled at how his dad let him watch a film with so many swearwords in it, loving that feeling of trust and maturity. Walking the pier felt like something Jesse ought to do to honour Dash. To honour his dad.

Jesse often thought about his dad's revelation: that people can inspire you. The snarl of someone you know; the laugh of a person you love. A madcap character in a film about a man on the edge. The font of a soda brand; a newspaper headline typeface. It made Jesse realise, in an industry where it was difficult to have a completely original idea and concept, you could be inspired, you could make something your own, you could make it better. Dash Draxler was brilliant and original and people all over the world loved reading about him.

Jesse walked down the pier, looking at the fishermen standing patiently at the end. He remembered his own meltdown. Not quite as catastrophic as Michael Douglas' in *Falling Down*, but at Bondiga's Books, the day Minnie had reappeared like a genie out of a bottle.

* * *

After lunch in a past-its-best diner, Jesse took a cab back to the hiking trails in the hills and walked the shorter route to Griffith Observatory. When he arrived at the summit, he went up to the West Terrace, which gave a panorama over people arriving; it overlooked the Hollywood sign. From his vantage point, leaning against the edge, Jesse remembered: this was where he'd stood as a child. This was the spot he had taken in the sparkling Los Angeles skyline with the security of his mother and father behind him, leaning, elbows propped on the pristine white wall.

Six o'clock came and went and Jesse watched the sun lower behind the city, beyond it, an ocean.

She clearly isn't coming.

Just after 7 p.m. Jesse dared to look at Minnie's Instagram. A new story! He clicked tentatively on the small circle with the pink and orange glow around it. Four hours ago. 'Getting red-carpet ready!'

Three hours ago: Minnie in the back of a car, hair and make-up making her look like a movie star. Red lips. Her black hair smoothed into a soft wave against her face.

Sixteen minutes ago: a shared story someone else had posted, of the cast, director and producers of *Summer of Siena* on the red carpet. One of the producers was a Hollywood A-lister who had stumped up the money to get the book made. Her showbiz smile echoing Minnie's more cautious, smouldering one. Minnie looked sensational.

No, Minnie definitely wasn't joining him tonight.

* * *

With a heavy heart, Jesse went to catch the second half of LA Galaxy vs. Vancouver, which he thought might help his World Cup research, but the flat goalless draw at the stadium in Carson City was so uninspiring he came out with a foam finger and no ideas.

He thought about Artie Donner's proposition the night before. After their *moules frites* she'd invited him back to her place for a nightcap as her fingertips touched the edge of Jesse's, and he'd considered it for a second, before saying he had to get back to his hotel.

'Can't blame a girl for trying,' she said, her tongue sticking out the side of her mouth.

'I don't.'

'Well call me if you change your mind,' Artie said as she planted a kiss on Jesse's cheek and skipped off, in the direction of her condo.

As Jesse came out of the stadium at Carson City he looked at his phone.

He realised Ida would be up and dressed and heading out to school.

'Hey sweetpea, how are you?'

'It's dark there, Daddy!' Ida said, utterly surprised.

Jesse pointed the foam finger he had bought her, up to the sky. 'Yes! It's still last night here!'

Ida giggled as she held Henrike's hand and clutched her nanny's phone. 'But how can that be?'

She looked closer at the screen, in awe of her father, as if he were a magician who could time travel.

'It's very clever and I will show you how one day!'

51

JESSE

Now

Wednesday was Jesse's last day in LA, and he decided to spend it more leisurely. He was done with research, and he had given up hope of meeting Minnie. So he decided to go easy on himself, to rest his tired feet, to lie in and go downstairs for a relaxing breakfast just before the service closed at 11 a.m.

As he stepped out of the elevator into the bustling reception area, he thought he'd better find out what time check out was and ask whether he could leave his luggage in a baggage room. His flight wasn't until tonight.

'Yes, sir,' a woman behind the desk said. 'Check out is midday and you can leave your cases in the *vestiaire* in the basement.'

Vestiaire, Jesse thought, laughing to himself.

'Thanks,' he said, as he went to the dining room, picked up a paper, and slid into a table for two. He ordered coffee and pancakes from a waitress, eschewing the buffet breakfast, and scrolled through the news on his phone. While he was clicking on a story about another Tory MP embroiled in another scandal, he heard a familiar voice. A British accent.

A man directing people: which car they should head towards and where and when they would reconvene. He dropped his phone on the table, looked across the restaurant and saw Devon Smith, the agent who looked like an actor, standing up, fastening the button on his jacket, extending a confident arm as if to say *after you*. The woman he was letting out of a large round table wore a white blazer slung over her shoulders and short black bobbed hair.

'Minnie?' Jesse whispered to himself, delighted. 'Fuck!'

He threw his napkin down, bounced up and then froze, paralysed in the middle of the restaurant, as he watched the group of men and women, about six or seven of them, air kiss each other and say their goodbyes.

Fuck! Why didn't I come down earlier?

Jesse opened his mouth to call out her name. To shout, 'Nice to meet you, I'm Jesse!' To see if he could eke out a long-forgotten joke.

But it was too late. He watched the group head off onto the street to awaiting cars.

Fuck.

She obviously hadn't wanted to see him anyway. Maybe the agent hadn't even bothered to convey the message. Jesse was just a distraction in a tightly packed schedule. Or if he had, why would she want to see him? She was busy. She was having the time of her life after everything she had worked hard for, after some shit-rotten luck, after she'd made the leap and jumped on a plane to get there. Minnie Byrne did not need Jesse Lightning to rain on her parade. She was being schmoozed, dined, directed. She was the talent. Jesse was just a small part of her journey; she was a small part of his. Perhaps they would one day both look back on their six-week friendship, their five magical days together and their one-night fling, with gratitude, he hoped.

Jesse looked at the floor, shook his head, and went back to his table, as agitated as he had been that first day in Bondiga's Books, only this time Minnie hadn't seen his beautiful, flustered face.

* * *

After Jesse packed, checked out, and put his case in the luggage store, he decided to walk all of Hollywood Boulevard, to find Angela Lansbury's star on the Hollywood Walk of Fame, and to finish his LA odyssey in the most LA of ways. Saraswati was in his pocket, so the trip had been a success at least. Saraswati was the reason he had come, and he could delete the plane tracker app on his phone, go home, and get on with his life.

* * *

The September sun made Hollywood glisten as he walked among the stars, laughing to himself at this most touristy of things to do. Artie had called him a tourist for walking to Griffith, if only she could see him now. As he strolled, stopping at Starbucks to grab an Americano – extra hot – he looked down at the stars, wondering which way Minnie's car had gone when she'd left the hotel. What was the next stop on her busy schedule? He called Ida again, trying Hannah's phone rather than Henrike's because it was a midweek evening.

'She's asleep already...' Hannah answered.

'Oh, OK. Everything all right? How is she?'

Hannah sounded tired. Distracted. Jesse pictured her sitting on the sofa. *That* sofa, watching TV with a glass of wine, and all the memories of tension and deceit bobbled back to the surface. It made him yearn for *his* flat. He had already made the rental feel cosy yet light, warm yet open, a *home* he and Ida could be happy in. He would make the flat he was buying next door even more so. For the first time, as he clutched the phone to his ear and *felt* Hannah, he felt a sense of relief that he didn't have to live with her any more. He was liberated by her actions, and he could be OK with that.

'I'll tell her you called,' Hannah said.

'Thanks.'

'You'll be back in time to get her from school on Friday, right?'

'Right, I fly tonight, overnight.'

'Great because I have a – I have a *thing* on Friday night.' Hannah wasn't sure what her dinner with JP was about when he'd suggested meeting up, when he'd said he wanted to 'check in' with her.

Jesse smiled in the glorious September sunshine.

'Don't worry, I'll be there.'

wisest guess what her turn out with. It was an that Ken had bargained meeting up when she could have opted to check in with her Jesse smiled in the glorious September sunshine.

Don't worry, I'll be there.

52

JESSE

Now

> Jessica Fletcher! Your dad's hero!

Jesse wasn't used to his mother replying to a message straight away; she must have been out in Arles, perhaps at the theatre with a friend, so she had phone reception.

Jesse had sent his mother a photo of himself, crouched down at Angela Lansbury's star on the Hollywood Walk of Fame, giving a big thumbs up, and what his dad ascribed to Dash Draxler as a 'shit-eating grin'.

> I know right!

Jesse added a star-struck eyes emoji afterwards. He didn't know Caryn had actually laughed out loud when she'd opened the photo. He followed up with:

> Are you OK?

Yes thank you darling. Just in Marseille with Marcheline.

Cool. Give her my best!

Likewise to Angela! Safe flight home darling.
Love you.

Love you too Mum x

Jesse pocketed his phone, smiled to himself and walked a few steps further until another star caught his eye.

Geraldine Byrne.

Minnie's mother.

How had he not noticed that? The same light green eyes and wild beauty, even if Geraldine was older, wiser, with Titian-esque hair. Jesse thought of all the films and plays he might have seen her in. He thought about how Minnie's childhood might not have been that different from his own. Noisier perhaps. Less long-distance travel. Not many people knew the Venn diagram of pride, prejudice and total embarrassment that came with having a famous parent. At least Jesse's childhood could be more anonymous. He imagined it must be hard for anyone who'd been in a Harry Potter film to grab a quiet coffee anywhere in the world.

He wondered if Minnie had been on this spot this week, to see her mother's star. She'd come all this way. Had she crouched down and taken a thumbs-up photo too? Did she even know it was there?

He went to take a photo, in case he could one day share it with Minnie, but then he realised that was weird, so he left his phone in his pocket and carried on his way.

* * *

At the corner of Hollywood Boulevard and Franklin Avenue, Jesse looked up and saw the Hollywood sign in the hills beyond the buildings, Griffith Observatory on the other side of the canyon.

Do I bother?

He thought about the same disheartening wait, the unlikelihood that

Minnie would ever come, even if he had 365 sunsets in which to wait for her. Then he felt the weight of Saraswati in his pocket, almost as if she were prodding him in the thigh. This was what he had come for. Saraswati and his dad. If he could ask his dad his advice right now, he would tell him to climb the bloody hill and go see that view again.

* * *

The trail's terrain felt familiar, even though Jesse was taking a third and different path to the top. He had the sensation of déjà vu, as if he were revisiting a dream from a different angle. The dry brush. The warm sunshine. His thirst. The winding steps. Greeting hikers, overtaking them or smiling as they passed, as they went about their days.

It was 5.40 p.m. when Jesse got to the Observatory and walked to the Astronomers Monument. The serene men still stood guard and welcomed him with an imaginary salute. He walked past the sundial and its neat lawn, looking at all the faces he passed, which were all different, but every face blurred into one. He found the staircase to the upper West Terrace, which he crossed, heading to the wall that had the best vantage point over the lawns.

Then he saw a figure, leaning against the white wall, her back to him. Hair slicked to the side, an incredible black sequin suit, vertiginous gunmetal heels.

It can't be.

He thought his mind was playing tricks on him; maybe that wasn't her at breakfast; it definitely wasn't her now.

Except she turned around, as if she knew he was standing there, his expression agog. Finally, he cleared his throat.

'I didn't think you'd ever come.'

53

MINNIE

Now

'Nor did I.'

Their eyes locked as the sun seemed to drop suddenly in the sky. Minnie looked stunning. She wore a black loose-fitting sequin tux seemingly with nothing underneath it, and black trousers with a gunmetal side stripe. Her green eyes were painted smoky grey, her lips blood red. She looked like a fucking movie star, not a TV actor chasing her first dream. She was astonishing.

Jesse glanced at his feet. Then back up.

'You made it. You got on a plane! You made it out to LA. That's amazing.'

Minnie nodded and smiled knowingly.

'The buzz about the show is insane. Everywhere I look I'm seeing you, about twenty-feet tall, on billboards all over the city.'

'Creepy huh?'

'Mesmeric.' He paused. 'And nothing less than you deserve.'

Minnie smiled awkwardly but didn't seem to be able to find her words.

'The premiere last night – I saw pictures. It looked incredible.'

She blushed.

'*You're* incredible.'

Minnie looked up at him sharply, but still the words couldn't come.

Jesse put his hands in his pocket and dared to take a step nearer.

'I really am genuinely sorry, Minnie.'

Minnie scowled as Jesse felt time slow down; the sky darken further.

'Sorry? Sorry for what?'

'I'm sorry I upset you. I'm sorry I didn't tell you everything. I'm sorry you're angry with me. I really didn't mean to—'

'Don't worry about it, fair dos...'

'Huh?'

'I'm angrier with myself if I'm honest.'

Jesse was taken aback. He approached the wall and leaned against it, facing Minnie.

'Why?'

'I was shocked about you – what you didn't tell me – but to be honest, I was angrier with myself. You held up the mirror to me that I was failing.'

'Failing? How? Look at you!'

'I was failing the Bechdel test of my life. A real howler you could say.'

She raised her eyebrows as if to concede.

Jesse didn't understand.

'I can't believe I tried to get over a broken heart by falling in love with another man.'

Jesse felt it. The punch of love, hope and disappointment, all coiled into one tight spring, slammed into his stomach. She was with that slug JP.

Love?

He was speechless.

'I was so focused on the optics: how my career looked, how I wasn't going to be a success, I forgot about the metrics. I failed the metrics of the Bechdel test of my own life. I suppose I realised that in France. And then Tony helped me chew it over.'

'What does a stupid test mean if you got what you wanted? Isn't that empowering at least?'

'What?' Minnie scowled again. Jesse thought she really did have the most beautiful scowl. He'd seen it when JP dumped her. He'd seen it in bed the morning she'd run away from him. He could see it tonight.

'You got what you wanted.' Jesse said it as casually and supportively as he could manage. 'The TV show. You got JP back. You made it out here without crashing; I assume you didn't crash...'

Minnie shook her head.

'I'm not with JP.'

Then she looked disgusted.

'Eww! Why would you think I was with JP?'

'Oh, I just thought...'

'No!'

'Someone saw you.'

Minnie looked a little like she had in the bedroom that morning back in Gordes. Spied upon. Outraged.

'It wasn't me – Kip from the cafe. I went in, asking after you. He said someone saw you out with a man, I suppose he assumed it was JP...'

'It was JP. We went for dinner. Once! A consolation dinner apparently. He does it with all his girls. Likes to check in with exes a few months down the line, just to make sure they're not *too* cut up over him. Sort of like an exit interview, I imagine.'

Jesse shook his head.

'Gross.'

'Yeah, I think it's just an ego boost. He's probably due to take your wife out any day now!' she added cheerily.

Minnie saw the hurt in Jesse's face and felt instantly wretched.

'I'm sorry, I'm so sorry. I was trying to be funny—'

'It's fine.'

'It wasn't funny.'

'Blissfully, I don't care if he does,' Jesse declared. And he meant it.

It was Minnie's barb that hurt more than the thought of Hannah with JP, but he could see the remorse on her face. He nodded. 'It really is fine...' He leaned an elbow on the wall and looked at Minnie pleadingly. 'I just didn't want us to end how it did.'

Us. It had sounded nice to both of them.

'No, I know. But it had to. I had to be on my own.'

Jesse nodded. Minnie sounded sensible, more mature. It made him love her even more.

'But I made it!' she almost shouted into the evening. 'On a plane. Out here. Without JP, without Wim Fischer. I don't need anyone to get me my next job or to coax me onto a plane or to mend my silly heart.'

Jesse felt the punch.

'I know.' He fiddled with his watch while he galvanised himself. 'But I need you.'

'Huh?'

'Minnie, please.'

She looked at him with the light of Downtown glimmering like a reverse night sky behind him, leaning on the wall.

'*You* rescued me, Minnie.'

She studied him.

'*You* rescued *me*. From Orson's mum...'

They both laughed, breaking the tension that lingered in the dusk.

'You rescued me from my drudgery. From my grief. From couch surfing. The moment you came up to me in that cafe and suggested your ridiculous game, you illuminated my world.'

Jesse looked to the dots sparkling on the hills behind her as she smiled and put a palm on Jesse's cheek. The touch of gratitude, of friendship.

'Jesse,' she said, as she leaned over and kissed him, carefully and precisely on the lips, so as not to blur her lipstick. 'You know I have to walk away now, don't you?'

Jesse felt sick. They'd come all this way.

'Please, you are more than the sum of the Bechdel test. You are brilliant. And I want my time with you.'

Minnie gasped. 'You saw it?'

They were both transported to St Pancras station. Neon art glowing pink. The start of their fourth day together.

'Yes.'

She looked sombrely at her heels, then back up at him intently. 'It made me think of you.'

'It made me think of you. I want my fucking time with you, Minnie. I want to introduce you to Ida and to travel with you and to go see the Northern Lights in Scotland – or fuck it – Finland now you can fly, or wherever we can! And drive along the Côte d'Azur with you and show you my new flat and support your meteoric rise, and show up and meet your family and...'

Minnie put a bejewelled finger to his lips to shush him. 'Not now.'

'Why?'

A figure from down below got out of a sleek black car and shouted up.

'Get your skates on!' the man shouted. Jesse narrowed his eyes and saw Devon, standing on the asphalt, as he took his hands out of his pockets and raised them to the night sky. Minnie nodded back at him.

She looked back to Jesse and levelled him with a palm on his shirt.

'You have a flight to catch and I'm going on *Jimmy Kimmel Live* – we were due at the studio half an hour ago.'

'*What?*'

'But listen...'

She leaned in again and kissed him wholeheartedly this time. He kissed her back, under the encouraging gaze of the astronomers. She didn't want to break his heart; she never wanted him to break hers. The reassurance she felt from his warm gentle kiss, from the touch of his hand on her cheek as if she were a work of art he would treasure until the end of time, was reassurance enough.

'I'll see you back in London,' she said with a slight mischievousness in her smile as she walked away, across the terrace, down the steps and towards the car.

He heard the muffled conversation of Devon hurrying Minnie along.

'All right, all right! Small matter of the heart to fix!' she said, looking up with a backward glance.

'And we need make-up to fix your mouth, you look like Weird Barbie.'

'Fair dos,' Minnie said proudly.

As Jesse watched Minnie glance up again as she got into her car, he waved, unaware – or unbothered – that he had red lipstick all over his mouth. As he watched the car speed away he pressed both palms onto the white surface of the terrace wall, leaned on it, and smiled to himself. Relief rolling away into the canyon. It was then that Jesse felt a strong palm press his shoulder blade and his smile widened even more.

EPILOGUE

DAY ONE THOUSAND AND FIFTY-FIVE

The Not-Too-Distant Future

Minnie Byrne and Ida Lightning stood at the panda enclosure and watched Xing Er chew bamboo while Mao Sun pawed at a ball swinging from a tree branch.

'Panda poo is teardrop-shaped,' Ida said. 'A greeny yellow.'

'Wow,' Minnie said, looking more sharply into the foliage. 'I wonder if we'll spot any today.'

Jesse came back from the kiosk clutching two coffees and a slushie for Ida.

They hadn't made it in time to see Yang Guang and Tian Tian at Edinburgh Zoo before they went back to China, but for Ida's tenth birthday, Jesse took Ida and Minnie to Copenhagen so Ida could see a giant panda in person.

Jesse had also decided to put a panda in the next *Remy* book: a cute story about identity when Pom-pom the giant panda arrives at Paris Zoo and confuses the hell out of little Remy, who had been expecting a bigger version of himself. He was planning to press on with an early idea, a book about all the monochromatic animal friends of Remy.

Lenny the Lemur was proving popular, and Jesse knew he needed to up his part.

The Amazing Adventures of Remy the Red Panda series was now a number-one children's bestseller, dominating the charts and, more recently, the children's TV schedules. And although Lars Lightning's name hadn't been on the cover since the first original edition, every Remy book bore a photo and dedication to the man who came up with the idea, inside every single jacket.

'Ooh thanks,' Minnie said, as she took the cup and kissed Jesse on the lips. He looked at her, as mesmerised as he had been the day he'd put his palm to the window of Bondiga's Books. He then handed Ida the slushie, who beamed at the prospect of a blue drink, before the family continued towards the bison and elk.

Ida linked her arm inside Minnie's and huddled in.

'Is that not too cold on a day like today?' Minnie said, wrapped up and toasty in a scarf and hat. Ida shook her head and slurped happily.

'Nuh-uh.'

* * *

'Excuse me, miss,' a Danish woman with wide brown eyes and a hearty, friendly voice said. 'My kids – and I – we're big fans.'

'Oh!'

'I'm sorry to disturb your family time...' The woman nodded to her daughter and son, as if to say *I get it*. 'But, can we get a picture with you? And maybe an autograph please?'

Minnie stopped, startled. She still wasn't used to this.

Marvel didn't ever call back, but just as *Summer of Siena* aired three years ago, Minnie was offered the part in a kickass new superhero franchise, *Artemis*, based on the Greek goddess whose twin brother Apollo was out to wreak havoc on a world she was trying to save. More emotional than *Black Widow*; more striking than *Wonder Woman*; and as strong and clever as Shuri. It was directed by Xanthe Dabiri, the hottest female director in Hollywood, and a dream to work with. Minnie learned so much from her, every day.

Xanthe Dabiri had also been one of the early voices calling out her mentor, Wim Fischer, for sexual assault. She had worked with journalist Zahara Zaman, on an exposé about Wim Fischer for the *New York Times*, and he was currently awaiting sentencing. Minnie slept better at night too knowing that Wim Fischer was behind bars.

Critics said casting Minnie Byrne and Timothée Chalamet as twins was perfect and she loved working with him, and the older Hollywood heavyweights in the cast – but even more than that, she loved going home to Jesse and Ida at the end of a shoot.

For the past two years, Minnie's face had been *everywhere*, and given that she was about to start filming the third instalment, *Artemis: Ascent*, in Morocco next week, her star didn't seem to be waning any time soon.

While Minnie was on location or lucky to be shooting in a UK studio, Jesse would keep everything ticking over at home, which was now a much nicer and more spacious apartment in King's Cross. Ida even got to visit her stepmother on set a few times, the way her father had visited film sets when he was a child.

* * *

'Of course,' Minnie said, smiling to the woman and her children, who seemed to be cowering behind her, either desperate to meet Minette Byrne or dying of embarrassment, Minnie couldn't tell. 'Do you have a piece of paper? We can do a picture after.'

The woman took out her Copenhagen Zoo tickets, printed on one side of a sheet of A4, and a Sharpie she had nestled at the bottom of her bag, while Ida stared at the children, who looked at Minnie in awe. Actual Artemis in the flesh!

'Here, can you take this?' Minnie handed her coffee to Jesse who looked on, proud, bemused, accommodating.

'Who do I sign it to?' Minnie paused, Sharpie poised.

'Oh if you could make it to Alina and Alex, that would be amazing, thank you!' the woman said, happily flustered. 'They can fight for whose bedroom it goes in.' She gave a loud and nervous laugh. 'Guys! Don't be so shy! Say something!' the woman admonished. The kids shuffled out

from behind their mother, flushed and shy but happy. Ida smiled at
them.

Their hero.

Minnie signed the paper, a blousy scrawl, and looked at each of the
kids, before shooting her husband a quick smile.

'Nice to meet you, I'm Minnie.'

ACKNOWLEDGEMENTS

Enormous gratitude and appreciation goes to you, my readers. Without you I really am talking into a void, so thank you for choosing this book, and my previous six, and for all the messages I get on social media telling me what you think (some of you are still angry with Harry in *Fairytale of New York*, and I hear you!). You can reach me on Instagram @zoefolbigg or sign up to my newsletter there to stay in touch.

Heartfelt thanks to my editor Sarah Ritherdon – whose wisdom, wit and brilliance makes me feel like I'm always in safe hands. What you have achieved with Boldwood is incredible and I'm in awe. Thank you again for believing in me and my characters. Thank you to my agent, Becky Ritchie, back from mat leave for this one with a beautiful bonny boy to add to the team – thank you for being so amazing at articulating what I'm thinking. You're the best. Also thanks to Florence Rees for holding the fort so beautifully and being the very first reader of *Five Days*.

Thanks to the wider Boldwood team: Nia Beynon, Claire Fenby, Niamh Wallace, Jenna Houston, Marcela Torres, Issy Flynn, Emily Ruston, Tara Loder, Isobel Akenhead, Rachel Faulkner-Willcocks, Caroline Ridding, Emily Yau, Leila Mauger, Ben Wilson and Amanda Ridout. You have sold 22 million books in less than five years (not *all* mine ;-) what a team!

Behind the scenes are the copy editors and proof-readers who make me look less stupid: huge thanks to Candida Bradford, Sandra Ferguson and Sue Lamprell for your wordsmithery and grammar genius. And to Alice Moore for my favourite cover yet. Who would have thought that

Beryl and Meryl, the bit-part scarlet macaws from my book-within-a-book would look so glorious on the cover? Thank you!

I would like to thank a few people for helping me with my research and little extra ideas they unwittingly give me when we're casually chatting. To my friend Justin, who told me he tracks a small temporary memorial plaque from his mother's grave, which he left on a plane once, to see where it is in the world. Rest in peace Maria Start, I hope your travels are wonderful. To Sophie Rutschmann for checking my French midway through writing an immunology paper (sorry, science!). To Vinamra Misra, for gifting my husband a keyring with an Indian deity on it (it holds the key to my garden office where I write). To Erin Kelly for enlightening me about the Bechdel test and *My Little Pony* being worthy pieces of feminist fiction. To Charlotte Luxford for being so lovely, and for sharing with me what it's like to be a jobbing actor. To Tony Carelli for the empty chair therapy idea and the therapist inspiration (as well as the late-night MAFS Australia texts). And to James Williams for lending me Bingley the Border terrier for a scene or two.

Thank you to my author friends and cheerleaders: Olivia Beirne, Lorraine Brown, Jo Carnegie, Caroline Corcoran, Ian Critchley, Nicola Gill, Janet Hoggarth, Caroline Khoury, Lia Louis, Shari Low, Jacquelyn Middleton, Laura Pearson, Holly June Smith, Samantha Tonge, Paige Toon and Kathleen Whyman. I've said it before and I'll say it again – you make this hustle fun.

And finally, heartfelt thanks to my family and friends. I have fiercely loyal beta-reader friends and family I adore. Get a bunch of Smiths, Folbiggs, Baileys, Lanes and Mitchells around a Black Forest gateau and happiness ensues. I love you all. Especially Mark, Felix and Max – fine men I am fortunate to live with and treasure every day.

ABOUT THE AUTHOR

Zoë Folbigg is the bestselling author of many novels including *The Note*. She had a broad career in journalism writing for magazines and newspapers from Cosmopolitan to The Guardian. She married Train Man (star of *The Note*) and lives with him and their children in Hertfordshire.

Sign up to Zoë Folbigg's mailing list for news, competitions and updates on future books.

Visit Zoë Folbigg's website: www.zoefolbigg.com

Follow Zoë on social media:

X x.com/zoefolbigg

f facebook.com/zoefolbiggauthor

⊙ instagram.com/zoefolbigg

BB bookbub.com/authors/zoe-folbigg

♪ tiktok.com/@zoefolbigg

ALSO BY ZOË FOLBIGG

The Three Loves of Sebastian Cooper

Fairytale of New York

Five Days

LOVE NOTES

LOVE IN EVERY CHAPTER

WHERE ALL YOUR ROMANCE
DREAMS COME TRUE!

THE HOME OF BESTSELLING
ROMANCE AND WOMEN'S
FICTION

 WARNING:
MAY CONTAIN SPICE

SIGN UP TO OUR
NEWSLETTER

https://bit.ly/Lovenotesnews

Boldwood

Boldwood Books is an award-winning fiction publishing company seeking out the best stories from around the world.

Find out more at www.boldwoodbooks.com

Join our reader community for brilliant books, competitions and offers!

Follow us
@BoldwoodBooks
@TheBoldBookClub

Sign up to our weekly deals newsletter

https://bit.ly/BoldwoodBNewsletter

Milton Keynes UK
Ingram Content Group UK Ltd.
UKHW042323290724
446180UK00002B/5

9 781804 269534